Life Lessons

"Dr. Apple's deeply probing book, Forgive To Live, *looks at a world divided by shadows and light. She cuts through the darkness, with surgical skills and exposes its dirty little secrets; gender bias, glass ceilings for women, and the privileged male driven by greed and a need to win at the expense of others.*

"Then, Dr. Apple balances the darkness with her compassion as a female doctor, who through the microscope of goodness and light reminds us that we do not live by bread alone, and that true wealth is not found in things, but they are found in love, serving humankind, and forgiveness...not in exacting revenge on an unenlightened society. This book is not to be read. It must be studied, as it contains a wealth of life lessons."

— Charles Johnson
Professional screenwriter, speaker,
recipient of the Christopher Award,
and author of *Prayer, The Power Beyond Belief*

Forgive to Live

Forgive to Live

"Father, forgive us our debts,
as we also have forgiven our debtors."

Sophia K. Apple, MD
The Unseen Doctor

"This, then, is how you should pray, 'Our Father in heaven, hallowed be your name, your kingdom come, your will be done, on earth as it is in heaven. Give us today our daily bread. And forgive us our debts, as we also have forgiven our debtors. And lead us not into temptation, but deliver us from the evil one. For thine is the kingdom, and the power and the glory forever. Amen.'"

For if you forgive other people when they sin against you, your heavenly Father will also forgive you.

— The Holy Bible, Matthew 6:9-14

Foreword

Notions of fairness, particularly toward women, are built upon our perspectives of the other person. Even in medicine, I have witnessed thousands of physicians who speak about bias and discrimination as broad topics that are known to exist, with minimal emotional connection to their hearts and minds. We create ideas and opinions about other people without taking time to understand the other person's reality. Hurt, anger and misunderstanding are intensifying, and the concept of forgiveness is vague or seen as irrelevant.

I met Dr. Sophia Apple during my interview with her after reading her first novel, *Covid-19: A Gripping Novel Inspired By Real Events*. Dr. Apple's powerful and lucid storytelling again captures my distracted, busy mind as I give in and quickly become immersed into the story that carries such depth in meaning and emotions. This second book, *Forgive to Live*, immediately illuminates a central theme of what many humans must encounter: hurt, despair, loss of trust, sickness, death, and then, forgiveness.

The most intriguing part of this book unfolds not just behind the storyline of a young girl's suffering through loss of a love affair, the shame and physical challenge of teenage pregnancy, and ensuing sickness leading to premature death. What is fantastic about this book just starts there. The author then allows us to experience what we often don't contemplate and try to understand: the perspective of four people in the middle of a heated struggle where the stakes run high, and the emotions run wild.

The parents struggle to deal with the death of their youngest daughter due to a potentially missed early detection of cancer from pregnancy, the daughter's last words to her mother begging her parents to forgive the doctor and not to pursue a malpractice suit, and the female doctor, who in her chaotic pursuit to perform as the interim chair of the pathology department, struggles to deal with the malpractice and restudies the pathology slides. In the midst of all of that, we understand the story behind each person: the life of a teenager and her desire to be loved and understood; the wife's discovery of her husband's infidelity leading to a heightened distress level, which secondarily brings the husband's undeserved force and vengeance upon the doctor being sued; and the discrimination which an Asian American female doctor faces both internally and externally, as she pursues the position of Chair of the Department of Pathology during the time of this painful lawsuit.

This, Dr. Apple's second novel, *Forgive to Live,* unravels our preconception of justice following human error and tragedy. Dr. Apple's startling portrayal of a series of events from the perspective of Daughter, Father, Mother, and Doctor ring true. The emotions are intense and details of the four storytellers abound with pain, humor, loss: and finally, forgiveness. Only a female physician could write this book. The emotional effect of experiencing gender and racial bias is raw and descriptive, underpinned by certain medical facts and true-to-life situations. Dr. Apple's stories emotionally connect with our hearts and minds. She makes vague ideas painfully clear and believable. A dramatic courtroom scene in the novel brings tears to all people in the courtroom, and to me. An unusual act of forgiveness with God's help becomes personal, and a force to be contemplated.

I have coached, trained, and spoken with thousands of leaders in medicine and in other professions. This book uncovers leadership skills through storytelling. We feel and see how opening ourselves to the story behind each person or party is crucial to the success of having crucial conversations. When a heated debate or conflict arises, we need to stop and ask ourselves: Are we judging or basing our ideas on facts? Where can I remove the judgment and put down the facts? What am I missing here that I may not be seeing? What other possibilities are there that I am not seeing? Who can I talk to about this?

Instead, those leaders who lack skills in Emotional Intelligence, may take action based on their emotions without self and social awareness. Dr. Apple uncovers the story behind each person in the lawsuit. When we learn to dive deeper behind the story, we can learn to be more resilient, open-minded, and understanding. We can learn to FORGIVE to LIVE. We can also learn to be accepting of people different from us, provide more diversity in our leadership teams, try new and unfamiliar ways of approaching new and old initiatives, and be able to flourish in a rapidly changing and challenging health care environment.

In this book, Dr. Sara Choi's struggle to be accepted into the leadership position she temporarily holds is common. When I spoke with Dr. Apple, she told me that this book is intended to help the reader to realize, experience and understand what minorities, women, and disadvantaged groups undergo with the hope that the messages will help influence change. Every person's action, large or small, makes a difference in allowing a cultural shift of diversity and inclusion.

Another theme we often discuss in leadership development is fear. Often this takes shape as denial, self-doubt, procrastination, and avoidance of change and having *crucial conversations*.

Sometimes it originates from painful or "unjust" experiences; in this story, a fortune teller tells Sara Choi that she should not pursue leadership, fueling the uncertainty and insecurities of Sara's own capabilities. Many of our biases and hidden paradigms come from our upbringing and life's journey, with significant influences from childhood. Some say they come through our genetics.

Dr. Apple shows us how fear can be overcome, and, in her novel, she boldly includes religion and God as her strength, which include topics that many in the field of medicine are timid to mention. We feel and experience these crucial conversations through her characters, perhaps more vividly than a film.

To forge ahead, to live in contentment and to lead effectively and successfully, I encourage everyone to read, digest, and contemplate the carefully crafted, moving story and consider what Dr. Apple has written applies in your own life and circles.

— Elsie Koh, MD, MHL
Chief Medical Officer at American Endovascular
and Amputation Prevention, and CEO of LEAD Physician
leadership program for physicians.

Preface

Young 15-year-old Julie Freedman is pregnant, unmarried, and unexpectedly faces a metastatic cancer to her brainstem. A pathologist is blamed for her unfortunate event. Doctors blame each other. Families want justice. Lawyers want money. In contrast, Julie finds peace by God's power and her mother repeats Julie's remarkable plea during a dramatic and shattering courtroom trial.

The story involves four characters providing subjective, alternative, and even contradictory versions connected by the same incident intertwined by their own circumstances. Daughter, Mother, Father, and Doctor are each unable to assume or predict the others' perspectives, nor their own battles to forgive each other.

Mary, the mother, has lost her youngest daughter amidst her husband's marital affair. Her courageous battle understanding how to forgive her daughter's doctor and her husband during her own suffocating pain comes from the necessity of caring for Greg, her grandson who Julie left in this world.

Martin, the father, is a famous trial attorney who knows only how to revenge, an eye for an eye approach to life. He transfers his painful loss toward fearless energy—winning the lawsuit against his daughter's doctor and paying back what the doctor deserves. He is dumbfounded by his wife's wisdom of forgiveness toward both the doctor and him.

Dr. Sara Choi's tragic pathology diagnosis for Julie occurs as she battles a silent war through the unbreakable reality of an older white male privileged society of medicine. Can Dr. Choi, whose young patient ultimately dies, learn how to forgive herself, receive forgiveness from others, and finally, extend forgiveness toward others to sustain life and stop the poisoning power of unforgiveness?

This book is a compelling story, to reveal overall inequity of women in the contemporary society administered by the indoctrinated reality of prejudice; spoken honestly and plainly. But instead of recoiling, retreating, shrinking, fleeing, or fighting with angry voice and violent acts demanding justice, the story tells us the underlying spirituality of why forgiveness is needed to live; to decontaminate the poisons in the world of unforgiveness. However, act of forgiveness is unnatural and not humanly possible. God needs to intervene.

— Sophia Apple

Table of Contents

I: Julie's Story

II: Mary's Story

V: Dr. Choi's Story

Prologue

Dr. Sara Choi's Diary

I was told by the fortune teller never to be a leader. He also said I will get married very late, if at all. I don't believe in fortune telling. And I was sure to prove his fortune telling is bogus. Strangely, and unfortunately, the fortune teller was right about his prediction of my love life.

Now, about leadership, I wish I had asked the fortune teller why I should not be a leader. Is it because I will be a poor leader, or becoming a leader will be detrimental to me? Not knowing the answer to this question is haunting me. At times, I wonder what exactly defines the leader. This irritating voice in my head asks, "Are you sure you can handle this leadership position?"

Maybe I am not a born leader with great skill sets and I would fall short leading other people. Or maybe I am not such a poor leader per se, but the leadership position is not good for me with inherent long hours and troublesome situations which may cause me to have a high blood pressure, compounded by difficult people I deal with, further causing me frustration and unhappiness. The real reason the fortune teller told me not to be a leader was probably for my own sake because taking such a position would surely decrease my life span.

So, why will I accept this position as the interim chair? First, I decide not to listen to the fortune teller saying I should not be a leader. I decide to not magnify his voice inside of my head but to take a chance to prove for myself and to others that I can, and I will become a good leader. I decide to trust in God who tells me otherwise and I am listening to the voice of the Holy Spirit who tells me that I can do anything and everything with Him who gives me the power to do so. I tell myself to live one day at a time, not to live in the future, worrying about what will happen if I fail. I also do not want to say to myself later in life "I should have, I could have, why didn't I?" I will take on this challenge and live day by day with the attitude of learning. Indeed, I love to learn which gives me more pleasure than anything in the world. I can learn how to be a good and effective leader. I will ask God how to live as a leader and I know He will answer me or show me what to do one day and one moment at a time.

At nights, however, there is a small voice in my head still tormenting me that says, "Who do you think you are? What makes you think you are so special and not to be eventually demoted as was the current chairman? Look around you. You are the only one with colored skin, all other leaders are white, some are Jewish, and you are the only woman in the society of chairman club in your hospital. Chairman is called chairman because men only do it, and you are not a man! There is no such title called chairwoman! You should just quit and live your life in an unassuming way and peacefully with the general population of being among females as you should. There are reasons why so few women are in the position of leadership. Who do you think you are, fooling yourself? You are an introvert who is really shy to be seen by people. Admit it! All you want to be is invisible and dissipate amongst the crowd. You are really nothing, nobody and insignificant. Just shrink and die or be quiet at least. Or else, you will ruin people's lives and you should have listened to the fortune teller who told you not to be a leader."

This voice is tormenting me to despair and self-doubt; a deceiver clothed in the name of reasoning in my head, and I am foolish to buy into it.

I: Julie's Story

Chapter One

I am only 16 years old and told that I am dying. A doctor, my oncologist, said that, and I didn't believe it. But when I saw my mother crying in my hospital bed, I realized something bad might really happen to me. I don't really understand the concept or meaning of death. The only dead person I have known is my grandma from our dad's side who died a year ago from old age.

She was 72 years old. She was in the nursing home and we visited her only occasionally after church, mostly on Christmas and Easter. We went to church only those two times each year, so grandma's visit meant we also attended a church service. I hated to visit our grandma because we had to drive a couple of hours to visit inside a depressing and smelly nursing home, a place where mostly older people live with urine stench smell. To me, dying is tied to the nursing home old people.

I saw my grandma in a coffin at her funeral. I wish they closed the casket but unfortunately it was open. Everyone who came to the funeral had to line up and kiss her forehead and say goodbye. I became scared to approach her when it was my turn. I came close to her and I just closed my eyes pretending I was praying to God and quickly turned around. I did not kiss her forehead. As far as I am concerned, that is how much I know about the death. Someone lying in a casket, not moving, not breathing. They look gray-white and old. I am not that old and don't smell that bad, so I don't understand my own death.

They told me that my death has something to do with my recent pregnancy. I had a son three months ago. His name is Gregory Freedman. We call him "little Greg" and he is gorgeous! He looks just like his father, Pete. Oh God, Pete was in big trouble with my family and his own family when they found out about our secret relationship. Well, it's no longer a secret because Greg is born. I knew better not to sleep with Pete, but one thing led to another and besides, I was deeply in love with him.

We were in high school together in Beverly Hills, California. In 9th grade I saw him. He was a year ahead of me, a sophomore, handsome football player. The fastest runner and a receiver for our football team, an all-star! All girls, even senior girls, liked him. I became a cheerleader just to see him more. Pete did not even notice me, but I had a crush on him the first time I saw him. We never had the same classes. I rarely had a chance to have a glimpse of him except when I was working on cheerleader routines with other girls in the same field where the football team practiced.

I ran into him one day. He had picked up all kinds of sodas for his teammates and had them stacked high in his arms. Suddenly he came out from a corner and ran into my breasts, spilling everything on my tightly fitted cheerleader uniform. I was already somewhat embarrassed about my ever so growing breasts, but he just *had* to crash into them. He apologized profusely and started to wipe my breasts with his bare hands, not realizing what he was doing. I was in shock. First, because his forceful collision, then the cold ice drinks on my chest and finally, his hands touching my breasts. When he noticed what he was doing, his face became red, like the hills way behind our school that burned all summer long. He didn't even say "sorry." He ran off and I had to clean up all the spilled cups and sodas scattered all around me.

After that incident, he started to look at me as I practiced my routines with other girls. He was running around, sometimes close to me just to look at me when we were in the same field during his practice. I was sure he didn't even know my name.

My best friend Chloe who was also on the cheerleader team told me he was asking for my name and she told him my name is Julie. Then I knew he was really interested in me. I could not believe it because he is so cute, tall, and handsome; all the girls are in love with him. It wouldn't be such a stretch to say he is the most popular guy in our high school.

He started to hang around me after school and we began to exchange our phone numbers. He called me almost every day. We hung around with his friends and my friends in all kinds of places. Sometimes friends' houses, my home, and his home, sometimes in the Starbucks coffee stores, libraries, in the practicing fields, and in his car. I didn't have my car, for I was not yet 16 years old.

My parents, mostly Mom, embarrass me when they drive me to school and pick me up right in front of my school. Recently, I told my mom that my friends are picking me up after school, so she doesn't have to pick me up. Besides, I was attending all kinds of after school activities including the cheerleader practices and my mom couldn't keep it straight which day of the week I am doing what.

Pete begins to introduce me as his girlfriend. He says this to his friends shortly after we began seeing each other. I am incredibly happy and proud of being his girlfriend. We hold our hands in public and kiss each other occasionally when we are with friends. He makes me feel so special as if I am a princess.

All the girls are admiring me and jealous to the point of hurting me—like sticking legs out when I run to make me fall so that my face is on the floor, bleeding. I am angry at certain girls but soon forget why I am angry because I have Pete who wipes my bleeding spot and once bandaged me with his gentle hands. He hugs me and kisses my cheek afterwards which makes these girls hate me more with passion.

I really like Pete's embraces and protection. He totally focuses on me, not those girls who adore him. He knows that, but still shows his affection toward me in front of them.

For two months we were together. One day, Pete asks me if he can have a more intimate relationship with me than just kissing and snuggling. I know what that means. I have seen what he means in movies, and my girlfriends often talk about it in detail. I am very curious about what it will be like to be with a boy, especially with Pete. He tells me he was never with a girl and this will be his first time too. I am at his house, in his room on a day when his parents are gone and we go all the way.

I remember he comes out very quickly. I don't feel much except his penis is pressuring down there. I begin to bleed and blood spills out and stains his white bed sheet. His arms shake and his eyes look everywhere but not at me. I can tell the blood makes him nervous and he quickly yanks the sheet off the bed and runs to the laundry machine down the hall. He is in a hurry to cover up the scene. I see him in panic. His parents may detect what happened and he seems afraid and not as concerned what I feel. I feel hurt by his lack of affection and love toward me. I walk home and feel disappointed at Pete. I wonder if he is going to see me after this since he had me now.

I never tell Pete how I felt after that incident and I don't call him that night. Neither does he.

We have sex a couple more times, once in his car and once in my bedroom. Each time, he comes out fast. I could never understand why girls do sex because I really did not feel much. All the sounds women make in the movies seem bogus. I never had a desire to make such sounds.

The act itself is somewhat disgusting to me, to tell the truth. I am embarrassed to admit that I was in bed with a boy. I had to open my legs for him to penetrate me. And the way he moves makes me feel like I am an animal. It makes me feel cheap, unappreciated, and totally used by a boy.

Thank God it is Pete who I love and adore. I cannot imagine doing this with anyone else and all the grumbles about sex are not a big deal but a bunch of deceptions. I feel shameful. I don't want to share what I did with him to any of my sisters, parents, not even my best friend Chloe.

I consider myself a good girl and behave as expected by my parents. I get good grades in school, never do drugs. Well, I did try smoking marijuana with Chloe one time in her house when I stayed overnight with a bunch of other friends. Pete was there too, trying it out with me. The only thing I remember with that experience was we all got so hungry and we ordered large cheese pizzas that arrived in stacks of boxes and we gulped them down with sodas.

Fortunately, Pete never abandons me after our special experiences. He is more affectionate, and he even gives me a cheap ring made of fake titanium when we were at a mall roaming around. It costs only $9.99 but it is so special for me because he gave it to me. I wear that ring whenever I am with him, mostly after school. I make sure to take it off before I enter classrooms and when I am home. I do not want my parents to find out I have a boyfriend.

Chapter Two

Then my period stops. For three months I feel nauseated, especially when I smell the breakfast cooking. I run into the bathroom gagging one morning, again the next day, and now I can't recall a day without nausea. I vomit until I am dizzy when I see the pancakes and eggs on the breakfast table. My reaction to breakfast is puzzling to my family and they make fun of me.

I am the youngest of three siblings, all girls, only a year apart from each other. My big sister, June, is a senior and my middle sister Jane, is a sophomore who has the same classes as Pete. Jane likes Pete also, but she knows that I am his girlfriend. She argues that she was the first one to love Pete, even before I had noticed him.

Jane stops talking to me and she is very cold to me. I think Jane is sad and feels hurt because Pete chose me to be his girlfriend. Both June and Jane love to make fun of me because I am their scapegoat and little sister they can abuse. They laugh at me whenever I gag during the breakfast, but it is Mom who notices something is not right with me.

One day, Mom tells me to stay home and see a doctor with her. She works at some office, doing some job as a realtor but she calls in sick for the day. That morning, we see our family doctor. I am afraid and nervous because I think everyone will know and figure out what is wrong with me. The family doctor doesn't ask me whether I am having sex with a boy and never asks me to do a pregnancy test. He just tells me about anti-acid medication which Mom picks up from over the counter in a drug store. Mom just drives and tells me to rest for a few days and skip school. I feel relief, and know I fooled everyone, even a doctor.

Now my belly has become more swollen. My jeans no longer fit, and I am eating more than my usual portion at every meal. My sisters are laughing at me again saying I am getting fatter and must quit the cheerleader squad. There are no fat girls who are cheerleaders. I am worried that people notice my fat belly. I have missed my period for a little over five months. Now I must go shopping with Mom and get bigger sized jeans and blouses. I tell her I can wear June's clothes, but June will not have me wearing her clothes. Her jeans do not even fit me, and I am getting larger than my big sister.

This is when Mom asks me if I am pregnant. We are in the car and I admit everything. She begins to scream at me, she is beside herself, and waves her arm in anger. I can't deal with Mom like this. She turns so fast and stops the car in the mall parking lot to scream more at me. I am not sure what she shouts because I just tune her out. I just want to get out and not look at her face, but she locks the car, and I can't escape her screams. She is mad as hell at the boy who I was with and asks me to reveal his name.

Eventually I tell Mom about Pete. We never make it to the mall that day. We just drive back home, and Mom insists to see Pete immediately after school. I call Pete and tell him what is happening and what is about to happen to him. My dad quickly leaves work and comes home early.

I remember the painful day so clearly.

All my family is sitting on the living room sofas and Pete is on his knees on the floor. I sit next to him, kneeling also. They all attack him and ask when this happened, what, where, how many times and why. He tries to answer as politely as he can, but the attacks are so severe, as of the machine guns firing in all direction without stopping, and we both end up crying rather than answering. My parents demand to see Pete's parents the same day, but Pete's dad is an airline pilot who is out of town this night. So, we are to meet again with his parents the next day, skipping school and work.

We all meet the next night, late evening after dinner. It happens again in our house but this time the attacks come from Pete's parents toward me. At least Pete doesn't have any siblings to add on to the attacks toward him, like my sisters did to me.

After all the screaming from all the people, we have a more constructive discussion of what should be the next step; abortion or keep the child. My family is adamant about keeping the child because we are Catholic, and abortion is not an option. Pete's parents want me to have an abortion because they don't want responsibility for the child.

Pete just keeps quiet, mainly because he is just a 16-year-old kid himself, and I am 15. We just hold hands together and cry. We never mention what we want to do with the child. We have no idea what to do. I never ask Pete about his opinion or tell him what I think.

My dad threatens to sue them because he is an attorney, but he is not asking for money or anything. He is just mad as hell and says anything he can think of to say to hurt them for their son's irresponsible behavior.

Pete's parents are blaming me for tempting their son to have sex by wearing a skimpy short dress and a cheerleader uniform revealing my underwear every time I jump. I had no idea how much either side can scream at each other and say such hurtful words.

After all the madness, it is decided to keep the child and Pete's family will pay all the medical expenses and some money for the damage to my reputation. I will have to stop going to school with an excuse of my "illness" to preserve my reputation while my belly is getting bigger to hide the pregnancy.

Pete and I are not to get married, which is the mutual parents' decision because we are too young and unable to take care of the child. Pete will continue attending the same school but hide the fact he is the father of our child.

After my pregnancy, I must go to another high school to finish. I will never see Pete again from this day on. Our parents make all these decisions without consent from me or Pete. It seems we don't have any choice in this matter, and they will not have it.

I want to keep the child, but I don't want to separate from Pete from this day on. I cry and yell out my opinion but to my surprise, Pete doesn't join me. He just looks down and doesn't even meet my eyes. He is going to obey his parent's wish. Everything is settled. Pete and his parents ignore me and silently walk out of our house.

I'm not going to the same school and will quit the cheerleader team, and told to never see my friends, including Chloe without saying the reasons. My job is to fool them to think I am sick and need to be in the hospital or somewhere else to rest during the next four to five months. This is what I have left.

Beverly Hills is such a tight community with nosy neighbors, so Mom and I are leaving soon for our vacation house in Lake Tahoe for the rest of my pregnancy. She left her job because of me.

My parents have a story. When the child is born, they will say they adopted a new baby or had an "oops" moment and finally had a son, and Julie got better from her "illness" and is returning to some other high school to catch up her lost time in education.

I am to start my sophomore year, or maybe repeat freshman year in a different high school after the delivery. I am expected to get the high school diploma and continue my education in college. My son, little Greg, is never to be claimed as my own, ever.

I rely on my parents' decisions from this point on, knowing they must know what is best for me but adults always have to fix things in their neat little boxes and their stories must be made to fit in, regardless how I feel. The pain and hurt of leaving Pete overwhelms me more than facing the reality of pregnancy.

I try but can't even grasp the idea of having a child through me. I only care about being separated from Pete. It's not fair. I miss him, his sweet breath, kisses and talking to him hours and hours at night over the phone.

My phone charger is missing next to my bed this morning and I realize Mom took away my cell phone. My sisters are not to let me borrow their cell phones. Everything is strict and my life is under unrealistic expectations from my parents. I have no voice in these matters. I am put to shame for my own behavior.

Everything changes when Pete and his family left our home. I no longer have freedom of my own. Why will Pete get to continue going to the same school and nothing really changes for him?

Why am I the only one to face all these changes as punishment? Is that because I am to carry this child in my belly? Why is it that only the girls are put to shame when the boys are equally responsible for the act of sex? In fact, I was only doing it because Pete really wanted it and I just went along with it because I wanted him to like me. Mom told me it is always the girls who lose everything. I guess she is right about that.

Chapter Three

The next morning Mom is on her way to my high school principal to tell him I am sick and unable to attend school for a while. She takes care of all the necessary paperwork for me to drop out from the high school. Mom and I pack a few suitcases and we drive to our Lake Tahoe vacation house.

I feel sad my sisters will not see Mom for a while, and I miss my dad. Both sisters are not happy about the situation and neither of them come out from their rooms to say goodbye to Mom and me. Dad promises that he will drive to Lake Tahoe when he is able to take his vacation, and definitely as my delivery time gets closer.

Suddenly he says the delivery must be in Beverly Hills hospital because he has connections with some famous doctors. So, we need to be back home when I am about to deliver a baby, which will be sometime in early August or late July.

Mom will homeschool me, but hasn't the faintest idea how to educate me while we are at Lake Tahoe. We also pack some books and computers for the next four months. We drive away. Mom never yells at me anymore. I think she is tired of yelling at this point.

While Mom and I are at Lake Tahoe, we settle in as well as we can. We are tired and don't fight too much. My room is lonely. I have no way to contact any of my friends. At first, I cry a lot because I miss Pete. When I walk around the lake, I cry alone because I don't want my mom to see me cry.

It is very calm and quiet here. We seldom talk about anything important. We watch TV and read books. We occasionally go out to eat at the restaurants in town, and sometimes I see Mom cry. I am afraid to ask her why.

Dad and my sisters arrive in Lake Tahoe before July 4th weekend and plan to stay with us for three weeks. That is our routine for the family vacation. My belly is really big. I am not able to do many activities like going out for boating, swimming in the lake, chasing my sisters and all the fun things I was able to do before the pregnancy.

My sisters update me on how Pete is doing. He is doing as usual and is becoming more popular because he always makes several touchdowns playing football. Girls are more in love with him now than ever before. Jane, who liked him before, even says he is a jerk because he is seeing someone else in the school, this time, a sophomore girl in the same class as Pete.

I am in shock because we separated merely three months ago. Every day I am thinking about him, wondering how he is doing without seeing me and hoping that he misses me as much as I miss him. I begin to love him more in Lake Tahoe, thinking and imagining his lovely face every day. Must I believe he is seeing someone else when I am carrying his baby inside my belly?

Jane tells me to just forget about him because he is not worthy of my attention and affection. I certainly feel betrayed. I am wasting my life for a stupid boy like Pete and mad, wanting to terminate the pregnancy.

I have a temper tantrum for the first time in my pregnancy and everyone thinks that I am so uncomfortable with the back pain and the huge belly. Jane tells Mom why I am in such a sour mood, so Mom calls me out to take a walk with her. She says boys are commonly like this and are never to be trusted. She hugs me when I am frustrated by the circumstances I face because of Pete.

She looks at me and tells me to face this situation by looking forward to face the child, and revenge to Pete by having a successful life ahead of me. I don't quite understand what this means and how to revenge. Nothing seems sufficient enough to revenge him. All I want is to go and crash into him to hurt him physically somehow. I don't know how best to revenge him.

Somehow the world is not fair for a girl to carry out the pregnancy. Even all the shames are dumped onto me, a girl. And meantime, a boy can continue his life as usual, succeed in his popularity and gain another girlfriend while someone else is carrying his child.

Three weeks into July, Dad and my sisters drive back to Beverly Hills. It is back to school time. My big sister is accepted into UC Berkeley and is so excited about going to college. She is going back home to pack, then fly to northern California to start college.

It is good they focus on my sister June instead of me for a change. The conversations are gloomy and dark when they talk about me but with June, they are excited for her and everyone smiles. I am sad, no longer the one to make my family smile.

I used to be the one who made them happy because no one expected much from me to achieve anything. I am okay to just be happy and silly because I am the last child. In many ways, the pregnancy makes me sad all the way around.

My mom and I are left in Lake Tahoe again by ourselves. Quiet, lonely and nothing much to do. We visit a neighborhood church on Sunday and sit way back so no one can see us. A preacher invites anyone who would like to trust in Jesus to raise a hand. I raise my hand. Mom is shocked and says, "We are Catholics and this is not a Catholic church!" But I don't care what she has to say. I want to answer to God that I am broken, lost and I want God to come into my life now.

I pray the prayer for God to accept me as His child. Nothing much happens after that. No thunder, lightning or Jesus saying anything to me. The only thing different to me is I decided to surrender my life to God and I trust that He accepted me.

I am so big now. I can't see my own toes or believe how much my belly skin can stretch. I have white streaks all over and my belly looks about to pop. I am so scared to look at myself in a mirror. I ask Mom what she felt when she had us. She explains it is her most beautiful experience when having each of us girls.

Only the women can experience miracles of birth because we are special. No boys can ever carry another life into this world. They just donate their sperms, and we both laugh. At least I see that something is more beneficial and special to be a girl, and Pete can't have it.

The due date is around the corner and Dad is coming back to Lake Tahoe the first week in August to pick us up and go back home. I am so big and my legs are swollen, I have so much trouble walking and moving around. Baby is kicking inside constantly at all times, even at night when I am sleeping. It is the strangest thing I ever felt; someone is inside of me, moves independently without my consent.

I eat like crazy. I never eat like this. I am hungry all the time and peeing all the time. I feel like my baby is constantly pressing my bladder. Dad drives, and we stop every hour for me to pee.

Suddenly I can't wait not even a minute and I have an accident in the car. I feel miserable and now I smell my own urine in the back seat. Thank goodness the seat is leather. Mom quickly turns and her eyes tell me it's okay and she stretches her arm out and wipes it off clean.

I am so hot. It has been five hours, so Dad cranks up the air conditioner. They are both wearing wool sweaters in the front seat while I am burning hot with red face in the back seat. This whole drive is very unpleasant for me.

Chapter Four

Finally, the baby is to come out today on August 7th. Dad is driving straight to the Beverly Hills hospital. Finally, I am being admitted. My dad knows a famous Obstetric doctor, Dr. Kline, and is requesting I have caesarian section because my dad can't bear to see me go through excruciating pain of natural birth.

Dr. Kline advises against my dad's wish because it is highly unusual practice for him not to deliver my baby naturally at my age. Dad insists that I have the surgery because of significant swelling in my legs. Dr. Kline mentions that I have a pregnancy induced high blood pressure; he calls it pre-eclampsia, but a mild form.

Mom is somewhat confused and doesn't express her opinion strongly one way or another. I am still a minor and don't have any voice or choice in the matter. So, I have a caesarian section, and deliver little Greg. I was out and never felt any pain.

I wake up from the surgery; I don't see my baby. I am so curious to see the baby—what it looks like, is it a boy or a girl, and does it look like me or Pete? My parents think it will be better if I don't see or hold the baby until I get discharged from the hospital and I am to see the baby for the first time at home.

Mom says the baby is a healthy seven-pound six-ounce boy and they name him Gregory. The intent is for me not to feel too motherly toward the baby. Two days have passed, and now the baby goes home, and tomorrow I get to go home.

I hold him for the first time as I come home. He is so tiny in my arms. He doesn't look like anyone. He is a little wrinkled, somewhat ugly thing. Mom and Dad are so happy to see the baby and they are smiling constantly. They decide that Greg is their "oops" baby in their late age.

Jane is happy to see Greg also. It is too bad June can't see him until she comes back home, maybe in the Thanksgiving time. I can't give Greg my breast milk, even though my breasts are bursting with milk. I must go back to school and giving breast milk is not in our discussions.

The school already started a week ago. I am starting my sophomore year even though I lost more than six months of my freshman year. Mom and I tried to do some homeschooling while we were at Lake Tahoe. I am afraid that I am unable to follow other students in my classes.

So, I am back at school. It is another high school, a little farther than my original school. I haven't seen any of these kids. They don't know me and I don't know them. That is a good thing. No one knows I had a baby boy. Pete is not here. Somehow, it is comforting to know I will not face Pete, even accidentally.

My mom religiously picks me up and brings me to school. I become 16, but my parents don't throw a sweet 16 birthday party or buy me a car like my other sisters.

Having Greg seems to interrupt normal flows of our lives. I don't join any activities like cheerleader or any other after-school events. I keep myself private and don't make friends. I come home straight from the school and see Greg. He gets a little bigger and stronger every day. And it is good this way.

A month after the delivery, I lose consciousness at the school bathroom. I am all by myself in the bathroom. Even after delivery, I notice bleeding and my underwear is soaked with blood as if I am having a period. It becomes frequent and I go to the bathroom during classes because I am afraid to leak the blood through my pants. I also feel dizzy, more often as days pass.

I must have passed out but I don't remember. No one sees me because I am inside of the locked bathroom with my underwear down, sitting on the toilet seat. I fall on the floor but no one detects I am missing in the classroom for I don't even have one close friend at this new school.

My mom is picking me up at the school. As usual she waits for a while outside at the street near the school entrance. After 30 minutes or so, she parks the car and is looking for me. She finds me in the bathroom. I am out maybe two hours.

She takes me to the hospital ER and they admit me into the hospital. Nobody knows what is going on with me and they can't figure out what tests to do. I pass out, then wake up, and now I pass out constantly. They do an MRI on my head finally and find multiple huge masses in my brain and even my brainstem.

They do more testing and find multiple masses all over my body. By this time, I am not able to breathe well. My brain is swelling up quickly and they need to put in some kind of shunt. My face is swollen up to the degree that I would not recognize my own face. I am passed out most of the time.

My mom and dad are frustrated with so many doctors not knowing what is going on with me. The doctors are talking nonsense and no one seems to tell me or my parents anything we can understand. They are all shaking their heads, recommending this test or that test.

They do the blood test and say my HCG level is extremely high, just like when I was pregnant. The doctors do a biopsy in my liver because the liver mass is close to the surface and easy to target under some machine called a CT scan. It is painful during the procedure but nothing unbearable.

We wait several days to get the result back from the lab. Mom stays with me day and night during my hospitalization. She calls sick from her work again for me. Mom is going back and forth, taking care of me and Greg. Fortunately, we find a nanny who can live in the house and that is very helpful. At least Greg is constantly with someone and looked after.

Three days later, we finally get the name of my problem. It is called a "*choriocarcinoma*." No one knows what this means. We are all looking at each other wondering what is next.

Dr. Kline is our main doctor again and explains that it means I have a cancer, high grade, an aggressive cancer, but luckily one that is quite treatable. Unfortunately, the cancer is in my brainstem, pushing down the head and neck, blocking major functions such as breathing.

I must have the chemotherapy as soon as possible to shrink down the brainstem mass, otherwise I will lose my life quickly. Within the next hour, I must get a minor surgery to connect a pump near my heart to get access for the chemotherapy drugs. I am now connected to many bags of chemotherapy drugs. I must look like a zombie hooked up with many lines to stay alive.

The doctors are discussing to put me on the ventilating machine if my oxygen level drops down in the near future. But for now, they are thinking the chemotherapy will significantly reduce the sizes of the tumors.

After chemotherapy, they discuss the possibility of radiation therapy. Surgery is not an option especially for the brainstem mass. All the masses in my body are somewhat treatable and shrinkable except the brainstem mass and that is the one the doctors say will determine whether I will live.

Dr. Kline speaks to my parents and explains there may be an error in missed diagnosis when I delivered Greg and they removed my placenta. The lab doctor examined the placenta and may have missed a diagnosis at that time. They look into the situations of what exactly happened.

Both my parents are surprised to find this out and ask all kinds of questions to Dr. Kline, like how is the tumor a missed opportunity in diagnosing something in the placenta related to what is happening to me now? The baby is healthy now and should we worry about his life as well? All the unknowns are out of control for all of us. New questions arise as we live daily.

The main focus for now is my prognosis which is directly related to shrinking my brainstem mass. Dr. Kline asks to bring Greg in for a thorough check-up because this particular cancer can also affect the infant. My mother brings little Greg and he is poked with needles for many tests. It appears little Greg is all right for the time being, which is a relief.

I am unable to walk. The main embarrassment is to pee and poop without ability to go to the bathroom. I do everything in my bed—eat, sleep, poop and pee. My mother is almost always by my side attending and helping with all these embarrassing activities. Most of all, she changes the diapers to clean up my constant bleeding.

I don't want anyone to visit me. I am still swollen to the degree no one will be able to recognize me, mostly due to high dosage of steroid. My hair is greasy because I lie in the hospital bed for weeks. The doctors tell us that the tumor in the brainstem is smaller but the fluid, they call it edema, is producing the mass-like effect, essentially the same effect as the mass itself and I am getting worse in symptoms.

I no longer can focus as I look at things. I see double visions. I have constant headaches, and dizziness. I vomit uncontrollably and suddenly. The doctors put me on more steroids which make my face swollen up even more. My cheeks look like a chipmunk's. Because I am unable to eat, they put the feeding tube in—what's another tube from already complex wiring going into my body?

Normally, my cancer is very treatable with chemotherapy but my situation is getting worse. The only inclination I am getting worse are the added tubes into my body and my mom's reactions. She often cries when I see her.

I am not conscious too many hours. When I am able to wake up, I see her crying near my bed. I overhear the conversation between the doctors and my parents as they discuss about the end-of-life issues; whether to intubate me and continue plugging me into the machine if I go into a totally vegetated state. I guess things are not working well with me.

They say that they detected my cancer in a late stage which makes it difficult to cure. I see my dad crying out loud which I never saw in my entire life. It breaks my heart to see him lose his cool. He is always the cool one, even during a disaster. He always knows what to do and takes care of all us girls.

He is the only male in our family who knows how to take care of all kinds of problems in our house. Now, I guess Greg is another male in the house, but it will require some years for him to help solve problems with Dad.

When I see my dad crying out loud, I realize I am really dying. Mom is beyond crying, she is hysterical.

Chapter Five

I have a dream tonight. I am going into a place that is so peaceful. The place is very bright, clean, and smells wonderfully fresh. I see the green grass, a perfect pasture that is unseen from the earth. I am with someone who I may have seen before. He looks very familiar. He is gentle, wears pure white cloth, so bright I can barely open my eyes. He has small round puncture wounds in his hands as light shines through the holes. He hugs me and lets me sit on his knees.

We are talking and playing. Nothing seems unusual or out of place as though we have always known each other. It just feels natural that I am with him. There is no more pain, no more tears and no more agony of not knowing about the future. I look into his most beautiful and gentle eyes as he looks down at me with a smile. He is so pleased to see me.

There is infinite understanding and fullness of complete love. He sings to me, saying how much he was looking forward to holding me like this. He tells me that he knew me even before I was born. He formed and knew me way before the universe even existed. I was to be born in this time and this era and was to give birth to little Greg for my family.

Greg will be an instrument for him and he will use Greg in a special way to give joy to my family. Greg will give smiles to my family's face more than the tears when they lose me, and he will comfort my family with unspeakable peace. And I will be with him forever. He will wipe every tear from my eyes. There will be no more death, mourning or crying or pain. The old things have passed away and I will be in his house forever.

I wake up, so disappointed that I am still in the hospital bed in pain again. Immediately I want to go back to my dream world. The smell of the hospital is almost unbearable. All the tubes around my body are so cumbersome and I want to be free of all these attachments as I was in my dream.

I see Mom and Dad talking to each other intensely and I over-hear they will sue the lab doctor who missed and delayed the diagnosis and caused my tumor to go everywhere in my body including the brainstem. They are mad and painfully angry, say-ing they will let this doctor pay for my pain and suffering and possibly my loss of life.

Tens of millions of dollars! Even that won't be able to replace what they are facing, and the losses. Dad being an attorney, this kind of conversation is not unique, and I hear these talks hun-dreds of times at the dinner table. The only difference, this time it is no longer someone else but his own family member. Dad is always so mad and unhappy at everything.

I call out to Mom. My voice is not as strong as before and they do not hear me at first. It is hard to get their attention these days. They are self-absorbed, talk too much in their anger and loud voices. Finally, Mom sees my arms going up a little and she comes to me. Dad runs toward me. It is difficult talking to them with all the oxygen tubes and mask so I gesture to remove them.

I whisper to be peaceful for I am at peace. I had a dream and I think I met Jesus. I retell everything Jesus told me including little Greg and why he was born.

I say not to be angry at the lab doctor. No one means to do any harm to the patients knowingly. The lab doctor must feel so bad right now for the pain and suffering that I and our family are facing. The lab doctor needs to be at peace also. Mom and Dad need to comfort the doctor, forgive and let it go.

God is using the lab doctor in His infinite designs and it has to be this way. Everything will work out and Jesus will take care of everything. All we have to do is just trust Him. Live one day at a time, knowing that He sees everything we do and think.

I am going to a beautiful place, the place where I belong and I want to go. We shall see each other there one day and embrace each other once again. I am at complete peace with myself.

I give them a big smile, my last, and I let myself go. I see Jesus opening his arms toward me. There are angels surrounding us welcoming me to the heaven.

II: Mary's Story

Chapter One

I married Martin when I was 31. After graduating from UCLA as an undergraduate, I began work at his law office as a secretary. It is disappointing only getting a mere secretarial job (now more appropriately titled as an administrative assistant) after graduation. Job opportunities are rare for women at the time.

Martin is the youngest hire at the law firm at age 26, a new rookie who is supposed to be an all-star attorney from Harvard Law School. The firm is immensely proud of their recruit with the highest bar exam score among Harvard Law grads. I am quickly promoted to become his personal assistant, a big leap and an exciting opportunity for me. My position as a general secretary only requires me to run errands, copy documents and clean up the break area as I stock coffee and refreshments.

Now with the promotion, I am expected to be an actual professional assistant to Martin. He is a gorgeous man, in a dark navy suit, green polo necktie against his white shirt, wearing shiny black shoes as he walks toward me; my first time to see him. I pause to see his slightly long, wavy brown hair, then his sparkling blue eyes that look into me as he introduces himself as

Martin. *How did I get this lucky in my life, to work for such a hand-some man?* All our firm's female assistants are jealous.

The law firm has over 100 attorneys, the largest and most lucrative trial law firm in Los Angeles. It takes just over four years to convert Martin to be my man. It has been a bit of work to convince Martin to pay any attention to me, especially at first. He works hard without intended distractions from me.

Fortunately, our time together begins to increase as our long work hours become longer and extend late into nighttime, and then into weekends. As it approaches 100 hours per week, we have moments to relax and even laugh, to know each other in a natural way instead of awkward dating situations that are typical. Instead of nice restaurants with drinks, I create more practical meals together.

One night I call for takeout fast Chinese, and other nights I pick up burgers or discover other creative takeout meals so we can continue our work. We work well with each other, like Bonnie and Clyde or yin and yang. I am able to read his mind; what he needs. He looks at me in awe sometimes, even when I already have what he needs placed on his desk. We work closer in proximity lately, especially evenings. One night I feel a soft silence, it lingers, and his eyes are swiftly in front of mine and he kisses me. Then things get a little hotter in the office.

Some time passes, and he continues to take his sweet time asking me to be with him. Patiently I wait for his proposal, yearn for the moment to see a breathtaking diamond ring inside a turquoise box with the capacity to contain such a dazzling gem. I know the amount of money Martin is billing since I manage his accounts.

He is 30 years old so I explain he is not getting any younger and needs to settle down and have a couple of kids of his own.

Martin can be romantic if he really wants to be. I relish our beautiful wedding on a hilltop in the Sonoma wine country with all his attorney friends as guests. An extravagantly large and spectacular wedding. I feel as if I am above a carpet of white clouds, a dream come true life.

His senior partner offers his personal private jet for our honeymoon and his yacht in the Bahamas "for us to spend time to make a baby," according to his wedding gift note. I never realized how a rich trial attorney actually lives. For us, everything is awe, so far out of our expectations.

Soon after, we have three beautiful girls, a year and a half apart. I always feel pregnant during these four to five years as June, Jane and Julie are born and we make a happy family. Overall, these are good children, successful in achieving superb grades, obedient to our guidance and happily obliging.

Martin makes it to senior partner during these times and generates significant money for us all to move into a two-story home in Beverly Hills. A year passes quickly, and we are closing on a vacation house in Lake Tahoe as we make plans to spend every summer there for at least three weeks. We are slowly making our own dream life in joining the rich and famous trial attorney reality.

I resign my secretarial job at the law firm after our first child June is born and become a stay-at-home mom until all three kids begin grade school. It is boring to stay at home and decide it is time to change this. I begin hard work to achieve and receive a real estate license in a medium-sized Beverly Hills real estate office.

Most of the time I answer calls, arrange meetings for the sellers and the buyers and occasionally show a house in Beverly Hills. For the most part, I enjoy showing expensive houses in Beverly Hills, occasionally touring homes of the rich and famous celebrities. I always make sure to count the number of zeros before I quote the price of a home to make sure I do not accidentally and mistakenly quote the wrong dollar amount. It takes me awhile to become familiar with the appraisal amounts of these outrageously expensive homes, especially as I begin my real estate career.

Chapter Two

I can say my life is wonderful until Julie becomes pregnant. She is the sweetest child of all three and the last child I expect something like this to experience.

June is a go-getter, a serious and competitive student who never stops studying until she achieves the highest grade in her class. Everything she touches she excels at, and I am overwhelmed and surprised how well she can surpass others.

She is extremely competitive, mostly toward herself, which makes her overly critical, irritable and unhappy most days. I learn to stay out of her way because she knows exactly what she wants to do. I experience only rare situations when I can coach her to do better.

Jane, the middle child, is into beauty. Applying makeup is essential even before June is remotely interested in her own physical beauty. Jane shudders to wear hand-me-down clothes from her big sister. No, she will not have that.

Her happiest days are when I take her to the malls for shopping. She is not satisfied with just one mall. She requires several malls. Jane is very particular and trendy, worries about her body image, and constant dieting is a part of her life. Everything she wears requires a brand name—bags, shoes, and clothes.

As we shop one day, she casually mentions a boy she likes in her class named Pete. Jane becomes more aware of her looks after she mentioned Pete, and noticeably begins to wear makeup every day. Often, I see her apply dark red lipstick that looks beyond her age. I discourage her to use such a visible lipstick and teach her how to apply makeup for a more subdued and sophisticated look. Her preoccupation with fashion and design are always on display, and I begin learning new things and new looks from her.

Then Julie, the last child. She is so sweet, gentle and quiet in her spirit. She is like a teddy bear I like to hold when I am down. She is more of an introvert and she keeps everything to herself. She meets a boy and begins to change.

She wants to be a cheerleader and asks for money to pay for multiple uniforms. Time with her friends, especially during evenings, is now common and tonight, she asks to spend the night at another friend's home. She is keeping her grades up so I am not too worried.

I do not make a connection that Jane likes a boy named Pete and Julie likes a boy with the same name — not until one evening at our dinner table when both girls argue over him. Jane and Julie do not talk to each other for months after this incident.

I assume they will get over it so I never pay much attention to their argument. Looking back, I am surprised that their silence toward each other lasted at least six months, if not more.

I see Julie's belly increase in size, perhaps signs of morning sickness. *There is no way Julie can be pregnant.* I cannot imagine my sweet daughter Julie sleeping with a boy at her age. If it were to happen to one of my three girls, it will most likely be Jane, who is very much into boys and beauty. I dismiss the idea of Julie being pregnant.

Well, a part of it is my fault and I feel guilty.

I am busy with my work, distracted as we shop and buy a reasonable but nice car for Jane as she turns 16 years of age, then prepare for her to pass the driver's license exam, then prom night, and now college for June. June is anxiously waiting for a letter of acceptance from her favorite colleges, namely UC Berkeley and UCLA, and runs to get the mail every day as the mailman approaches our home.

There is enormous pressure of living in Beverly Hills, and many watchful eyes. It is all about who buys what for their kids. It is essential to consider how I dress and present myself at the monthly tea party for ladies. I do not attend regularly, and recently make an excuse that my work is rather busy.

Even though Martin is earning a remarkably high income, somehow, we find there is not enough cash to buy the goods for my three girls. It is not about their necessities but their ego as we purchase better and more expensive things to show off.

Well, perhaps it is more of my and Martin's ego. We buy a 300 series BMW car for June as she turns 16 and we look to buy an equal if not slightly better car for Jane. We finally settle on an Audi for Jane. During this time as I busy myself with shopping and test driving with Jane, I discover Julie is pregnant.

I stop shopping for Jane's car and attend my focus on Julie. Jane complains and asks why she must always give in for Julie. "My baby sister even gets my boyfriend Pete, and now Julie is blocking my car purchase and driver's license lessons with Mom."

With my full-time work, and the demands of three girls and their transportation logistics and Martin's affair, I have my head barely over the water, and I am drowning.

Martin works late and sometimes says he must work all night. He comes home early some mornings to change and go back to his office. At first, I have no suspicions. When I find an American Express bill that includes a charge at a jewelry store,

Tiffany's in Beverly Hills, I assume Martin bought me a gift for our upcoming anniversary. I anticipate a special night with him to open the blue box from Tiffany he just purchased.

Martin takes care of all the finances and paying the bills but for the last six months or so, he is so busy and preoccupied with his trial cases, so I decide to receive and pay our bills. He must have forgotten I would see the bill for a jewelry purchase.

Our anniversary date passes and nothing happens. He even forgets about our special date and is on a last-minute business trip to Hawaii. He never asks me to join him.

After the trip, he spends another night working at his office and comes home early in the morning, around 5:30 a.m. to take a quick shower and change clothes as he often does. I take his cell phone from his suit pocket and look at his messages.

Martin does not realize I remember the password on his iPhone I bought him long ago for his birthday. Messages are filled with dates, times, and places to meet with a woman named Beth. Later I find out she is a new paralegal. About a year ago she came to the firm to be his personal assistant and paralegal, and he began seeing her soon after she arrived.

I leave his cell phone where I found it in his pocket. I am shaking in my anger but do not quite know how to address him. Of course, I let him go to his office as usual if nothing has changed. Maybe I overly react to his messages between co-workers. It is possible they need to meet at night and in hotels to discuss private matters of clients. After all, his messages do not say anything like "I love you" or "I miss you," or any personal comment.

But recently, he buys colorful clothes, funky neckties and fancy shoes that are not his usual style. He was never a fashion-sensitive person but now he often goes to expensive departments stores and boutiques, buys his own clothes, and fills his wardrobe with many new looks.

One evening I decide to follow his car. Martin came home and then quickly left to go back to his office. I pre-arranged to borrow an old Honda Civic from my neighbor's nanny to chase after him. I wear a dark cotton hoodie and dark jeans.

As I follow, he drives through residential streets and is not going to his office. He arrives at a Beverly Hills hotel. He is seeing a young woman, probably Beth, and I see him kiss her at the entrance to the hotel lobby. They walk inside the hotel shortly after.

I leave the Honda parked on the driveway of the hotel without giving the concierge boys the key and follow them. Martin is holding her hand and then he puts his hand around the woman's waist as they approach an elevator. His hand begins touching more than just her waist as he slides it down onto her buttock.

I don't know why I am not satisfied with them kissing at the entrance and why I have to confirm what I see.

They turn around in the elevator and Martin sees me. I stand directly in front of him, watching as he turns around while holding Beth tightly. The elevator door is closing slowly. It takes a moment for Martin to notice I am here, staring. Frantically, he tries to stop the elevator door and shouts, "Honey, it's not what you think!" after I turn around and run back to the car.

Martin shouts my name four or five times from the elevator and soon runs out to the driveway, confused why I am inside an unknown car, a Honda Civic. I drive to get away as quickly as possible to go back home. This is how I find out about Martin's affair.

I feel utterly alone. I am amidst my daughter's pregnancy; my husband is cheating, and my life is crumbling down. I cannot focus on my work. I am sure to get fired. Everything is crumbling down.

I lose my control when I go shopping with Julie in search of large-size jeans. She continues to eat enormous amounts of food, highly unusual for a girl her age, particularly a cheerleader. I am a stupid person, not knowing that she might be pregnant because I am preoccupied with myself, feeling betrayed by Martin.

I start to have what people might call a mental breakdown and I am screaming at my daughter in the car until I lose my voice. We never make it to the mall. Later, I order online. Three larger sized jeans for Julie.

I want to see this teenager boyfriend Pete and bring him down to his knees. Bastard! I transfer my anger and frustration to Pete while screaming what I want to say to Martin. He is a good scapegoat for my devastating situation since I have not had an opportunity to speak with such passionate anger toward Martin.

I avoid all discussions with Martin and ignore his repeated attempts to speak with me after that elevator incident. I cannot talk to him. I give him silence, regardless of how much effort he makes to connect with me.

Chapter Three

It is a good thing for me when I move away from Martin for a while, to our Lake Tahoe vacation house with Julie. I make a quick decision to have Julie drop out of high school to lessen the damage of teenage pregnancy stigma, away from the nosy neighbors' eyes.

It can be a matter of seconds when the entire neighborhood finds out my youngest daughter is pregnant and gossip spreads which will become a doctrine: we are not good parents after all. The pressure exists to display the ideal American Dream Household Parents in Beverly Hills Image more prominently here than anywhere else I ever lived.

Beverly Hills is not such a good place to enjoy freedom as do usual Americans. The curious eyes and sharp tongues of judgment from our neighbors is unbearable at times, and the preponderance of gossip they share is annoying, to say the least.

I do not wish upon my worst enemies to face judgment from my neighborhood. It is almost a sin not to buy a brand-new car; no, not just a brand-new car but it should be a Mercedes, BMW, Audi or Porsche when a child turns 16.

Our child's 16th birthday is monumental. Not only for our child, but for all parents who need to measure up and show off to others. At times, I have wished to live elsewhere, actually anywhere in Los Angeles except Beverly Hills. We have, in fact, recently begun planning to move after Julie finishes high school, three or four more years until we are free from judgmental eyes.

I do not address my own thoughts about Martin. After the elevator incident, I quickly pack up and drive off with Julie. The reason for this is simply because I do not know what to say or do.

The only thing I can do during this period is stop any significant conversation with Martin, except telling him on occasion to pick up dinner. I have trouble organizing my thoughts and find myself daydreaming extensively.

I no longer perform well at my workplace, either. I am unable to talk with trusted co-workers about my problems at home for they may be a source to spread juicy gossip about my pregnant daughter and my husband's affair.

Maybe they all knew about my husband's affair and I am the last one to know. I will quit my position at work before any of the gossip spreads and preempt any screw-up with appointments and prevent the possible loss of millions of dollars from a sale. So, I deliver my resignation letter, explaining I quit because my daughter has an illness, and I will take her to an out-of-town hospital for treatment over the next four to five months.

To my surprise, I am offered an extended vacation and a leave of absence status because I am taking care of my family member due to illness, which is protected by California law. I should have known this because my husband is an attorney. I am grateful for their nice gesture and accept the leave of absence option.

I do not divulge my daughter's illness. Most people just assume that she has some kind of bad cancer and needs several rounds of chemotherapy.

Coldly I say goodbye to Martin and leave. He promises to visit often, maybe on weekends and during our usual three-week vacation period in July. I do not even properly acknowledge him. "Whatever!" I say to Martin.

When we arrive at the vacation house, I get busy and preoccupy myself with cleaning the place, dusting the furniture not used for the past year and prepare to make this a home. Numerous chores and Julie's condition keep me from thinking about Martin.

At times, I have moments to think through things and feel sad and miserable. Why am I facing these tragedies? I feel like I am not a good mother to Julie and failed my husband. I must not have been a desirable wife to him anymore.

I should have done more for Martin, paid attention to his needs and been available for him. I thought about the time in his office, before we got married and were courting. In the same office, he must be having sex with Beth.

Beth is practically 20 years younger than Martin, a few years older than our oldest daughter. What the heck is he thinking? Well, he is not thinking. That's the problem! There is no way I can compete with her beauty, her youth and soft silky skin, full of energy and excitement. How can I possibly compete with women's beauty close to my daughter's age?

And Beth was beautiful when I saw her in the elevator holding Martin's arm. She was leaning her body toward Martin and tossing her shiny blond hair. Long skinny legs with high heels, tiny waist in her professional dark business attire—and a low-cut blouse to reveal her cleavage. Surely, she dresses like that to entice men in her office. And my stupid Martin had to fall for it.

We once had fun and excitement together, eager to see each other after work. Was he having the same fun and excitement with his new paralegal girl? Is she pretty to him? I did not have time to look at her carefully in that elevator. Is she someone who

Martin is willing to close the chapter with on our marriage, and damage his image as a father to his three lovely children? Is Martin going to marry her?

I think about my options, well, two options. One is to leave Martin and live with the girls. That choice comes with selling the house, moving into a new smaller house, getting a stable job to feed my girls and getting child support income from Martin. Well, maybe I can get alimony from Martin and go through a lawsuit which will take some time to settle.

The second choice is just stay with him. Nothing much would change except my trust toward Martin is broken and I will live in the hell. I regret not having a law degree which I was going to obtain after working in the law firm for a while. I got distracted from my path by a charming man, Martin, who promised me he would take care of me with his job and persuaded me not to pursue my own dream of becoming a lawyer.

Just like my daughter Julie who is losing everything because she has to carry the pregnancy, I lost my opportunity to become a lawyer. My dreams had to settle with raising three children instead of a JD degree and successful professional job as a lawyer. Why do men not have to compromise their career dreams? They gain everything; career, degree, family and wife. And now, when I am all wrinkled up with old age, he gets to have a young girl and still have fun in his life. Well, who said life is fair? Maybe and hopefully men suffer in a way I do not know.

Once Julie and I settle with organizing living conditions at the Lake Tahoe house, there is nothing to distract my obsessive thinking about Beth and Martin. I imagine all kinds of scenarios, their body twists, and positions, probably worst in my imagination than the reality.

I come to the breaking point of despair. My pain of betrayal is becoming bitter and unbearable. Thoughts of evil wishes against Martin grow to a monstrous level. I enlarge all thoughts of self-pity, faulting myself that I must have caused this tragedy because I am not good enough. No longer do I measure up to the standard Martin desires. I became boring, a mundane house-wife, not sexy enough anymore especially with an ever-growing muffin top wiggling around when I walk.

Before stepping into the shower, I look at myself in the mirror and notice how grotesque my body has become, wrinkling, drooping, cellulitis around my thighs and varicose veins popping out. I cry out in my misery looking so old without any makeup on my face, and thinning hair. How can I possibly compete with Beth?

I once had youth like her but now look at me. Who would possibly want a perimenopausal woman like me? I fall down onto the bathroom tile, sobbing my soul out. Why, why, why, I cry out. I cannot stop crying, making noise in the bathroom, naked, and unable to come to my senses.

Julie knocks on the bathroom door. She hears my cries. "Mom, Mom, are you all right?" Her knocks become desperate, louder. Getting to my knees, I manage to get my bathrobe, push myself up, and open the door for her.

"Mom, what's wrong!" She reaches and hugs me and cries louder.

"Mom, why are you crying? Is it because of me? I'm sorry, I'm so sorry I made you sad through this pregnancy." Julie uncontrollably cries and sobs as she desperately holds me tight.

"No honey, that's not it." I cannot tell her why I am so miserable. Julie's assumption and misery comes from believing my sorrow is caused by her! How can I possibly tell her about my complexity in feeling helpless? This burden of despair leaves me unable to stand and hold my daughter, and my strength gives away as I become limp and collapse to the floor sobbing as Julie holds me tighter, bearing my weight and together we sob. The bathrobe became untidy, showing my ugly and embarrassing cellulitis. But who cares? It's just my daughter seeing it through her clouds of tears.

"Mom, please stop crying, please…" Julie pleads and adds, "it's going to be all right. We will be all right. Mom, please don't cry. God is watching us. He knows your tears and mine."

"Oh, baby, my sweet baby!" I cry out, thinking is God really looking down at us? Would God really know what it feels like to be betrayed, abandoned, trashed, and ruined by pregnancy to have innocent dreams that we once had? Does God really understand the misery, despair, and hurt of infidelity?

Chapter Four

When Martin and our two girls come out to Lake Tahoe, I am somewhat well settled living quietly with Julie. I am watching her baby belly become remarkably big and remembering the times I was pregnant. My memories of pregnancy are beautiful, full of anticipations and in love with Martin.

I feel so devastated that Julie is not in a similar situation where her husband is taking care of her. She is without her lover to watch the glorious and happiest moments during the pregnancy sharing the experience of a baby kicking and moving inside the womb.

I try to be there for her, to be her mom and her lover. But I know I cannot be Pete. I see her tears many times when she is alone. She usually takes a long walk around the lake when she misses Pete. I feel miserable for such a young girl to experience solitude in pregnancy. A girl in her age should have fun, running around, receiving attention from boys her age and be innocent.

Once Martin arrives to live with us for a while, we mostly discuss what we need to discuss. Whose child is Julie's child? Would it be Martin's and mine, or Julie's? Can we fool the child that he or she is adopted? What if the child looks very much like Julie, me, or Martin? People soon will find out the child is ours or Julie's. We cannot go along with the adoption story for a long time. In just a matter of time the child will find out he or she is related to our family.

After a long discussion laying out all the possibilities, Martin and I decide to tell others that the child is ours and not Julie's. That will make more sense. Then the question is, what if Julie resists our suggestion? What if she wants to be called the child's mom? How will she continue her education and live a somewhat normal life with her child who needs Julie's constant care?

What if I get a divorce from Martin? Then, I will have to raise the child by myself. The girls do not know I am even contemplating a divorce. So many complicated questions and there are no realistic solutions, especially for me.

I am pretty much antagonistic toward Martin's ideas, whatever he says. The girls must notice my cold reactions toward Martin. We do not even sleep in the same room. He sleeps on the living room sofa.

Whenever he approaches to talk, I escape. He begins by saying at some point we need to talk about it, but I refuse to face him. I am just angry and nothing I might say will be pleasant or constructive. I avoid speaking to him as long as possible.

Perhaps in denial, I bury the memory and think maybe I really did not see them together going up to their hotel room. Maybe Martin will convince me since he said, "It's really not what you think."

But in case it is what I think it is, I am afraid to face it. By not talking to him, I still have a hope, albeit a small hope, that Martin is not really having an affair.

Three weeks pass rather quickly. Highlight of the vacation weeks is June's acceptance into her dream college, UC Berkeley. She has been on the waiting list for a while. She was accepted into UC Irvine but she really wants to go to either UCLA or UC Berkeley. She did not get into UCLA.

June is so happy, gleaming in her jubilation. At least one of my girls is happy. We need to prepare and buy so many things for her freshman year but Martin will have to do that for her when they go back to LA. I must stay in Tahoe with Julie until she is about to deliver.

Martin and I also argue about her method of delivery. He wants her to have C-section and I want a natural vaginal delivery. In my opinion, she is too young to have a scar in her abdomen with C-section. And as a woman, having the severe pain of vaginal delivery is an experience, an important milestone in a woman's life, which Julie will never forget. Maybe the delivery pain will deter her from sleeping with boys in the future. But Martin will not consider it. So, Julie is to have the C-section.

I resent the fact that whatever Martin says goes. I feel ill equipped to defend for my girls as a mother. Whatever the decision is, if it is a big decision like buying a house in Beverly Hills, Martin always has the final say. Sometimes I regret marrying a lawyer who is constantly involved with disputes and has to win all the time. There are really no discussions or compromises with Martin.

My memory of driving back to Los Angeles when Julie was about to deliver is rather blurry. I had to do so many things, packing, cleaning, and taking care of Julie who faced many challenges physically. She had severe swelling in her legs and face. I felt so guilty preventing proper prenatal care for her.

Because this pregnancy is secretive, we decide not to see obstetric doctors during her pregnancy. This is why we do not even know the sex of the child she is carrying. Thank God Julie has no significant issues during her pregnancy, but I know the swelling in her later trimester is rather dangerous. Maybe Martin had a wise idea to deliver as soon as possible and alleviate any problem for Julie.

Chapter Five

As little Greg is wrapped in a tiny blue blanket and handed over to us, Martin and I look at him while we laugh and cry. He looks so much like Julie and Pete, a perfect combination of those two. The boy is undeniably one of us, our family. How can we lie about little Greg, our adopted baby because even at birth, he resembles so much like us?

It is important to detach Julie's motherly feeling toward little Greg as soon as possible, so, we choose not to show little Greg to Julie when she wakes up from her anesthesia and continue to keep them separated during her three-day stay in the hospital. I feel cruel to do such a thing but we both agree it will be better in the end for Julie to live her life without little Greg as her own.

Quickly we become more occupied raising little Greg. At once I look for a full-time nanny. Luckily, our next-door neighbor employs a nanny, whose Honda Civic I borrowed, and the younger sister is looking for a job after recently finishing her two-year college education. I quickly interview and hire her. She soon stays with us in the extra bedroom so she can work every day and night. She goes to her home during weekends, and if she works over the weekend, I pay her extra. This helps us tremendously.

The neighborhood people have many questions and confusions; how did a baby show up so suddenly? How did Julie get better from her cancer? Whose baby is this "Greg"? Most people probably figured it out, connected all the dots, but I have no time caring what they have to say. I am busy dealing with all kinds of immediate issues to carry on living.

Soon after we bring Greg home, people begin to figure things out and proclaim Greg is indeed Julie's son. The truth always reveals in time and there is nothing I can do to stop the spread of the words from people's mouths. The hidden criticisms and judgments increase by the day, and the only thing I can do is ignore what others say and pay attention to my own business in living.

I am most bothered and react furiously when people criticize my daughter Julie for her intended promiscuous behaviors which led her to have a baby in her teenage years. I might bear any kind of criticism toward me but I cannot bear it toward my daughter. This must be the mother's instinct to protect the offspring.

I start back to work and Julie begins attending her new high school. Over the next month things become somewhat normal except we have little Greg in our home as an addition.

Today I pick up Julie from school, and she is not at the curb. Soon I rush inside and find her passed out in the school bathroom. God knows how long she has been stuck in this tiny, isolated bathroom, on the floor. No one noticed she missed classes for hours!

Julie has been bleeding since she had her baby but she had not told us. After we arrive at the hospital, she continues to pass out frequently and no one in the hospital can explain the cause of it.

I quit my work again, and this time, I do not have any more excuses or chance to go back even though my daughter is truly sick, without a diagnosis.

Despite all the technology in medicine, and even in Beverly Hills, no doctors know what is wrong with my daughter. Test after test, my daughter Julie endures her pain and suffering, not knowing what will happen to her.

My loss of control is unbearable. I no longer restrain my suffering. My fuse is short with Martin and with all the people around me. I often scream in frustration, unable to bear even the tiniest stress.

Dr. Kline finally announces the name of the disease as a choriocarcinoma and I do not even know what that means. Doctors use such a jargon language, not even understandable English words. I hear him say it is "treatable but deadly" at the same time because "one of the tumor sites is in her brainstem…her cancer is related to her pregnancy…a pathologist may have missed the diagnosis one month ago in her placenta."

Dr. Kline also explains if it had been detected earlier, Julie may have gotten the proper treatment and her prognosis would have been particularly good but because there was a delay in detection, the cancer is now in her brainstem and her prognosis may be rather poor. They will try everything because Julie is young and may be able to win her fight with cancer.

Immediately, Martin begins to call the friends and colleagues at his office who are experienced medical legal trial lawyers and he threatens to sue the lab doctor, Dr. Choi. It seems Martin is checked out, doing his stuff that he knows how to do so he can handle the problem and I am left with all the other issues but I do not know what I am doing, unlike Martin. I still cannot even digest what is happening around me because all I really care is, will my daughter live?

People go through sufferings in many different ways. For Martin, he basically checks out on Julie and the family, and enters his comfort zone, his fighting mode, and proclaims someone will pay back the pain he is facing. I fall back on blaming myself, not being a better mother to my daughter or a better wife. Neither of us can face our sufferings in a healthy way; Martin in his fight-or-flight mode, mostly fight without focusing on what is the best for our child; and me, in hopeless-and-helpless mode, doing nothing but cry.

Chapter Six

Julie is hospitalized under the care of Dr. Kline and I watch as Julie is hooked up with more types of lines that carry multiple bags of toxic chemicals through her body, often for hours. She repeatedly loses consciousness, and most of the time rarely opens her eyes.

Days pass and she makes groaning noises. She must be in severe pain. But I do not know how to comfort her, to lessen the pain for my daughter. All I am able to do is cry next to her. So helpless and hopeless.

I am not able to recognize my daughter's face. She is swollen up so much, her cheeks have expanded to the degree of reflecting shiny light even in the gloomy fluorescent-lit room. The last dose of Decadron, a steroid injection, is making her face more swollen and cracking her already dry, wrinkled skin. I put lotion constantly on her face to ease the white flaky skin.

It must add pain, as her pink raw skin is exposed all day. This pain is probably the last and I hope the least on her pain list. She endures constant and severe headaches, nausea and vomiting, and dizziness. She has not been able to eat for weeks but I am unable to detect if she lost weight because she is swollen up everywhere.

To live to see one of my daughters get to the point of this suffering and pain. It is unreal and devastating. I wish that I am in the bed suffering instead of Julie. I will do anything to exchange the positions between us.

My whole head and heart are with Julie now, I could not care less about Martin's affair at this point. I am losing my daughter and I see it coming. It is frustrating to watch her dying right in front of the most famous and capable doctors in Beverly Hills. They are supposed to be the best medical doctors with the best care in the world. Death is truly inevitable for everyone, including my young, once vibrant and energetic Julie.

But I just want to *not* face this. Doctors are already discussing end-of-life issues and ask us to prepare for the worst. Martin and I talk through the worst scenario of losing her, and another scenario of putting her in the hands of machines to support her life in a vegetated state.

If there is any hope for her to come back to life in some degree of normalcy, we will sign the paper for her to live, however long it takes for her to come back to life, but doctors are not hinting to us if this might be a possibility.

Doctors are not God and they cannot guarantee anything, naturally. Why do we even think that doctors are remotely close to having power like God?

After intense thoughts, Martin and I sign the paper "Do not Resuscitate." Looking at Julie's peaceful face as she sleeps, we know not to prolong cruelty and more pain, and to help her go peacefully.

In a moment of my darkest point, I discover a chapel in the hospital and enter, take a seat and talk to the Lord. I am raised as a Catholic but never take my faith seriously till this point. I want to talk to God but He is not talking to me. I say whatever comes into my mind and speak out loud in the chapel for no one is here to listen. I pray to God for a sign of miracle, to cure my daughter, so I can see her running and laughing again. If I can just have Julie smile again, I will give up anything. But God is silent.

I yearn to hear God's voice, someone I can talk to, so I visit a nearby Catholic church one morning before Julie wakes up. To my surprise, not only is the church door open but a priest is in the church praying an early morning prayer.

Not wanting to disturb him, I pause at the back row and kneel down to pray. Shortly after, I feel a tap on my shoulder. "Would you like to come and confess your sins?"

"Yes, Father!"

I follow him to one of the boxes and see inside a wooden door separating the priest and me. He opens the curtain to expose a small, lattice window for me to see him.

"What is on your mind and tell me about your sins so God can forgive you."

"Father, I have sinned. I have not come to the church for decades."

"The Lord was there with you and He will be with you now and the future."

"Father, my daughter is dying and I want to talk to God."

"He is here listening to you, speak!"

"My daughter has a cancer and she is in the hospital, dying. There is nothing more the doctors can do. They are a bunch of worthless beings right now. One of the doctors made a mistake and caused a delay in my daughter's treatment. She killed my daughter!"

"What else is in our mind?"

"What do I do so that my daughter can live? What shall I do?" I cry uncontrollably. The silence persists until I regain my composure.

"My husband is cheating on me. We have been married 19 years and he is destroying our family for another young woman. I never said anything to him as of yet for I am afraid to admit his affair in my reality. I don't know what to do with that also. My life is in shambles and I don't know what to do. Can God tell me what I need to do?"

"My child, God is with you and will give you strength to forgive only if you ask."

"Are you asking me to forgive? How can I forgive who hurt me? And why am I to forgive? Why can't they kneel down and ask for forgiveness from me?

"I have done nothing. I was a good mother and wife. I never cheated on my husband. I never asked this doctor to misdiagnose my daughter's cancer because she is a careless, pompous and negligent doctor who was lazy to do her job.

"Why am I to lose my daughter and my husband for their mistakes? Why am I getting all the punishments when I had nothing to do with any of this?

"Why is God so unfair? What did I ever do to God to deserve these punishments? Is it because I have not come here to confess my sins for decades? I have not done anything so sinful to deserve my daughter's death.

"Where is God when I am suffering so much? Are not children supposed to die *after* their parents? Why is my child dying before me? How am I supposed to live through this much pain?"

Another bout of crying spills out. Again, the silence. The priest is quiet before my pain.

"My child, God sees your tears and your pain. He is with you as he has been always." He opens up a Bible and continues, "In the letter to the Romans, chapter eight verses 35 through 39, God says, *'Who shall separate us from the love of Christ?'*"

"My child, does it mean he no longer loves us if we have trouble or calamity, or are persecuted, or hungry, or destitute, or in danger, or threatened with death? No, my child, He still loves us." He continues reciting the passage.

"As scriptures say, *'For your sake we face death all day long; we are considered as sheep to be slaughtered.'*"

"My child, it is here that God replies and says '*No, in all these things we are more than conquerors through Him who loved us. For I am convinced that neither death nor life, nor angels nor demons, neither the present nor the future, nor any powers, neither height nor depth, nor anything else in all creation, will be able to separate us from the love of God that is in Christ Jesus our Lord.*'"

Another silence and the priest speaks, "This is what the Lord says to you, my child, the doctor who made a mistake is not able to kill your daughter for she is not God or has such power to let your daughter live or die. It is God who can give such power. If the Lord is willing, He can resurrect your daughter like Lazarus even after the fourth day of death, with stench.

"For your husband, you will need to exercise the power of forgiveness also, and God will perform His miracle which will give you the power of forgiveness. And you shall see how God will reveal His purposes in your life. Go out there and see how God will answer all your prayers in agony and turn all of them into blessings. You shall go in peace and let God reveal to you His plans in your life. Bless my child in the most Holy names, the Father, the Son and the Holy Spirit, Amen."

With this statement, the priest walks out. I sit to regurgitate what he just said to me. It is if God has spoken to me in voice. I asked God to talk to me and He did answer my prayer in human voice.

Chapter Seven

Leaving the church, I go to the hospital and find Martin already sitting beside Julie's bed. He sees me walking in and we sit across from each other at the bedside table. He rambles on with specifics about how he will sue the doctor.

He is going to formulate and gather the top medical trial lawyers, his friend Jeff Grey, a senior partner who will head up the team, and Tony Spiro, Mavis Hill, Jennifer Watts, and Virginia Chang, all ruthless and aggressive attorneys will be on the team and fight to win the case worth millions of dollars. "The lab doctor has to pay the price for misdiagnosing Julie's misfortune in pain and suffering and we will bring her down to her knees and strip her pride, expose her to be a negligent doctor in the courtroom."

She should be lucky if Martin does not approach her, slap her cheek, or even choke her but instead lets her pay with embarrassment in the open court. Vengeance and justice according to human understanding is what I am hearing from Martin, a quite different message from what I just heard from the priest.

Martin is getting red in his face, heated with his anger in loud voice, which leads me to join in his anger. My head is getting hot as I imagine the scene with the doctor in the courthouse as he puts her into the position of defeat and humbleness.

I can see how sweet that moment will be to revenge all the pain and suffering for all of us, not just Julie. But no amount of money can actually replace the pain and suffering we are facing. Millions of dollars will not exchange Julie's life. It is strange to think that our sufferings can be exchanged for monetary goods. How can the sufferings or people's lives be equated to money?

We are so angry and busy with our hearts filled with plans to ambush the doctor, and we hear Julie's faint voice calling my name and raising her hand to get my attention.

I run to her. She says she had a dream this morning. She saw Jesus. She was sitting on his lap and He sang to her. She said she wants to go back to her dream. She is at peace with herself and her life.

She asks that we forgive the lab doctor because everything was meant to happen by God's design, and everything happens for reasons and God is behind every mishap, even death, and we need to forgive to live in peace.

Julie speaks an almost identical message to the one the priest said this morning. I become dizzy with the same voice from God speaking to me twice in the same morning.

My baby passes away. She gives me a big smile before she is gone. I was asking God for me to see her smile again and He heard my prayers. That smile is locked on her face as she passes away.

The doctors must have heard the flatline alarms shortly after her last breath in peace. Peace that I never experienced is on Julie's face, as if she is seeing Jesus again.

Several doctors now push Martin and I away from her and begin to work on her body. Someone is giving an electric shock to resuscitate her heart, several times. Some doctor is on top of her pushing her heart, doing CPR. Some other doctors are trying to push oxygen into her lungs. Another doctor was called to ventilate her and is pushing a large tube into her mouth.

All seems too chaotic and I want my child to be left alone and die peacefully. It breaks me. I see all this commotion at the holy site of death.

The doctors are trying their best. In fact, we are all doing our best. Our intentions are all good in human eyes, but I wonder what God thinks of all our best activities.

I have a strong urge for the doctors to stop their efforts to resuscitate my daughter Julie, and yell out loud, "STOP!" The entire room becomes deadly quiet and they all look at me. "Stop, let her go in peace!" I plead.

One of the doctors reads out loud from Julie's chart, speaking "D.N.R., Do Not Resuscitate." All the doctors who are doing their things look at each other as if they are caught in a guilty act. Soon after that, the doctor pronounces Julie's death.

Everyone leaves the room except me and Martin. We touch her beautiful face, her hands and say goodbye. We kiss her cheeks and forehead for the last time. Martin and I hold each other and cry. Julie was our child, our unique creation in deepest love, blessed by God. She was a blessing and joy to have, to both of us for a short 16 years.

Chapter Eight

At her funeral, many of Julie's Beverly Hills High School students arrive, including Pete and his parents. It is late September and one of the hottest days in Los Angeles. The summer heat is persistent and relentless. It is supposed to be the first day of autumn soon but the resilient summer season will not let go of the heat as I will not let go of my girl Julie. She is still living in my heart, smiling to me every morning with her unique and pretty scent spreading around the breakfast table.

I have not put on my makeup because there is no point applying mascara since I am tearful all the time. With the heat of 104 degrees, I see no point to put on skin powder either. Instead, I am wearing large dark sunglasses to cover my swollen eyes and to match my black sleeveless dress.

My long brunette curly hair is loose to cover my wrinkled neck that is ever so sagging these days. I have no appetite and lost almost ten pounds already. Hence, my honeymoon-year black dress fits nicely around my waist today and I wear it for Julie's funeral with matching black heels.

I still look good, reasonably attractive woman in early 50s. I want to make sure Martin will still look at me in awe, in case he forgot how I used to look and why he was first attracted to me. I also dress for the occasion in case his paralegal lover happens to be here at my daughter's funeral. How dare she show up on my saddest day of life!

The funeral is held in the Catholic church where I saw the priest who spoke to me in my darkest hours before Julie passed, and this same priest will be conducting the funeral service. We are not members of any specific Catholic church and so it was rather difficult to arrange Julie's funeral in this church. The service was approved only because the priest I met with to request the funeral recognized me and had compassion toward our grieving.

We also are paying an enormous amount of money for the funeral service and the purchase of a burial site near the church. Everything is expensive around Beverly Hills, even one single burial site. We could have bought a nice sized house or at least condominium in the Midwest with the amount of money we spent for a tiny piece of land for the cost her small casket. But what is the money when we are talking about our daughter? We are lucky to have a space for her to be buried.

Selecting her casket, how to dress her, whether to have an open or closed casket service, where and when to have her funeral, where to bury her—all these activities are smothering me to properly grieve my daughter.

On top of this, Martin is constantly discussing the lawsuit against the lab doctor and is preoccupied with all kinds of meetings with his lawyer friends while I deal with the funeral arrangements. He is not really here to help; neither the physical nor emotional needs for me.

Martin is unable to control his anger toward anyone. He moves so close to Pete, forehead to forehead, fumes in his anger and says, "It's your fault that Julie died."

Pete's father is upset that Martin is attacking and intimidating a minor inappropriately and they soon get into a fist fight during the funeral. No one knows why they are fighting except the immediate family members but now, our nosy Beverly Hills folks will surely talk about it and gossip, knowing who for sure is the father of little Greg. At this point, I really do not care if people find out what happened to my daughter.

Pete's mother quickly comes to me and apologizes for both her husband's behavior and for Pete. They likely found out that my daughter's death was related to Julie's pregnancy. I do not say anything back to her. There is nothing she or I did which resulted in this calamity, really. We are just mothers of children, a bystander, who want the best for our children and there is nothing to apologize.

I become numbed to any more feelings of pain, unable to cope with the life anymore. I just want to go back to bed and never get up. I withdraw from the life, unlike how men cope with pain which is by physical fights in fury.

I find it strange that neither Pete nor his parents ask about Greg. Greg is not attending the funeral. He is with the nanny at home. Pete must be so young to comprehend the situation now, but in the future, I am sure he will be curious about his son Greg.

Chapter Nine

After the funeral, I seldom get up in the morning to attend for the family's needs. I stay in bed, depressed and unable to stand up for the life. I eat something from the refrigerator for a late lunch and go back to bed. As Jane comes back from school, I hear her enter from the garage. She was driving my car to school. I still have not completed her car purchase. So many things happened during the process of buying Jane's car and now I have no energy to even get up.

When Martin comes back from work, I do not get up to say hello to him either. I stay in bed. The curtains are never open even during the day and my room is always dark. Little Greg is doing well with the nanny, so I don't have to worry about him. Besides, I care less about anyone including myself.

Anhedonia sets in and I feel nothing is worthy of getting excited or cared for. I tear up quickly. I feel like a failure in all things. I am not a good mother to Julie. I am not good enough for Martin. I just feel like I caused all these misfortunes in my life and burdened all the people around me as a worthless being. The irony is, this is all I have and I tried my best, but my best was not good enough.

Jane tries to console me some days saying it makes her sad to see me like this and that she also needs her mom. "You can't give up and you are not just a mom for Julie," is what she said.

Martin encourages me to get up and live like before. He often tells me he is sorry for everything. I do not know if he is apologizing for having an affair or that he is generally sorry for all the sorrows in losing our child Julie.

Martin is just disgusting these days. I do not want to see him or talk to him and I wish he will just move out with that bitch of his.

While down amid darkness, it is little Greg who wakes me up from the dark clouds one day, crying uncontrollably loud. The nanny says he has started to throw up and has diarrhea for several days.

He is slightly warm to touch and probably has a low fever. I remember the doctors warning me that Julie's disease can be found in Greg. The thought of losing little Greg dawns upon me and I quickly get up, change, and drive him to the ER.

It was three months ago I last drove and it seems unfamiliar how to handle the driving. The ER doctor informs me that Greg is just having a colicky symptom most likely due to recent changes in his milk formula. I tell the ER doctor the story about Julie and that she had a placental choriocarcinoma. The ER doctor tests Greg's blood and calmly explains the HCG level is normal and therefore Greg is okay.

Our nanny admits she recently could not find the same milk formula and bought some other brand. I am so relieved that Greg's illness is not the same disease that killed my daughter. I realize then, I need to get back and address many things in the house. I cannot just let other people take care of things that are still important to me and needing my attention.

I go to the grocery store to buy the right formula and buy fresh vegetables for my family. I notice they eat so poorly these days, ordering pizzas, fried chicken, and hot dogs. No one has been cooking fresh meals.

I now cook fresh food for Jane when she comes home and I begin preparing dinners for the family. I decide to live with the responsibilities that are uniquely my portions to do.

To my surprise, Martin comes home on time and works no nights or weekends. I guess he decided to end the relationship with his paralegal. I pretend nothing ever happened to him and we live what appears to be a normal couple's life from unknown people's eyes. I never address his affair and neither does he.

The only visible change since the night I saw them together in the hotel elevator is that I never share a bed with him. He sleeps in a different room, his study room sofa every night since the hotel incident.

Martin focuses on the lawsuit against the lab doctor incessantly and tells me he and his partners completed the process of filing. The court date is set for just two months from today.

I do not quite understand all the cause-and-effect analyses of how the doctor has assumed the error in the diagnosis for my daughter and I do not really care to know any details. I just go along with Martin, hoping and thinking that he knows better.

All I want to do is move on with life and not be consumed with angry thoughts of what-if. My daughter is gone and no matter how much we focus on could-have or should-have or what-if, my daughter cannot come back to us.

It is hard enough to live without her, but to have a constant thought and agony of, "We didn't have to let that happen" is even more unbearable. What I see is little Greg who is a piece and a part of my daughter Julie, so I live knowing Julie is living her life through him.

What is left for my lap is little Greg, who I decide to accept as a gift from Julie and God and who I need to take into my care. Greg needs all my attention to fill my days. And his smiles, cries and voices of demands to be fed and attend him are joyful. It is good to know at least someone needs me desperately.

It is so much fun to dress him with different clothes, shoes, and hats for various occasions. When I had my girls, I had not enough money or time to do such things but with little Greg, I have all the leisure of time and resources to do so. I bring him to the Catholic church every Sunday to show off how I dressed him. In part, I am always holding on to Julie's life, at least what she left behind.

The priest who saw me to confess my sins never fails to encourage me and he brightly smiles whenever he sees me with little Greg. I find out he is called "Father Nicolas." He is unmarried, an ordained priest in his 40s, somewhat attractive and he knows exactly what to say to comfort me.

Martin does not go to the church with me on Sundays and neither does Jane. I did not really ask either of them to join me in church. Sunday church is a special date for just two of us. I enjoy being with little Greg in the church, somewhat free of all the expectations from home. So, I enjoy a weekly date with little Greg.

People from the church ask me if little Greg is my son or grandson. I tell them the truth. He is a gift from my daughter who died of cancer. People seem to sympathize with my loss of my daughter and rejoice with my gain in little Greg. Or at least that is how I have decided to see from the people in church. I decide not to care about the gossip toward my daughter any longer. The truth always reveals in time and the more I try to hide, the more exaggerated people become with the stories behind me.

So, I let the true story come directly from me. In this way I can control my own story. The only thing I choose not to divulge is the father of the child, for I want to protect Pete and his family's reputation.

As God promised, little Greg is indeed my savior to hang on to my life. When anhedonia and depression found me and I hit the rock bottom of my life, his desperate colicky cries jolted me and still help me. He reminds me of the reason to live, at least for him. He clings on to me and does not let me fall back to the darkness.

With his gentle smile, I see the joy in my heart. I see the beauty in this life as God said to me through the priest and Julie: little Greg will bring meanings and joy in my life much more than the loss. Of course, I wish that I can have both Julie and little Greg but it is the way it is and at least I have little Greg who makes me smile.

III: Dr. Choi's Story

Chapter One

I was told by a fortune teller not to be a leader. It was my first-year medical school classmate, a Chinese medical student who told me this after reading several lines in my palms, touching the skull of my head and examining my face. It was not my desire to be told about my life by a fortune teller. He just did it voluntarily. I didn't pay for his service either.

He said many other things such as I probably will not get married. If I do marry, it will be in my late age. He said that my first love will be tragic and I will then have a painful time forgetting and letting go of my first love for a long period of time.

He was right about my love life which irritates me. I do not want to believe any words spoken by a fortune teller, especially when I did not even ask for his thoughts. I do not seek advice from palm readers, astrology signs, zodiac predictions, seers, or horoscopes. I don't believe any of them. But I am still single, never been married and my first love passed away tragically.

We were engaged to be married when I completed medical school. And at that time, I was sure to prove the fortune telling is bogus. Dr. Yuri Kim was my first love. He was a first-year resident when I was a third-year medical student. I was doing gynecologic clinical rotation, delivering babies at all hours of the night, attending gynecologic cancer surgeries, and merely just surviving endless work hours in a constant sleep-deprived mode.

Yuri was beside me all the time and took a role of being a mentor voluntarily. I think he felt sorry for me not knowing all the pimping questions from our attending physicians. He helped me to answer questions and avoid embarrassing situations. He pushed me to study harder, mainly because he did not want any Asian medical student, especially Koreans, to receive bad reputations.

At first, I did not like Yuri because he was pushing me so hard to be a perfect medical student and I did not appreciate his high bar of expectations bearing down upon me to be the Perfect Asian Doctor. I was already sick and tired of trying to be a perfect student with a 4.0 GPA, perfect scores on MCAT, a model citizen and doctor because of this silly Asian stereotype image endorsed by parents and most of the Asian communities.

I followed his general directions and recommendations in life because he actually cared for my wellbeing beyond just pushing me to be a perfect Asian doctor. Yuri and I spent many hours together in the hospital even after the gynecologic rotation in my third year. We were dating for more than a year when he was diagnosed with a late stage NK-cell lymphoma originating from his sinus and spreading to multiple sites including his brain, eventually killing him within three months. He could have survived from this illness and lived many more years if he had not ignored his symptoms.

But doctors are the worst patients; he just ignored his symptoms until he could not see from his left eye one day. And by that time, it was too late to get successful treatments. He passed away quickly while he was getting the second of six rounds of chemotherapy treatment. Our engagement never fulfilled and the shattered dream of having our lives together devastated me when I was graduating from medical school.

Yes, my fortune teller was correct about my love life. I have not met any other man I loved as much as Yuri. I scarcely had time to meet people or become romantically involved during my residency, fellowship, and now attending doctor life. And I never forgot and let go of my first love. Strangely, and unfortunately, the fortune teller was right about his prediction of my love life.

Now, about leadership, I wish I had asked the fortune teller why I should not be a leader. Is it because I will be a poor leader or becoming a leader will be detrimental to me? Not knowing the answer to this question is haunting me, especially when I have this wonderful opportunity to become the interim chair for the department of pathology in the large and prestigious Beverly Hills Hospital.

At times, I wonder what exactly defines the leader. I am director of our women's health fellowship and a division head of breast/gynecology, and also cytology chief in the department. Do these positions qualify me as a leader? To be chair of the department definitely seems like a leadership position.

This irritating voice behind my head asks, "Are you sure you can handle this position?"

When I was younger, I thought that I should not be a leader because I would make a terrible leader. Maybe I am not a born leader with great skill sets and I would fall short leading other people. But now, I am thinking maybe I am not such a poor leader per se but the leadership position is not good for me with inherent long hours and troublesome situations which may cause me to have a high blood pressure, compounded by difficult people I deal with, further causing me frustration and unhappiness.

My biggest fear is hurting other people under me, or even ruining the organization due to my inability to be a good leader. The last thing I want to do is take a position of leadership and lead the people in a wrong direction. But as I judge myself through my leadership experiences and leadership style I lived up to this point, I am actually not a bad leader.

My leadership style is not as a traditional charismatic leader, but rather as a transformative and collective team leader. I feel more comfortable being quiet, introverted and not a publicly outspoken person. The real reason why the fortune teller told me not to be a leader was probably for my own sake because taking such a position would surely decrease my life span.

So, why will I accept this position? First of all, I decide not to listen to the fortune teller saying I should not be a leader. I decide to not magnify his voice inside of my head but to take a chance to prove for myself and to others that I can and I will become a good leader. I decide to trust in God who tells me otherwise and I am listening to the voice of the Holy Spirit who tells me that I can do anything and everything with Him who gives me the power to do so.

I tell myself to live one day at a time, not to live in the future, worrying about what will happen if I fail. I also do not want to say to myself later in my life "I should have, I could have, why didn't I?" I will take on this challenge and live day by day with the attitude of learning. Indeed, I love to learn, which gives me more pleasure than anything in the world. I can learn how to be a good and effective leader. I will ask God how to live as a leader and I know He will answer me or show me what to do one day and one moment at a time.

At nights, however, there is a small voice in my head still tormenting me that says, "Who do you think you are? What makes you think you are so special and not to be eventually demoted as was the current chairman? Look around you. You are the only one with colored skin, all other leaders are white, some are Jewish, and you are the only woman in the society of chairmen group in your hospital.

"Chairman is called chairman because men only do it, and you are not a man! There is no such title called chairwoman! You should just quit and live your life in an unassuming way, and peaceful with the general population of being among females as you should. There are reasons why so few women are in the position of leadership. Who do you think you are, fooling yourself?

"You are an introvert who is really shy to be seen by the people. Admit it! All you want to be is invisible and dissipate amongst the crowd. You are really nothing, nobody and insignificant. Just shrink and die or be quiet at least. Or else, you will ruin people's lives and you should have listened to the fortune teller who told you not to be a leader."

I know this is a voice of devil who is tormenting me to despair and self-doubt; a deceiver clothed in the name of reasoning.

When I was young, this devil's voice was more convincing and I often bought into it. My cultural upbringing also was in total agreement that women should be quiet and obedient to men, to the elderly, and even to their own sons. Even though I was born in America, I was taught this by my mother who is a Korean American who could not brush off the traditional Korean values and culture. My church also had the same voice. Women should be quiet, an invisible servant and subservient in the church. To talk back at someone, particularly to more authoritative figures or to men, is seen as the most unattractive and inconceivable thing to do as a woman.

It is my natural tendency to think I should be more accepting of how other people think of me as a woman and not to cause scenes or inconvenience to others. Their opinions of me were more important than my own opinion in defining who I am. I would even care to learn and to hear what they had to say about me.

As I get older, I learn that no one really cares about who I am and who I become. People are generally busy with their lives and never think deeply about others, including me. Their opinions are at a minimum, haphazard and fragmented in knowing who I really am. I should not care about how others think of me. I realize what I feel and how I think of myself is more important than any others' opinions about me. Not only that, but no one even takes time to think about me to begin with.

This understanding is a significant one and gave freedom in the mature age which I am enjoying, a definite benefit of getting older. As long as I am not tangled in the misconception of my own insignificance, the people around me are perfectly comfortable with who I am as a leader, a woman and a person.

I realize what I think, feel and experience are more important than how others think of me. And to work for the reputation or popularity from others is the silliest thing. My life and my time are ticking ruthlessly, and to spend the precious hours to care how others think about me seem futile.

My life should not be given so cheaply for others' sake. In the end, when I am lined up in the heaven to answer the question, "What have you done on earth?" and to answer, "I was worried about my reputations and lived according to others' expectations of how I should live and that's what I have done," will be the most pathetic and tragic answer.

Chapter Two

I am given the opportunity to be interim chair by the new president, Dr. Louis Bernard, who recently joined our hospital a few months ago. The first thing Dr. Bernard does is decisively demote several chairmen from several departments. One of the departments with such misfortune is ours. I am not sure the reasons why our department chairman is removed from his position.

Dr. Bernard's usual methods for demoting the chairmen are first, meet with all faculty members in each department which I thought was a promising idea; then, meet with an individual doctor who might replace the chairman and bestow a temporary title as "Interim Chairman," and then look for the actual replacement from both inside and outside of the institution.

I did not know this was his usual method when he first approached me.

Dr. Bernard arrives at our monthly departmental faculty meeting, so I introduce myself as, "women's health care director with focus on breast, gynecology and cytopathology fields," as one equal to other pathologists. We have a large department with 40 pathologists, 26 residents and 20 fellows, and work within a pathology subspecialty sign-out system. *Subspecialty* means pathologists do not look at all organs at all times but only one or two organ systems, and in my case, my expertise is breast pathology, gynecological pathology and cytopathology.

I cover more diverse specialties than many of my colleagues. Some pathologists are focused on only one organ type. I am the division chief of women's health care. Under my umbrella are six other pathologists who practice the same subspecialties and two women's health fellows and two cytopathology fellows.

I am in charge of generating the quarterly work schedules for myself and six other pathologists. So, my job requires some administrative skills, dealing with other clinicians and hospital staff when it comes to women's health care issues, and interviewing and choosing the women's health fellows and cytopathology fellows each year. I have quarterly meetings with my chairman Dr. Daniel Ross to report updates about any changes or issues in my fields.

Three months after the first faculty meeting with Dr. Bernard, I am called to meet him at his office by his administrative assistant, Dorothy. I have no idea why Dr. Bernard wants to see me, a mid-level person in our department. I arrive without knowing what exactly the meeting is about. I find myself alone in his office for the 45-minute meeting. I look around to see if there will be anyone else coming to join the meeting.

"Have a seat, Sara, and call me Louis," he begins in his French accent.

I sit in front of him on his new sofa, which is low and uncomfortable, without back support. My short body sinks deeper, a disappearing person of small stature. *Is this the place where so many people come to do the politics with him?* He looks at me up and down as I sit uncomfortably. All I can think of is that I should have worn better shoes as he stares at my shoes for a while.

"What can I do for you?" he asks.

That question is weird, comes to mind. "What is this meeting about, Dr. Bernard?" I ask.

"Call me Louis, please."

"Okay, Louis, why did you ask to see me?" I hesitated to call out his first name. I am not familiar with the American tradition or culture to call a respected person like him by calling out his first name.

"Well, I am here to serve you, so you can perform your job better," he says with satisfaction, manifesting he is a humble leader, or at least trying to be a humble leader. I do not answer his question but rather I ask, "What are your goals and directions as president in our institution?"

In short, he wants me to come to work happy every day. In so many words without actually saying exactly the words, I gather Louis is not happy with my chairman Dan, and Louis is looking to see if I fit as a replacement.

"I would like to be loyal to Dan because he hired me."

Suddenly Louis becomes terribly upset, which I do not expect. His voice and demeanor violently oppose my idea of being loyal to Dan.

"What do you mean by being loyal to Dan?" he asks as he looks at me with piercing blue eyes.

I mumble a few words, "He is the one who hired me," and I begin to imagine what happened between Dan and Louis in such a brief time, and how can Louis be so vehemently negative toward Dan and what else will trigger him to become so disgusted?

I soon realize there is no constructive conversation on an honest level with him. I recognize he is seriously thinking about removing Dan from his position and Louis is checking to see if I can step up for the position without really saying any of his thoughts clearly. There is another obvious person in our department who can assume the position, director of research Dr. Margaret Asher. She is a more natural person for the job because she is more heavily involved in administrative duties and is my senior. So, I mention her name but to my surprise, Louis is even more disgusted when I bring up her name.

Cleary, she is not a serious contender. Louis says we need to talk more and suggests we go out to lunch, a two-hour meeting to talk more frankly. He recommends I talk with Mr. Tim Cobalt, our pathology department operations director to discuss what the department should look like in the future. I am surprised to see Tim has such authority to shape our department.

I am very confused after our meeting. He said so many things without actually saying anything specifically. Nothing Louis and I spoke about make any sense. But we talk as if we understand each other perfectly.

Two months pass and finally Dr. Bernard and I meet for a two-hour lunch at a local small Italian restaurant. He orders a pasta dish and I order the same. Louis appears much more relaxed this time and expresses his thoughts without abstract words. He considers our pathology department the center of all medical care and critical for essential patient care and research endeavors.

He tries to describe a vivid picture of what the new pathology department should look like. I ask about the current chairman and the executive research director, and he says Dan as a chairman does not fit his vision because Dan does not listen well and nobody wants to work with him.

Also, the executive research director, Margaret, is highly intelligent but possesses the worst leadership attributes, none he considers respectful. The number one attribute he looks for in a leader is, "Are you nice?" He takes a bite of pasta and says, "Margaret is downright mean and condescending to others with her superiority and blaming attitude."

Louis must have talked extensively with others to obtain these personal attributes about Dan and Margaret because I do not think they actually had many personal encounters or meetings with Louis in such a brief time. People in leadership must talk and gossip among themselves, some true and some not true and it must travel fast.

One thing I am glad to hear is that Louis, the president of the institution, thinks the department of pathology is the center of all departments and thinks our roles are important. The second thing I am pleased to hear is that Louis is looking for a leader who can build a good relationship with others. This includes mutual respect to others, humble and kind, regardless of their status including upper management, lower-level workers and even janitors and others at this service level. Louis will professionally survey all the chairmen and based on their responses and feedback, he "will act accordingly to cover his behind in case he has to fire someone and avoid any lawsuit," he says during our lunch meeting.

This time, Louis is a toned-down version from the very first meeting we had when he asked, "Who do you need to fire?" He must have had a coaching session with human resources personnel. The old style of machoism does not cut it these days to fire doctors.

Louis never really asks me if I can fill the chair position. He never flat out asks me anything or inquires who would be a suitable candidate. The title of interim chair is not discussed, and no candidate is mentioned at lunch. All along, I am thinking he will discuss replacing the chairman and I just presume that Louis is looking to see if I am interested in being the chair without really asking me. It is very awkward for me to sit here and discuss the department in general. Perhaps he is testing me to see if he can work with me.

During our remaining lunch time Louis acquires my personal information such as how large is my family, what did my father and mother do for a living and what are my hobbies. I go along with his casual conversation and ask about his family. The lunch ends after one hour and we each drive back to our offices and continue our usual work.

A few weeks later, I receive the survey via email that Louis mentioned during lunch. Basically, four or five simple, generic questions. How satisfied are you with your chairman? What things does he do that you wish he continues to do? What things do you wish he would stop doing? What things do you wish to see done in the future? Very generic questions with a lot of space to fill in without word limits, so I fill out my opinions knowing what this will be used for. I try to be honest as possible.

There are many attributes that I like about my chairman Dan and he had some areas of improvements he can work on. I am not nasty as others who were surveyed, which I find out later. My chairman Dan soon tells me what his report card looks like. He has average results from the pathologists, and worse scores from hospital operations staff and other departmental chairmen.

Another two weeks pass and Dan is called to Louis's office late on a Friday afternoon. Dan does not know the content or reason for the meeting. We are nearing fiscal year end, so Dan has gathered all the new publications from our faculty and makes a copy of each paper to show off to Louis how well the department is doing academically.

In a rather short meeting, Louis demotes Dan without any reasons. Dan never had a chance to show off all the papers he gathered.

Dan calls me two days later on Sunday when I am attending a conference in San Francisco to advance my knowledge in digital pathology and Artificial Intelligence (AI) capabilities in pathology. Dan is upset and breaks the news to me about his Friday meeting with Louis.

Louis had asked him who would be the most appropriate and best choice for the interim chair role. Dan told him Dr. Sara Choi, followed by vice chair Dr. Stephen Schwartz. He did not recommend his current research director, Margaret, for the position and they mutually agreed.

I am perturbed by this news. Louis has not called me or prepared me for what he was about to do. Yet, I am comforted Louis proceeds with his action without my prior knowledge. I am not trying to take Dan's job and have no premeditated plan. I really did not know anything and feel sorry for Dan who is obviously hurt.

Three days later on Wednesday, the last day of my conference, I still have not heard from Louis. For three days, without an email, phone call or text from Louis, I presume he has another person in mind. Suddenly an email pops up from our operations head Tim, explaining I am requested to make an appointment with Louis by calling Dorothy, Louis's assistant.

I call Dorothy and agree to make the five-hour drive back to LA for a five o'clock meeting tonight with Louis. Surely, I am the second or third person in line, otherwise Louis would have tried hard to contact me sooner.

On the drive down to LA, I call Dr. Stephen Schwartz who tells me Louis had asked him about my leadership style and whether I am a wishy-washy type, or too rigid, or unable to be flexible.

Stephen says he only spoke very favorable things about me to Louis. Stephen also told me Louis has never asked him to take the chair position, and that he would not accept the position even if Louis had asked.

He also warns me Louis is the type of person who cannot handle direct confrontation or blame, and I would have to work around him smoothly and make sure Louis can wiggle out at all times, especially "when push comes to shove" types of situations. Louis cannot handle a straight-arrow style like mine that is honest, and I must learn how to bend around him.

Stephen is very observant, mature and accurate in reading people and I agree with his analysis about Louis.

During my 5:00 p.m. meeting with Louis, he starts by asking me if I want to become interim chair at this time. "No, I will accept a permanent chair, not an interim chair," I say.

"I do not have the power to appoint you as a permanent chair and it needs to go through the committee and the board's approval which will take some time, maybe a year or two and they will need to open and advertise the position nationally." He adds, "If I had the power to do it, I would appoint you in a second but it is not up to me."

Then he asks, "Can you be loyal to me?"

Such a strange question he's asking me. "I will support you and your missions regarding advancing this hospital to be a better place." I avoid answering him.

"But will you be loyal to me?" he asks again, as if I need to pledge allegiance toward him personally, and I answer in a similar way as before. Perhaps Louis is worried about my loyalty toward Dan, which I stated during our first meeting. To me, loyalty comes with firsthand experiences like I had with Dan over time, who not only hired me but treated me with respect and personal care, with genuine interest for my professional advancement.

I look at him directly but do not answer his question, but ask him about the logistics of the announcement, the timeline, my salary, and how to decrease my current functions so I can be able to assume additional responsibilities required for the interim chair job. Louis replies without answering any of my specific questions, but does give me a timeline that I will be assuming the job as of this coming Monday.

I reiterate the importance that I will not assume the job unless I have a fair chance to be the permanent chair. This is extremely important to me because I do not want to do the job as an interim/acting chair with all the administrative stress, knowing I will be pushed around by people all around me, and that I will lose certain medical skills needed if I later must return to the current job that I do well. In the end, going back to my medical pathology job will result in me giving to Louis's new chairman all the towers of accomplishments I established as interim chair.

An interim chair will have to do all the challenging work with little respect or power, and I will not accept such a situation. I must have a fair chance. Louis assures me he will see that it happens. And so, I take the position and we shake hands. I felt obligation to guide the department toward a safe place during this rocky and unstable time.

Louis took a huge risk. What if I said no to his offer? He already made the current chairman resign from the position. He asked nobody but me as of yet. He waited three days after demoting Dan before asking me. He must have so much confidence that I will accept the interim chair position. What a gut he has!

Two days later, an official email from Louis says the current pathology chair has decided to step down effective immediately, and Dr. Sara Choi has accepted the responsibility to be the interim chair. Louis's content of the email mostly congratulates Dan for his work and celebrates his career accomplishments.

I am mentioned in the last paragraph, just stating that I have assumed the job of interim chair.

Dr. Dan Ross had sent an email to everyone a few hours before Louis's email, basically saying that he is retiring from the chairman position and will stay on as a practicing pathologist as one of the faculty members in the department. This arrangement of the announcement was already figured out between Louis and Dan so that Dan does not appear to have the position removed from him and it seems Dan volunteered to step down to protect his dignity. Everyone from the department knows what happened because Dan has never talked to anyone about his desire to step down from the chairman position—it was so sudden. Also, similar things are happening in the other departments; chairmen suddenly stepping down.

Shortly after, I meet with Dan to go over the department finances which are mostly hidden from staff. I discover Dan had considerable money in his control that he distributed to faculty. Money is the power and he had a lot of power as the chairman.

Now, he must disclose the entire departmental assets. As usual, he is straightforward and honest to me, revealing everything he knows and what he has done with the money in the past. I do not agree with how he spends the money, but I always trust him because he is genuinely an honest person.

I feel a heavy burden, my shoulders pressed down. The level of stress makes my stomach tighten up. It is not a joke. I constantly talk to God, whenever and wherever I am, to seek His help. The first day is okay and I decide that is all I can do, live one day at a time and seek God's help at all times. I am comforted that I have my Lord God.

I cannot trust anyone, and no one can be my friend, for I need to be impartial to all. Being a leader is truly a lonely process.

Chapter Three

It takes more than a month for my move into the chairman's office. New office is very large, and a round table that can seat at least six people is several feet in front of my large desk. The most exciting feature is the large windows. Pathology department offices rarely have windows and are usually stuck in the basement near the morgue. There is no reason pathologists should not have window offices because most of us do no autopsy work.

For me, the window office is the most attractive aspect of being the chair. It is my very first window office in 20 years of practice. It is very hectic to move while I am still on service duty, spending most of my time looking at the patients' slides with residents and fellows.

The office staff who were responsible to order bookcases failed to do the job, and all my books and journals are on the floor. I cannot concentrate well enough to do any job. Phones, computers, printer and microscope have to be moved and re-directed. Boxes are everywhere and all the accumulated junk with personal and sentimental value are on my desk and everywhere around the desk, but I have a tough time to toss them out. I am not a hoarder but when things are outside of the drawers or closets it looks messy and I am a person who cannot function well if my desk and office are not tidy.

During this time period I encounter a placenta case from a young mother, age 16, who had a cesarean section delivery due to pre-eclampsia. Pre-eclampsia is a pregnancy induced high blood pressure experienced by a mother, usually in the third trimester. The baby boy's Apgar scores are excellent at birth and he is discharged from the hospital after two days.

The resident and I look through my multi-headed microscope together in this haphazard office and notice everything looks as expected except one section at the corner of the slide of the placenta shows focal areas with many syncytiotrophoblast, intermediate trophoblast and cytotrophoblast proliferations, somewhat unusual for a 37-week gestational placenta.

A possible diagnosis of placental choriocarcinoma comes to mind but it is exceedingly rare to have that diagnosis. I need to attend my very first two-hour chairmen's meeting with Louis, who will be introducing me to the entire group in 10 minutes, and the location is not connected to our building. It usually takes 15 minutes so I need to walk there in a hurry. I am already late for the meeting.

So, I sign out and basically write that the placenta is unremarkable. After all, the focus is tiny and seen only in one of six slides we routinely submit for review for every placenta case.

I run, and soon join Louis's chairmen meeting for the first time, rather breathlessly. Very important people are present. I know their names but not their faces except the surgery department chairman. They are all males. The entire 15 chairmen are men, the president Louis is certainly a man, his chief operating officer (COO) is a man, the chief financial officer (CFO) is a man; and me, the only female in the room.

At the periphery of the room I notice two women, one is a transcriber of the meeting and the other responsible for our refreshments and drinks and she leaves the meeting shortly after it starts. It is intimidating to be among all white-haired men around me but I sit at the table as one of them, leaning in.

I have to move into new territory and must know my function quickly and pretend that I am comfortable in my skin; the only female, Asian American, the youngest and I forgot to mention, the shortest. I am uncomfortable especially with my personality being an introvert.

A minority is (reluctantly) accepted only when it is perceived as an underdog by the majority. And the majority often ask, "Why are you uncomfortable?" and deny the fact that they are biased or racist because "We really are willing to accept other races and genders." But to a person like me, who looks so different from them, feel that if they are truly inclusive, then we would already have more diversity among people in power.

I feel comfortable as an independent contributor, working alone and quietly doing my part. I am not used to speaking in the public, acting smart, fast talking and visible to others. I do not enjoy dealing with conflicts and clashing with people or commanding others what to do. I will avoid conflict at all costs. I am not quick in speaking — forget about humor or witty words. I never joke or enjoy joking in public. I do better in strategizing, thinking and planning to build things or creating something and studying; behind the scenes.

I can tell that I do not fit into this new position by my appearance or my personality and to top it off, I am not a good politician as well.

I feel so out of place.

As far as I can tell, Louis is a skillful politician who is set in his own ways with his leadership. He is not a person I can trust entirely because he can tune me out quickly if I do not follow his direction, as he has done already with Dan. The way he hired me; his avoidance to discuss my new contract as the interim chair, the way he asked me to demote our research director Margaret, and his lack of personal involvement in times of need are all signs to me that I should not trust him. He may spit me out as quickly as he hired me.

He introduces me to everyone at the table, then suddenly says with a smile, "We need more female chairs!" This statement makes me extremely uncomfortable. I respect the fact that Louis realizes I am the only female in the room, but to publicly announce an order to solve a gender issue is unprofessional. His words, tone and gestures imply it will be generous to open the door for a prestigious chairman position and extend offers to lesser qualified women just to fulfill an inclusion policy.

Women are rarely seen at the table of leadership positions such as company CEOs, department chairs or deans of medical schools. This is not because there are not enough smart and intelligent women out there who are more than qualified to do the tasks. Instead, men will not allow women on their team. Particularly in medicine, the structure of being hierarchical like the military with male domination is rampant even in current times.

Somehow, I survive the first meeting as I pretend to follow and understand all the agenda items. Thank God I do not have to talk or present during the meeting. I realize that I must quickly speed up my understanding of all agenda items that pertain to my department. There was no introduction or hand-me-down instructions from Dan, my previous chairman so I need to learn things fast.

Chapter Four

Getting agreement on my compensation contract is a painful ordeal. Louis has offered me less salary than I currently earn as a pathologist, simply because he does not understand our pay structures. He does not care to even learn basic information to provide a decent contract for me.

I work with his academic finance manager and hash it out back and forth. The chair's bonus structure has changed from the previous years and now it is tagged with strings attached based on my performance at the end of the year from three tiered categories, and these categories are never discussed with me personally and are handled through Tim, our operations manager who has never dealt with the chair's bonus.

Tim is absolutely not an appropriate person to handle a physician's salary and bonus, let alone chair of a department. His role is to make sure hospital employees in his area are performing well, and nothing to do with a physician's compensation who works under the separate physician's medical group. Furthermore, the prior chair never had his bonus tied to performance strings. My total compensation of salary *plus* 100% of a potential bonus tied to three performance categories is much less than the prior chair's salary. It is even less than a research director salary.

After much discussion back and forth it is still barely above what I earn as a faculty member doing service work. But I must realize it is just a one-year contract as an interim chair. In the end, I do not really work for the money and I am getting tired and disappointed in the piecemeal process negotiating for money.

No one talks to each other. Most disappointing fact is for six weeks no one has talked to me and Louis lacks interest and effort to make sure I am properly or even respectfully treated. Finally, I initiate an appointment with Louis and the academic finance person, to finalize my compensation package, and they both agree to meet. I hate to talk about money, but I must do it for my sake.

Remarkably, Louis emails me a new negotiated salary after this meeting. He simply went back to the original dollar amount for me to sign even after our meeting I had to initiate. At this point, I do not know who is dropping the ball. Perhaps Louis really thinks I do not deserve to be paid higher for the interim chair position than even Margaret, the research director.

I send a new email. "I am extremely disappointed and very concerned," since he knows I am about to say "screw it" and go back to my existing position and contract. I am not going to let Louis take advantage of me and I am totally fed up and disgusted with his lack of care in writing the compensation as we already discussed and agreed.

Later the same night I receive his revised compensation, an actual letter with a somewhat respectable contract and compensation amount which is slightly better than what we had agreed. The experience is pulling teeth one at a time. Clearly, Louis is busy but, ultimately, he is responsible to check the accuracy of his offer, understand the current compensation system and not depend on the finance person entirely. Of course, there is no indication of his apology.

Anyhow, I am curious to learn who is the actual culprit for all the confusions with my compensation package. Louis had made excuses and mentioned the academic finance person's name, describing her as "somewhat incompetent and careless in the past with other financial matters." But I think It might not be her after all.

During the weekend, I assemble the two large bookcases in my new office. It takes nine hours. I could not wait any longer for the workers to come to my office and do this. I know they might come during the day when I have meetings, or signing out with residents and fellows, or next week or next month when I also have surgery fellows to help train. I cannot have an interruption and make a mistake in our patients' care.

Fuming as I put together the larger-than-my-body bookcases by tightening screws and pounding with a hammer which I brought from home, the bookcases are finally erected, and I lift and put into place all the heavy medical textbooks. I am exhausted physically and frustrated. *What else must I do in order to take care of this department to compensate for inefficiency and incompetence?* I need a tidy place to work efficiently and am known in my department for an immaculately clean office even when I am very busy.

The schedule for the clinical work was done three months ago and I cannot make changes and I do not want to make changes that will add more responsibilities to my colleagues who are confused sufficiently enough with changes in their leadership.

People in my department ask me whether I am happy to have this new position. I find it hard to answer the question. How can I be happy with so many new challenges, learning a new stressful job, unassembled bookcases cluttering my office, organizing my belongings, and working exhausting late hours to create a decent place to function? I still carry 30% of my time designated for clinical work in addition to my role as interim chair. The previous chair only had 10% designated for clinical work. I do not even know what defines success or failure in the new position, I feel like a fish out of water and everyone watches me closely to see if I will survive.

I decide that what I like about my job are three things. My window and spacy office; Tim, the operations manager who truly helps me to function daily in my administrative role; and my personal assistant Veronica, who protects me from chaos. The challenges are many, including different languages in finance, countless abbreviations, and acronyms during meetings when I have no idea what they are talking about, unfamiliar territories and complexities among 2,000 people who are working directly in my department, and people who want more money from me.

People suck up to me, brown nose and try to manipulate with subgroup interests. At times, I feel like I am their Santa Claus. Their quick criticisms and misunderstandings, and unreasonable expectations drain me.

The most painful part of the job is the constant distractions and interruptions. Without my personal assistant Veronica blocking nearly all these distractions with her power, I will lose my sanity. My days fill with doing meaningless and menial things. I feel like a chicken without its head running around. The hours in a day go quickly.

It soon becomes apparent I spend more time with the negative people. The positive and encouraging people are rare to come by. Insecure people try to protect their own interests and need much of my time, and the negative and nasty people are never satisfied no matter what I do or don't do for them require much of my energy.

Constant watchful eyes, always quick to judge and criticize are all around me, seizing the opportunities for verbal attacks and verbal diarrhea. I watch what I say and not say, polite but firm and ready to defend the goals for our department and for Louis. The most stifling part of being interim chair is that I was told simply to keep the lights on. I cannot truly exercise my vision and direction as a leader for the department.

Louis begins a biweekly meeting with me which turns into a monthly meeting, and the main discussion point is always his agenda for the institution: to clone all the cancers. DNA fingerprinting from all cancer patients to receive specific treatments is his goal, I come to realize. The official name he uses is "Personalized Medicine."

His ultimate academic goal from this project is to provide researchers all the data to ask appropriate questions to answer, then publish their findings. Later on, I find out he has more than pure intentions. He has formulated a relationship with several high-tech companies to share the data for his own financial benefit.

Louis also has two or three of his own companies within and outside of our institution who can develop the cocktail chemotherapies based on the unique DNA fingerprinting from each patient's cancer cells under a project named, "Precision Medicine and Personalized Care and Treatment." The theory is good and sound, but it definitely supplies his own financial gain because he is the Principal Investigator for some of the companies who are involved.

The reason he is so interested in having a collegial or perhaps naive chair in the department of pathology is the fact our pathology department has access to the cancer tissue from all our patients. Louis most likely wants to control a naive and obedient chair who will not obstruct his goals in gaining access to the tissue without exposing his personal and financial gain from the processes.

Always behind the picture, Louis will never overtly push his agendas to others, but manipulates his power to have other doctors be the spokespersons for his goals. Some doctors have become company spokespersons for Louis's own companies.

These doctors are from our institution, and some are previously from Louis's former institution, and they most likely have financial deals or perhaps they are being forced to be involved with his work to keep their status, because some of them are departmental chairmen. None of his own companies are public knowledge. A surgeon tells me some of this information in secret and holds his phone screen for me to see a company's website which Louis has not revealed.

This explains many behaviors from Louis as he arranges to meet personally with many workers in my department who handle molecular pathology. Even my physician assistants, tissue bank staff, and IT people meet behind me so he can have infrastructures in place to fit his goals. I generally follow and support the leader's goal if it is more aligned with the integrity, quality, and value in patient care, but his goals are a little ambiguous at most. Is it more about research, or financial interest?

I become more suspicious of his motives. As soon as he develops the infrastructure from our department, he will likely abandon any interest in the department and throw me aside out to the trash, especially if I begin questioning him.

Now I see why the pathology department is essential and central to him. Louis never emphasizes his personal goal during chairmen meetings or any other meetings. No one really knows what he is about and the direction he is moving toward except a few people required to be connected to his needs.

He is very skillful in deceiving others by his presumed genuine care, including families of staff and patients. He is surprisingly warm and personable. He talks the talk and smooths out his path, while his real interest seems hidden and undiscoverable.

I also learn he will soon gain support from a director and designer of chemotherapeutic agents, who is a PhD and works on the research and development of drugs within our institution. I am told she must promise her control to be subsidiary to Louis and "pledge her allegiance to him." It is like we the people under him must kiss the King's signet ring to be around him and work for him. Loyalty, trust, and obedience are the critical attributes to display under Louis. It is hard to believe such leaders act like we live in the era of Caesar Augustus.

Louis likes to micromanage who I appoint and designate for specific departmental functions, which is a surprise. At least Louis likes Tim, the operations manager who is a God-sent person I trust and enjoy working closely with him. Without Tim, nothing is possible. We develop a true friendship by working long hours, side by side together. Tim tells me what he likes about me is that I was not looking to be a leader, the position was given to me without my ambition, and he can see I am able to walk away from the position of power gladly, without much ego. For that reason, paradoxically, he says I am the most effective leader because I am not afraid of anything or anyone including Louis.

What I decide to do more than anything else is listen to people without interrupting them. At times, it is painful to listen to all the negative and whiny complaints, but within such unpleasantly critical voices there are some facts and conditions I need to hear. As a leader, because of the pressure of time and lack thereof, listening to people is a monumental task. Often, people present facts in such a long-winded way, do not get to the point, do not have the whole picture in their mind and they are busy focusing on whining and complaining with their limited knowledge rather than trying to be helpful.

Asking self-centered doctors to be helpful and less selfish may be an impossible demand. I quickly understand that I was one of them just recently because I did the same thing to Dan. It is embarrassing to admit, and I appreciate Dan's patience. I promise myself I will try not to complain about the work to my future boss.

Chapter Five

I barely settle into my new position when I learn second-hand the national search for the pathology department chairman has begun. Louis proclaims there are already more than 10 people who applied for the position from outside the institution, and none internally. I have not seen the ads for this position in any of the official and usual publication sites, neither internally nor externally.

It seems Louis is not going to advertise the position to external public sites, so the search is by no measure a national search. The search is only among his well-connected circle, and other department chairs' words to their pathology friends. This explains why they have only collected around 10–12 applications.

Louis carefully informs me there will be a pathology chair search committee composed of 15 doctors headed by the surgery chairman and that I will have to apply formally by filling out the application including a personal statement as to why I want to be chairman of the department.

Second step will be a formal interview process with all committee members, followed by a one-hour lecture presentation on my academic research interest or papers I have published. Then the committee will select 3–5 top candidates and invite them for a second interview. They will then narrow down to 2–3 candidates. Louis will then choose the top candidate and work with the demands of the top candidate to be matched. If the financial or other demands are too high, then, Louis will contact the second candidate in line and hassle for a cheaper price according to the institutional budgetary restraints.

This is the specific process Louis explains to me.

Louis seems eager and adds, "I will personally help you draft a personal statement and help you get this position." He talks some more and says, "All these processes are merely a formality and, in the end, I will decide who will be the chair of the department." Smiling, he shakes my hand again. Louis says repeatedly I am "doing a great job!" He reminds me of the president Donald Trump who often said how great of a job he was doing, with his two thumbs up. I am glad Louis has confidence in me. I give the job my one hundred percent effort and work long hours, 10–14 hours a day, regularly.

At times, it is fun to be in this position, influencing to solve problems with people, making the path smoother and protecting our department from incorrect or untrue views and preconceptions. I am learning and perfecting the art of listening through this job.

Most people love to hear themselves talk and they get something out of a meeting with me even though all I do is just listen. I also notice that if I am talking, I cannot listen well because my mind is preoccupied with what to say, which distracts my ability to read others.

Most people talk and talk and eventually realize what they need to do for their next step, then thank me for taking time to talk with them. I feel like a psychiatrist and I should charge them to talk with me by the hour. But over time, things accumulate in my heart and I have to let it out to someone.

I often find myself talking to God in the morning quiet time to let go of all the pressures. I cannot talk to anyone about the confidential things people pour out to me. The benefit of listening with patience from my part is that I gain their trust and I have a better chance to express my thoughts next time when I need something from them.

Sometimes I wonder what our world would look like if we talk 50% less. Much more work could be accomplished in silence. One disadvantage of the *Listening style* in leadership is that the very people who are so busy talking and never give me time to speak, later say I had no strong opinions, or was too shy to express them, or they could not read me. Some even misinterpret my listening as agreeing with them.

Listening and agreeing are two different matters. There are indeed rare win-win situations in being a leader.

Chapter Six

Dr. Kline, Obstetrics and Gynecology chairman, calls and wants me to rereview a placenta case I signed out less than two months ago on a 16-year-old patient named Julie Freedman. Her father Martin Freedman is a prominent trial attorney, a good friend of his, whose daughter is now hospitalized with multiple masses in her body and ready to get her CT-guided liver biopsy for a diagnosis.

Dr. Kline wants me to look into the liver biopsy they will soon obtain and make sure I get the specimen and sign it out with special care. "Will do and I will have our liver pathologist read it ASAP," I reply, and the moment I hang up the phone with him I retrieve the previous slides from the patient case and begin to rereview the case.

It is the placenta I had thought about which had more proliferations of trophoblasts. I call the lab to see if they still have the remainder of the placenta. College of American Pathology (CAP) is the national pathology accreditation organization that sets up guidelines and protocols, including the pathology requirement of retaining wet tissue.

In general, two weeks of wet tissue retainment is required after a final report is generated. I know that our policy for retention is longer than this, but it has been a few months since I signed out the case and I do not have confidence that the placental wet tissue is still available in our specimen storage area. Sure enough, the specimen was discarded which means I have no opportunity to further examine the placenta or submit more tissue to confirm or rule out any other diagnoses.

I had once thought and still have some suspicion that I might have missed the diagnosis of placental choriocarcinoma in this case. Gestational choriocarcinoma occurs rarely, one in 40,000 pregnancies and placental choriocarcinoma is the rarest form, estimated to be less than one in a million and it is usually diagnosed in *symptomatic* patients with metastases like this particular case. Both maternal and neonates can have metastases.

Incidental placental choriocarcinoma is only documented in a few case reports published in the entire medical literature since it is so rare. So far, there have been only 32 documented reports in English literature. The majority of placental choriocarcinoma appear as a poorly defined lesion by naked eye and therefore it is difficult to make sections from the diseased areas.

The diagnosis is made only after mother or infant's symptom with metastases and submitting more sections of intervillus necrotic and infarcted areas of placenta. However, intervillus necrosis and placental infarcts are very commonly seen in the normal placenta, so it would be hit-and-miss and difficult to identify with a naked eye where in the placenta to submit.

Microscopically, placental choriocarcinoma shows the trophoblasts distributed as a mantle around villi with partial involvement and transition from normal trophoblast. The surface growth of trophoblasts is seen at the periphery of a central zone of necrotic confluent trophoblast and villi. In this case, however, we only have a tip of the iceberg and shows one edematous and focally necrotic villi with partial trophoblastic proliferation around the periphery and it is easy to miss seeing the lesion. The presentation is also classic, a mother presenting with multiple metastatic lesions of choriocarcinoma a few months after her delivery. I wonder if the baby is symptomatic also.

The next day, I receive the liver biopsy from the same patient and knowing that she already had a possible diagnosis of placental choriocarcinoma, it becomes rather easy to recognize the lesion in the liver. Without this prior knowledge, it would be more challenging to rule out other possible diagnoses such as a hepatocellular carcinoma with giant cell features, for example. I ask the liver pathologist to order the appropriate and confirmatory immunohistochemical stains. The stains are confirmatory.

I call Dr. Kline and tell him what the diagnosis is in the liver and that I rereviewed the placenta and there is a focal area suggestive of placental choriocarcinoma that I might have missed. I explain to Dr. Kline that the baby also needs to be examined for possible metastatic lesions and to have blood drawn from both mom and the baby to test for beta hCG levels.

I also tell him that detecting a placental choriocarcinoma is usually by this current scenario with late stage and multiple metastases. I will send him all the case study reports and literature electronically. He seems appreciative of my service and prompt phone call. He says he will bring the baby to his clinic and examine him also.

I remember the day I signed out the case as I rushed to attend the first chairmen meeting. I regret not holding the case until the next day to study it more thoroughly, or maybe submitting more tissue and reexamining the placenta myself. It is one of those things I wish I can go back in time to redo things. I had a few "only if" times in my professional life and this incident will add to that list.

How could I be so stupid?!

Why did I rush through the case? Dr. Kline said the patient's father is a trial lawyer. I am sure he is a medical malpractice trial lawyer and goes after doctors who make mistakes. What bad luck I had! Why me?

All those helpless regrets and self-pity pour out and make me miserable. And there is nothing else I can do at this point. I will admit all my errors and go from here. I will not make excuses of how I missed it and how others would have missed it or "it's the nature of the disease."

In the eyes of the court, they will not be sympathetic about my personal situation, how busy I was, my office looking like a tornado swept by, my new interim chair role, and arriving late to my first chairmen meeting. The only thing the lawyers will emphasize is the fact that I missed the diagnosis, caused a delay in treatment and that the patient is dying with a treatable disease due to a lesion in her brainstem which was too late to be treated.

Looking at her current medical records, I read about a large necrotic mass in her brainstem which is endangering her life. *They should be treating with radiation therapy and what are they doing with just pushing the chemotherapy?* is my question for the oncologist. But then what do I know about the appropriate treatments; I am just a pathologist. I picture the trial lawyers having a field day with me in court and during depositions. I am doomed.

So far, I am lucky not to be involved in any lawsuit; except one case I was involved in consultation with our dermatopathologist who showed me a nipple lesion in which I provided an opinion. The case was settled, and I was only involved peripherally, but it still took two years of misery.

I am preparing and ready for the patient complaint committee (PCC) to call me, the tissue committee from the hospital to evaluate the situation, the morbidity and mortality (M&M) committee to review the case, and all the lawyer meetings and depositions from our hospital defense and plaintiff sides.

This will take at least one year, if not two or three. The lawsuit case usually drags on many years for reasons I am not sure.

In the meantime, I must focus on being the interim chair, a leader and a pathologist when my mind wanders and worries about what will happen to me.

I know I should think about the patient but self-defense and self-preservation is heavier in my mind than anything else. How nasty will the patient's parents become to torment me? This is what I worry about. Clinicians pointing their fingers at me is a scene I should expect to see. When shit hits the fan, all the doctors point their fingers at each other and not toward themselves.

I already pointed my finger at myself by admitting that I missed the diagnosis of placental choriocarcinoma to Dr. Kline. For now, he said he appreciates my prompt service very politely, but let me see how he reacts when a lawsuit comes his way. All doctors may become bastards without exception as far as I can see.

We, pathologists, pretend to be cordial with surgeons to pass the time during their unpredictable temper tantrums in the operation room (OR). Now in my current time, the proper behaviors and professionalism are emphasized at all times and younger doctors are keenly aware of who is not following the rules. Surgeons are actually "called out" if scissors are thrown in the OR and are disciplined. Thank God for that.

It is understandable why surgeons are demanding of pathologists because the surgeon faces the patient and works on the front lines, not the pathologist who makes the diagnosis behind the scenes. If we make a good and correct diagnosis, they get all the glory and when we make a mistake in the diagnosis, they point the fault to pathologists.

The system does not allow a patient to see and choose their pathologist, unlike how a patient has some choice to select their surgeon. The only time a patient knows who their pathologist is when they get the medical reports and billings. We are indeed unseen doctors who actually make the most critical health care decision for a patient when we name the disease which all treatment options are then based on.

Dr. Kline calls a few days later to inform me that the patient, Julie Freedman, died. Her father is threatening him with a lawsuit and already talking to our hospital's Patient Relations and Grieving personnel. A lawsuit is imminent, with his key complaint being, "A wrongful death due to delay in diagnosis." Dr. Kline sighs, suggesting I talk to the risk manager and let the system do its procedures. My nightmare has come.

I hang up and call our risk manager Gail Waisman, an attorney I know well. She and I had several discussions about our department's involvement in earlier medical lawsuits. These were fortunately not my cases, but I was peripherally involved through our faculty members.

After several phone tags, we finally speak about the case. She already knows about the case from Dr. Kline who had spoken to her recently.

"Dr. Choi, we are only at the initial stage and must prepare for the worst. The best thing is to settle the case at the request of the hospital and hope for the best that the patient's family asks for just a few million dollars. California places a cap on damages in medical malpractice claims of $250,000 according to the Medical Injury Compensation Reform Act, but the patient's father is a trial lawyer, and for sure will wiggle around this reform act and bring us to a jury trial."

The whole incident sucks breath out of my lungs. It feels like the legal system will dry my blood out. I am suffocating with all the consequences and anticipations of what will come in the future. I think to myself I should just quit practicing medicine altogether. I am only a 49-year-old doctor, too young to retire. I am actually in the prime time of my career.

Once the medical legal process begins by a plaintiff filing a lawsuit, no one is allowed to talk about the case in all circumstances. Even though this is the policy, everyone will find out and know the case and will talk behind my back that I made a mistake. It will be embarrassing to face other doctors, both within and outside of my department. They will say the department chair made a mistake in patient care.

What a gossip that will be. Nobody will care to discuss how unusual this case is and that anyone can easily repeat the mistake I made. This is an active medical legal case that prohibits discussion. I will see how effective this policy truly is in the real time.

I have trouble sleeping after speaking with Gail. The next day, my first interview is scheduled for the position of chairman. The interview process is an all-day event, starts at 6:45 a.m. and ends at 5:45 p.m., and possibly an interview dinner afterwards. Preparing my personal statement, I reflect on what I already accomplished in a short period of recent months.

I equalized all the faculty salaries based on their academic rankings, restructured faculty bonuses based on their merit in academic publications, fulfilled more than what Louis expected in my amount of service work (patient cases), successively backfilled my departmental directorship, and more than fulfilled all administrative duties.

Everything about bonuses is now transparent and it is no longer based on the chair's favoritism. I hold regular monthly faculty meetings and inform our team about upper management goals and directions that are discussed in the chairmen's meetings and medical group meetings. I am much more hands-on to resolve daily systemic difficulties faced by our faculty to do their jobs.

Between Tim and I, we are doing our best to discover, implement and find better ways to improve our department by first listening to employees' feedback. Tim repeatedly says how much he enjoys working with me because he gets respect from others, he gets to be at the table because I invite him to most of my meetings, and his voice is being heard and things get done.

I ask myself; do I really enjoy doing the job or am I just fearful of failure? I work as hard as I can. Of course, in my culture, being Asian American, failure is not an option. And therefore, whether I enjoy my job or not is not even the question I will ever ask. In fact, I never actually sat down to evaluate whether I like this or that about my job. I just do the job, work hard and find the best way to expedite outcomes. I do not take time to ask myself, "Do I enjoy doing what I do?" I just run as hard as I can to be a doctor, the best diagnostician, and the best interim chair without reflecting how I got here.

I am busy looking at what is the next thing to accomplish without ever being satisfied with myself because I push myself too hard. So much to do and not enough time. What a nonsense this life is when tomorrow, my life can be taken away. I should enjoy today more, breathe more deeply and smell the roses, even in the midst of a lawsuit.

One encouragement is that Louis gives me a little recognition award and says in public how great a leader I am. I feel satisfied my boss recognizes all my time that I invested in this work. For me, the most fun thing about being a leader is to come up with the ideas and make decisions as if all the team came up with the ideas and decided upon the strategies and all I have to do is step back and let the team get excited about the decisions they think they have made.

Chapter Seven

My chair position interviews seem to go fairly well. Most people already know me well because I am an internal candidate and I receive compliments on my work as interim chair. I am the fifth candidate from a total of seven initial candidates. I do not have a privilege to interview the other candidates because I am a candidate myself, but I can attend each candidate's one-hour lecture to see how they communicate and predict their personalities. Of course, I am not given an opportunity to evaluate the candidates.

In my 30-minute interview with Louis, we talk about many future goals to meet. Louis thinks the oncology and pathology departments are dysfunctional and he first wants to start correcting things in pathology. Louis personally thanks me for my game-changing direction and cooperation to meet his goals which are now becoming institutional goals.

He says only three candidates will be invited for the second interview. He asks why I want this job and I give him a personal reason—to stretch and expand myself to learn new things, including learning about myself, leadership skills, and I want to leave a legacy. Louis states he did not interview all the candidates, except the most recent one from New Jersey, and he will not consider inviting that candidate for a second interview. He seems somewhat disgusted at the candidate's attitude.

A rumor spreads. Louis has been seeing and is interested in another candidate, perhaps his favorable one. In fact, Louis brought this other candidate to his house for dinner which I think is more significant than a 30-minute interview at the office. This candidate is from Houston and was invited by Louis himself to apply for the position, and Louis had tried to hire him for a vacant pathology chairman position at Louis's previous institution a year before Louis recently joined our institution.

Louis has changed his mind and now emphasizes that "research pathology" is now his focus for our department, so this other candidate probably fits very well into meeting Louis's goals. I am more of a clinical and practicing pathologist. Louis appears very tired, yawns several times and stretches many times in my brief interview. I do not appreciate his casual nature toward me during the interview and I feel disrespected. Maybe I am reading too much into it. Maybe Louis is actually comfortable with me to be himself. But I feel and see Louis is now colder and distancing himself from me.

During my one-hour lecture, I find myself fumbling a little due to lack of practice with my PowerPoint slides and everyone sees that I am unfamiliar with my own slides which I made a month ago. I have nightly lack of sleep and no time to practice my own talk. And the ever-present worries of a lawsuit take my mind away from everything.

The outside candidates are each invited to dinner but I am not invited to a dinner. It must be because I am the internal candidate, but I think this is not fair because many aspects can be evaluated during dinnertime when people are less uptight, especially with a glass of wine and food, where people get to know each other in a more personal way, but I am not given that opportunity.

A week later, I hear from Dr. Stephen Schwartz who is on the search committee. I did not make it as one of the top two candidates from the first round. There were two "abstain" votes from women (one from surgery and one from oncology) who decided not to vote. Women's votes are especially important to me because they are outnumbered by men on the search committee. The search committee is also composed primarily of research oncologists, and the reason for that is all pathology chairmen at our institution have always been researchers.

The first top candidate is the man who Louis had invited to his house for dinner. The second candidate is from New Jersey, the man Louis already told me he would not choose.

"The meeting was interesting to say the least," Stephen said. "There are strong opinions of likes and dislikes about this top candidate. Good news for you is that three members voted for you as their top candidate and no one spoke anything negative about you." Stephen says that the committee members are all political and selfish, wanting the new chair of pathology to accommodate their interests which are all different. The entire process is manifesting how dysfunctional our institution really is.

A few days later, Louis tells me that I am selected as one of three candidates who will have a second interview. Only one person is from the list of two candidates chosen by the search committee. The other new candidate is also a woman, definitely not among those chosen by the search committee, so Louis likely added this candidate to create an image that they truly are seriously looking into choosing a woman as the chair. But by the way it looks to me, Louis has decided on the person from Houston, a male, the top candidate from the search committee and also his top candidate.

My regular meetings with Louis become more infrequent and shorter, 40 minutes rather than one full hour. Formerly, he stayed longer because he wanted to talk to me more. Now, he looks down and avoids eye contact. I can feel he wants to distance himself from me. I can tell he has indecisive moments.

It is obvious to me that the other two candidates do not have administrative skills, the experience needed for the job, and they are both associate professors, rather junior, and without impressive records of publication or grants. My skills, qualifications and proven ability to perform in this job appears to make me a much stronger candidate than them. I feel much more qualified than them, a full professor, and on top of that, I am already doing the job well.

Louis surprisingly announces he will make his decision in six weeks. The timing is so aggressive to hold second interviews for all three candidates, get an offer letter out, and then negotiate. It appears Louis has already made a decision and I know it is not me. I feel very used and exploited.

The first time I met with Louis, I told him that I do not want to be an interim chair if I am not going to be the permanent one, and Louis knew that but still used me to carry out what he needs. I have been working so hard and spending all my energy into this job, losing sleep, but in the end, it is just the exercise of futility on my part.

Come to think of it, the decision to let go of my earlier chairman Dan was also not done properly. There was no warning, no chance to improve, and no assessment of his performance with proper time to improve; just Louis's decision that he would not take Dan with him to achieve his goals without clearly saying what are his goals.

Louis has fired or demoted three other chairmen within a brief period of time, less than one year. He lacks communication but is abundantly clear in his actions. He acts like he is king in the old century, with tyranny, a powerful leader without saying the reasons for his actions. Everything has become a guessing game.

He has hired so many new positions for his Precision Medicine goal without involving our department. We in pathology play the most critical role in the goal because all tissues come to us. In my opinion, Louis is very haphazard in his direction, if he had any direction.

There are seven ways to tell if one is a bad leader in my opinion:

1. You expect others to follow rules that you yourself do not follow.
2. You do not keep your word.
3. You do not genuinely admit when you are wrong.
4. You make promises you cannot keep.
5. You want to look good.
6. You criticize others but cannot take criticism yourself.
7. You believe your way is the right and only way.

For the most part, Louis checks off most of these attributes. By far the most striking attribute he demonstrates to me is not keeping his own word, which is the fastest way to lose respect and earn resentment as a leader.

My idea of characteristics for a *good leader* are approachable, humble, selfless, inclusive, good listener, fair, consider all perspectives before any major decision, team builder, work for the better of the group, communication, and non-dominant. These are typically easier to find in women and are not emphasized during the search for our new chairman.

As the title states, institutions like mine look for a *man* who is charismatic, commanding, confident, decisive, forceful, takes charge and always at the center of the table, a loud and deep voice. These are the attributes that this society as a whole are more accustomed to. Most people often confuse confidence with competency. For example, most famous cooks boast they were inspired to cook by their grandmothers (females) but why are there not more women chefs in Michelin-starred restaurants?

Chapter Eight

My second interview is with Louis's boss, our hospital CEO who is not a medical doctor but an accountant by training. He has been with the institution more than three decades. During the interview, the conversation goes something like this after a few pleasantries from each other.

"Tell me about what kind of person you look for as pathology chair? Are you looking for someone who has leadership, or a candidate more focused on research with significant NIH grants like the previous several chairmen from our department, or a well-known clinical pathologist?"

"I am looking for someone who has the leadership quality. The leadership comes from mostly acquired skills and some from inherited skills. You have the latter, the inherited leadership. I observed that you have multiple strengths and one of them is the inclusive quality, bringing the group into a unified team that works together but I have not seen you able to make the tough decisions and plans to serve the organizational needs by letting go of team members who are not on the A-team."

He continues. "There are two components in leadership I'd like the department chairman to have: operations and finances, and regulatory and compliance. The pathology staff needs to be an A-team and have a successful chair in the department. The pathology department chair is the most important chair in our institution, not the surgery or oncology chairs. You could be the chair at this time or next round. I want to see the old culture of pathology department gone," he adds.

I feel he judges me for not firing Dr. Margaret Asher which he and others had wanted done for a long time. I also know he rarely had a chance to know me. Everything he heard about me must be hearsay. I hardly talked to him, not even 15 minutes the entire time I have been working in this institution. Also, he himself never communicated to me that I must fire Margaret to show that I can make a hard decision. *How does he know I lack acquired skills to be a good leader?*

"And how does one get these so-called acquired skills to be a good leader and how do you determine someone has acquired skills or not in 30-minute interviews you have with candidates?" I ask somewhat perplexed.

"Acquired skills come from the experiences from actually doing the leadership jobs."

I wonder what kinds of acquired leadership skills the other two candidates will be able to bring when neither of them had the time or experience in a position to administratively fire someone? They are merely directors on a small scale within their subdivisions without power to hire nor fire.

"So, you judged that I lack this acquired skill because you have not seen me fire some of the faculty members in our department during my interim year?" I choose not to divulge the conversation I had with Louis. He and I had agreed not to focus on negative things like firing someone during a brief time as interim chair and focus on that after I become permanent chair. Perhaps Louis did not talk to him about this decision we mutually agreed upon.

"Yes, that among other things," our CEO states.

"How long have you been doing the job you are doing now?" I ask.

"Well, I have been here in this place for all my professional career, really, and I am the CEO for 20 years now."

"So, do you consider yourself having these inherited and acquired skills to be a good leader?"

"Well, let's put it this way," and chuckling, "I am well experienced in leadership with many years of practice." I can tell he is rather satisfied with himself and his leadership abilities.

"Then, how come you did not fire this faculty of mine when you had a chance and when I was not the interim chair? You have more direct experience with her than I have."

He is flabbergasted with my bluntness as he becomes red in his white face. *Why couldn't he do the dirty job himself when he had his chance?*

I am rather perturbed at the CEO for his hasty judgment on my leadership skills when he lacks simple communication skills to let me know his goals and desires if he was unable to fire one of my faculty members himself. He must have no acquired skills to be a good leader himself because he did not exercise his power to fire when the problems with Margaret were evident to him well before my time as an interim chair.

His face seems frozen for a while. To break this ice and his inability to answer my direct question, I change the topic and decide not to give him more tough time which I enjoy immensely. I literally punched him back and was able to think quickly on my feet. I did not let him bully me by his white male superiority and I let him have a dose of his own medicine.

My next question is rather abrupt and changes the topic.

"Do you think the cancer DNA cloning project is the number one institutional goal as Louis thinks?"

He becomes less flustered and answers, "Yes."

At the end of the interview, we shake hands and as he leaves, "Shall I close the door or would you like it open?" and I reply, "closed, please!" At this point, I realize I must have kicked his balls awfully hard and he probably did not know what kind of guts I really have. He either has to take it and swallow his ego if he is a big enough man or I merely killed my opportunity to become the next chair. I sensed they already decided upon the Houston guy as chairman because the CEO clearly mentioned maybe I could become department chair the next round.

Recently I am told that Louis describes me as a nice Mercedes car and the other candidate from Houston as a Ferrari. At once I say, "Do you know where a Ferrari resides most of the time? In a garage getting fixed, while a nice Mercedes is seen on the highway running." What a disgraceful and distasteful statement this is from Louis. He is not a refined leader for sure.

Another distasteful thing is revealed by one of my faculty who spoke with a surgeon who chairs the search committee. The surgeon spoke badly about me and why I should not be the chair of our department. This is oddly confusing since at the end of my second interview, I had gone to dinner with this search committee chair and other members of the search committee who are from my department. At dinner, this same surgeon repeatedly said "Congratulations!" and shook my hand as if I made the final cut.

Another search committee member told my faculty that the younger male candidate from Houston is being forced to sign a contract, pushed by Louis to close the deal. With this rumor, the whole department reveals their true faces, fangs and nails or genuine sympathy. It is interesting to see and just watch who shows their fangs and nails against me.

It is an ideal time to see who are truly loyal to me and who are my enemies or just opportunists. To be the leader is a lonely process. No one is truthful and honest. Everyone wants something from me.

A hospital operations leader tells me I should be compensated for all the work I have done as the interim chair and for the pain and suffering going through the process, saying, "You should ask for 20-25% of your salary as a separate bonus." I feel this is also strange how men often think so differently from me. Every pain and suffering have monetary price tags.

When I think through things, Louis has a masterful pre-planned game now being played out, and the game started without broadcasting the open position in the typical way of advertising the position and doing a national search, as our institutional policy is written. He also did not respect the search committee's recommendations and instead hand-picked candidates for the second round.

Louis always had a preferred male candidate in mind. He had many earlier encounters with this candidate and had tried to hire this man as chair of the pathology department at Louis's prior institution.

My earlier chairman Dan recommends that I not withdraw my application which I am tempted to do and avoid personal embarrassment of being second choice. "You should just stick around because in my experience, the internal candidate always becomes the chair. Louis's first choice may not work out during negotiations. The candidate may request extraordinary demands of finances, laboratory space and added lab staff with enormous fringe benefits, and expenses to move his entire family and maybe other staff."

Dan feels somewhat responsible for me as I go through the painful processes. He encourages me to stay put till the very end to see what will happen. "It is not over until the fat lady sings in the opera," he says.

Six weeks pass, and the deadline Louis had announced to make his decision is well past. In another meeting with Louis, he mentions the chair of the search committee is making a new list of names for the chairman position. He implies that I might not be number one on the list, but his nervousness tells me he may be afraid I might quit my interim chair role.

"You are under the microscope because you are an internal candidate, and it is not fair because the outside candidates will not have the same opportunity for criticisms." He continues and says, "If you do not get any criticisms, then, you're not really doing the job."

Louis tells me how impressed he is that I am doing a "superb job in such a dysfunctional department," and complements me for maturing into the position and how much he appreciates me for doing the pathology service work on top of already demanding job as the chair. Yet his delay to announce a new chairman for the pathology department clearly shows I am definitely not his first choice.

As Louis continues to speak, he clearly fears I might just step down as the interim chair and leave the chair position in limbo. His statements are unwise as the leader of a large organization. He is either too bluntly honest and naive, or stupid. Most physicians, like me, do their jobs because they are self-motivated with great responsibility and accountability, not because a fear of reputation.

Another sign I am not the top candidate occurs as I try to fill a vacant position and hire a faculty member and am told that new hiring should be stopped until the permanent chair is appointed. A clear and disappointing sign that I am not their choice.

By this time, I had already decided I will just finish a one-year term of being the interim chair, or when they announce the new chair, whichever comes first, and then leave the institution.

First time I mention this is to Stephen who has very much supported me. Whether Louis has to go back to his drawing board to start a new search if the top candidate decides not to join us is not really my issue. I have decided to leave.

Also, it is too late for Louis to come back to me with a job offer even if he begs me to take the chair job, although the thought of him begging me as I walk away from him is a pleasant one to imagine. My decision to leave is because of Louis, whom I no longer trust. It is usually the boss and not the institution when the employee leaves.

A couple more months pass, and it is now about five months past the deadline Louis had set to hire a new chair. News spreads that new search committee members are being assembled for selecting the chair of pathology, and days later faculty members are discussing the top candidate from Houston may not arrive until a couple of years from now.

The candidate probably thinks there are hidden agendas and is feeling forced to sign a contract in a hurry, especially since he is discouraged to meet with all the faculty members in our department. He is smart to demand that he meet with at least a few. When I volunteer to meet with the Houston candidate, Louis adamantly refuses. I am not going to discourage the candidate not to come, obviously. Anyhow, Louis denies the meeting.

By this time, praises about me are spoken to hospital leaders from many people in various hospital departments, and from many within the operations staff of how well I am doing as the interim chair. This appears to be a well-known fact. People are expecting the announcement very soon. But as Louis takes his time and months pass, people question Louis's ability to make his decision. His ability is questioned especially since he openly said he wants to hire more women chairs, and his own deadline to appoint the pathology chair is well past.

Louis becomes a less trustworthy leader and he gets smaller as each day passes. Even a recruiter who organizes the interviews and hiring process personally reprimands Louis, saying, "You are not treating Dr. Choi with respect, and you are not sincere." She even tries to put some sense into Louis, risking her own job.

Louis must think everyone else is stupid not to know and realize what is happening. He just buries his head into the sand, hopes for the best that his top candidate will just sign the contract. But when I ask him directly whether he has offered a position to the other candidate, he flat out denies. He looks directly at me and says, "It will be either you or the Houston candidate; in fact, a 50/50 chance at this point and I have not decided yet." He adamantly denies a fact the job was offered to the other candidate.

I do not talk about my situation nor take part in gossips among our department.

Most people often side with a victim and some people treat me with more respect at this point. Even my usually contentious faculty become more supportive of my quiet leadership.

I show up every day and stand where I need to stand and perform a daily job with all my strength. It takes much courage to just show up and do the work. I recognize watchful eyes all around me. People around me say if there is any intelligence left in Louis, he should do whatever is necessary to retain me because I am way too talented. It is indeed hard to work as hard as I do because the circumstances are demotivating and demoralizing.

Chapter Nine

Another three weeks pass and I receive a confusing email message from Louis. He writes that he has not made a decision to name the final candidate and he is gathering information to get a sense for the items needed by me and the department.

This is yet another, different process from what he said before. His initial plan was to have his number one candidate chosen, and then, work on the negotiation. If the candidate's demands are too high for our institution to meet, then, he will go down the list to the second candidate. Louis either changed his tactic and changed his mind or he is forgetful, showing a sign of early dementia.

I do not answer him back.

I choose to meet him during our next 1:1 meeting and tell him I am very confused. First, the whole department is expecting that his first-choice candidate from Houston will be the next chairman. The candidate already told many of the faculty that it is up to him to decide to come and the decision is entirely his. This means Louis gave him a job offer, at least verbally.

Louis adamantly denies giving him the job offer, either verbal or written in format. Louis is asking the same items from the other candidate as he is asking me. He will then take these two lists from both candidates, bring them to the hospital CEO and make a final decision.

I sense there must be a problem with the first-choice candidate making a decision, maybe it is his wife who is not too keen on moving. Louis seems to be in this awkward and ambiguous time, waiting for the decision from the other candidate and his wife, and Louis must have calculated the odds are not in favor to have his first choice.

"Louis, I will be totally fine if the other candidate comes and I will even help the new chair successfully formulate a list of things we need in our department, since he is an outsider and may not know what we need."

"Sara, I really appreciate your mature attitude."

"Louis, I just need your honesty and clarity."

Louis is impressive in his efforts to persuade me that I have a shot at this, and even offers to meet with his operations people to work on coming up with the list of future departmental needs. If I read him correctly, he even prefers me at this time, and provides me early guidance that our research lab can be expanded into a multi-million-dollar facility. Therefore, I would need to hire several faculty members to bridge academic and research endeavors.

He asks me to include in my list the following items: My desirable salary, the number of new faculty needed along with the bridging faculty, dollar amounts needed for enhancing the department, new equipment, and to include the new building we will need for the future. It will be no problem making the list because I made it when I applied for the position. I know exactly what I will need to be successful, and the amount is not cheap.

But I am not going to give the list to him because I already decided I am no longer interested in pursuing the position. I do not tell him that at this time, however. I am seeing how things will roll in the near future. I will be a spectator and see how things display in front of me as though I am not even involved emotionally and personally.

My emotion is detached from the whole thing and I am not hurt anymore. The only thing I notice about my mood is that whenever there are activities or talks about me not getting the job as chair, my strength and motivation to do the job for the day decreases significantly, as if all my energy escapes from my body. I cannot understand why I am so down, because I already gave up on the idea to be appointed as the chair.

The main reason I decide not to take the job is that I do not trust Louis as a leader. Maybe the degree of honesty and transparency I ask of him is not realistic, but I will not trust someone who is not able to talk straight and always makes a spot to wiggle out, who pushes someone under the bus when push comes to shove, a true political figure who does not even recognize how deceitful he has become.

His lack of leadership shows no clarity in his goals, lack of transparency and integrity, and this becomes truly clear to me and I do not want to work under him. I would rather eat less and have peace of mind. One thing a leader cannot afford to lose is their integrity. This is applicable even today regardless how modern the time we live in. Human dignity and integrity are the most important attributes as a leader to me.

Normal days are good to have, as ignorance is a bliss. A normal day is filled with many issues in the department. Clinicians complain about the turn-around-time of pathology reports, or someone is not making things clear in their diagnosis, outside experts differ in opinions that will alter treatment options, someone is not behaving professionally, problems with some of the division directors, internal fighting among faculty and staff, others file official complaints, another pathologist complains about the work schedule saying how unfair it is, someone asks for time off suddenly, someone calls in sick, someone retiring and requests to arrange departmental parties, some equipment malfunctions which shuts down parts of our lab testing, and so on and so forth.

I work closely with the operations manager Tim, who repeatedly says I am an excellent and impressive leader. The respect and awe from him are obvious. He says I lead quietly, effectively and maintain integrity at all times, and never disrespectful to anyone.

I learn that it does not take magic to be a good leader. It takes time, engagement, listening and supporting with firm and clear expectations. What I enjoy is this chance to know who I really am, what I am capable of, how I handle stressful situations, how people follow me even though some may have opposite opinions or different points of view, how I deal with people and their titles above me and below me, and what kind of leader I have become.

This is the first time a woman is chair of our department in 75 years of history and albeit it is just an interim position, I am happy to break the tradition of having all males as leaders. Not only a first woman but the very first Asian American race to be at the top position. Previous chairmen were all white males with white hair.

Chapter Ten

Louis's deadline to hire a chair is now way in the past. I open a letter Louis has mailed me. Louis writes, "I have decided on a new focus in hiring the next chairman and will be looking for someone who has a national recognition in molecular research pathology."

The shift has moved again. I am speechless and beyond disgust. There was a rumor a new search might be possible, but Louis had denied that adamantly to me.

"Why would I do that when I have two strong candidates?" said Louis. "It will be either you or the other candidate who will become the chair." He definitely backpedals from his own promises and decisions. I feel that I am thrown into the trash after all the goods are sucked out of me. The letter began to destroy what little self-confidence I have left and it erodes all my pride in my own work during the last nine months. This is a total slap in my face. I feel naked and being utterly destroyed and defeated in self-preservation of my value. My inner voice of, "Who do you think you are?" is tormenting me again.

The flip side is that finally, Louis is showing his intention clearly. In my next meeting with him, I tell him that he is making a big mistake and he will regret this decision.

"You misled me so I would take the interim chair position from the very beginning, and you never intended to hire me. I am disappointed that you never nationally advertised the position and did not follow our institution's policy in hiring a critical position such as department chairman. I feel discrimination of being a woman especially when you yourself broadcasted that you want to hire more women chairs."

Louis immediately blames the chair of the search committee for not following the proper hiring processes. And once again, I lose more respect toward Louis as he blames someone else and finds fault and shifts the responsibility. This reinforces why I should not work for such a person. Calmly I look directly at him as I think whether I should continue the job as interim chair. I feel in full control over the conversation, putting him in a position to be quiet and humble in front of me.

He even promises to find me another leadership position in our institution if I end up not becoming the permanent chair. I no longer believe any promises from him. I am shocked how he cannot motivate or retain his people and how in the world did he become a president? *He does not deserve to have a leader like me.*

Finally, I ask him, "What more should I do for the institution?"

"You are doing a great job," Louise says.

I did my best but my best is not enough for him. I am done and I am exhausted. My pride, my worth and values will not be defined by the limitation he sets before me. I will not be defined by what other people say what I can do or who I am but I will be defined by myself and God who created me.

To buy some time to exit, I ask Louis to compensate me for the loss in reputation of my name. He says he will work on it to make sure the amount will be attractive to me thinking that I will continue the interim chair job.

Now, I am misleading him and will let him chase around for things to work on while I look into other possibilities. I had a full intention to quit the interim chair job at the end of the year, if not exit altogether. I never work for the money but Louis does not need to know that.

I set up a meeting at a law firm with the intention of suing Louis and the institution for discrimination based on gender and race. These are very skillful lawyers who have represented both employees' and employers' sides. Some of the lawyers encourage me to pursue filing a lawsuit against Louis and the institution. They inform me our institution had multiple lawsuits from people like me and their firm has won settlements with good results.

The lawyers have read my diary books where I documented details of events ever since I began the interim chair job. They are impressed with the clear documentations and see the opportunity to pursue a case.

Amazingly, pain and suffering in discrimination cases have equated with monetary price tags in this country. The battles may take several years to prove the accuracy of my diary but the result will be a handsome millions of dollars in the settlement to live comfortably without working. I spend another few days and sleepless nights contemplating whether to pursue the lawsuit or not.

In the meantime, my former chairman Dan comes to visit me and says that he called the Houston candidate to ask him whether he is coming or not. Louis told the candidate not to talk about this and so he declined to answer. But with so many words, he implied without saying the words, he is not coming, and the reason is that he felt uncomfortable because he thinks everyone is hiding something.

Again, the same comment spoken by the psychiatry department chair candidate, who also has decided not to come.

Everything from Louis is so secretive, non-transparent and non-communicative so that he can orchestrate his plots.

To my surprise, Dan explains this is how the hospital CEO actually works, the boss of Louis; hiring consultants and sending surveys to plot and plan the future without talking to the actual persons involved or others in the department. Recently, the institution hired a consultant company for planning large scientific research initiatives and the consultants met with me twice, one hour each time. I met them without much thought they might influence Louis and our CEO's decision on who to hire as the chair in our department.

Dan speculates that Louis may not have a plot against me or ever had any intention not to hire me as the chair but may have been heavily influenced by the CEO and the consulting company's opinions. My interview with the CEO in which I told him maybe he has not learned how to be a good leader with acquired skills even though he was in that position for more than two decades probably backfired on me. I thought he was bigger than that as a man and a leader, but unfortunately, I must have fractured his fragile ego.

The consultant company does not know the holistic picture of what the department chair is required to do, and likely focuses only on the research part. I can see that if research is their main focus, a chair must have molecular research pathology expertise and the consultants are unaware of the other 90% of duties the chair of the department must oversee.

I ask Louis to come to our department faculty meeting to personally announce his new plan to search for a chairman from a fresh deck. My intention is to reveal who Louis really is, someone who changes his mind constantly, not treating me with dignity I deserve, sets his own dates he cannot deliver and how indecisive he is. Louis's reputation is murky to say the least.

Louis agrees to attend our faculty meeting and update us on the hiring plans. Louis arrives at our meeting and during his first sentence blames the search committee chair for the confusion of the entire process.

As he speaks, I promise myself never to become the chair of a search committee of any department because Louis pushes the envelope to others when he is in a sticky situation and never rolls up his sleeves to do the dirty jobs. He forgets that all our faculty and entire staff in the department know his intentions and exactly what happened.

One of the faculty members asks Louis a tough question. "Why can we not meet the chair candidates. Isn't it important that we meet and have our voice?" Louise fumbles a bit and says perhaps the recruiting personnel failed to make appointments. He is so clearly in denial to think he looks good at all times. Even Veronica, my admin assistant looks at me during the meeting, flabbergasted as she takes the meeting minutes and I wink at her.

Some of my faculty ask me why I allow humiliation of getting rejected in public. But from my perspective, Louis is humiliated, not me. I reveal his true identity when Louis says, "The chair of the search committee did a poor job communicating," pushing the committee chair under the bus in front of all of us in response to faculty members who ask him why they were not able to interview or even see the chair candidates.

Louis is like "Teflon," nothing sticks; all the negative aspects are due to someone else's fault and all the positives, he takes the credit. I want to show this part of him to my faculty in bright daylight so that no one will fault me when I exit this place. Everyone will understand my point of view, perhaps not now but later in time.

The atmosphere during the faculty meeting is hostile but Louis does not understand he is not among his friends. He asks me later, "How did I do?" This question says it all. How insensitive he has become when he is trampling all over me and not caring how I feel. All he wanted from me was to keep the interim chair position filled until he finds someone else. During his shopping and looking period, I maintained the stability of the department and received a little more money which Louis poured out from a little generosity.

He must be unable to self-reflect, which confirms the theory many leaders are narcissistic and have a trait of being psychopath, inability to feel remorse toward others and a sense of superiority.

After the meeting, expected chaos follows as most staff are surprised to find out the Houston candidate is not coming, and ask why I embarrassed myself in public and accepted such a blow of rejection. Mostly, faculty want to know what will happen to them individually. No one really cares how I must feel or come to see me or offer consolation. This reveals the reality people care only for their own interests and how things will affect them.

There are, indeed, no trusted friends when you are a leader. I never expect anyone to come and be my friend at this time. If I were them, I would be uncomfortable and not know what to say to me.

The next few days, I only tell a few people I will not be interim chair by the end of the year. I do this because there are a number of things that require official name changes and which will take a few months in licensing the laboratories.

Specifically, I ask Margaret to be the medical director because she is the most qualified to handle it and she wanted to be the medical director for the longest time. She has some personality difficulties but her competency is not an issue to be a medical director. No one questions her intelligence and competence.

I often felt bad no one has confronted her with the truth, mainly how she can improve her behaviors with others. She is one of those people who never learned to apologize because she is always right. Someone nicknamed her *Pit Bull* because they feel she is vicious, bitter, seldom gentle or forgiving.

At times, I felt sorry for her. She does not know how others feel about her, both upper management and even her own staff. She has a condescending leadership style with a superiority attitude and bullies others with her power. She seems sensitive enough to know the negative effects of her behaviors but she cannot control herself because things not getting done correctly are frustrating.

To her, things are either right or wrong. I quickly learned that in our business, it is not about right or wrong but how can we improve things by doing our best together and empowering others to do their job better. This is the best thing a leader can do. To point out what the staff did wrong and pounding on it is demotivating.

I decide to speak with Margaret about specific things that she can improve upon during the annual review session. I have rated her at the status of *Satisfactory Performance*, not *Excellent* as she presumes to deserve. It should take only 30-45 minutes, but she extends the meeting to more than an hour, which is exhausting and unpleasant. She argues every point that I make and disagrees with all my evaluations and feedback.

The status of *Satisfactory Performance* is not connected to her bonus amount at all, and I do not change my mind, regardless of her arguments back to me. She marches out upset and comes back to my office in two hours. She has "taken a walk around the campus to calm herself down," she explains. Margaret is relentless and persistent in her opinions about herself, unable to self-reflect and not able to receive criticism.

Typically, people think more highly of themselves and upgrade their performances. I am wondering if I am one of them. I listen to her, but do not change the status from *Satisfactory* to *Excellent*. I must be the first and only person to deal with her in honesty. No one had courage to tell her, which is sad. She could be a very decent and competent leader if she controls her mood and learns how to talk to others more professionally. I always feel sad when I think about Margaret because many people including Dan, the previous chair and myself, may have been demoted because of our reluctance to fire her as upper management wanted us to do.

It is much harder to deal with Margaret as a person and go through the process of writing her up in a stepwise fashion and provide her a chance to improve within a given time than just firing her or not extending her annual contract without providing her the reasons. There is a policy in our institution of "letting a doctor go" without cause and giving the doctor 90 days of pay, but that to me is not a decent thing to do to a human and physician colleague who really works hard to enhance our institution and gives 100% of herself during her career.

I realize once again how hard it is to fire someone. Hiring is easy and sometimes pleasant but firing takes so much negative energy. A threat of wrongful firing of a doctor is always behind my thinking and a lawsuit might take years to get resolved or settled. Another most distressing thing about being a leader is that I cannot talk about things with 100% clarity because there are so many components to protect, including myself and the institution. Lack of communication and clarity from the leader are criticisms we leaders often get, but by necessity we sometimes must be evasive, and it may not necessarily reflect our true desires.

Chapter Eleven

All these things are on top of complex legal activities I have been facing on the case involving the 16-year-old girl. Beginning three months ago, I undergo painful depositions with both hospital and plaintiff lawyers. Even our own hospital lawyers look at me with judgmental eyes. I can tell in their heart of hearts they ask, *How could you miss the diagnosis and kill a young girl?*

It does not matter how difficult this diagnosis is to make. I am guilty and they judged me already. All the law cares about is the negative outcome, the emotional aspects of the loss, exaggerated by the motivation of monetary gain.

This notion of *somebody has to pay for the wrong*, even if it is done unintentionally, accidentally, and accompanied by a specific price tag is an uncomfortable concept. The court of law does not care what is right or wrong but in a malpractice lawsuit, the judgment is based on the ability of the plaintiff to convince the jury that his or her injury is *more likely than not* the result of the defendant's negligence.

This standard is satisfied when the plaintiff can demonstrate a 51% or higher chance that the harm would not have taken place, but for the defendant's actions or lack thereof. The 51% is determined by *community doctors* who could make the correct diagnosis in the same scenario and situation in their standard community practice. This means 49% of the time, other so-called competent doctors can make the same mistake.

The plaintiff lawyers must demonstrate the injury was actually caused by the medical professional.

The concept of right or wrong is more like 100% versus 0% (all or none) in medicine. We need to be correct 100% of the time. It is like hitting the baseball for a homerun 100% of the time whether the ball is a strike, a curve ball, high or low, we need a homerun. There are so many difficult cases in medical practices. In fact, most cases are not straightforward. Pathologists are in the field of making the diagnosis which makes other clinicians react accordingly, based on the name of the disease we provide; indeed, a high stakes job.

I make no excuses on this case and admit my mistake at the very beginning. One good thing I learn later is that the baby boy did not have any signs of disease. Thank God for that. Because I do not deny my mistake, no other doctors are found to have faults.

Almost all doctors who touched this patient are involved in this case and required to give depositions which take tremendous time and sleepless nights with anxieties. I have not seen any doctor who actually enjoys doing a deposition. Doctors are generally not confrontational and avoid conflicts at all cost.

The plaintiff's attorneys make me feel like a piece of trash. They have a fun time making me feel small. They hired an expert in placental pathology from Boston who "lives and dies" practicing in only one field, Placenta. He wrote a textbook in this field and recently looked at my slides, saying I missed a slam-dunk diagnosis. This expert added many nasty remarks, which I discover during the reading of his deposition including, "She must be a novice and a naïve pathologist to make such an obvious mistake."

Such a hurtful remark against another pathologist to make a few more dollars in an academic setting with an ivory tower mentality. This expert only looks at placenta cases day in and day out and has no competency in any other field in pathology. How boring the life can be if I had to look at only the placentas!

So much for the definition of *standard practice*. It is supposed to be the *community practice* standard — not an academic placental pathologist who only looks at the placentas and wrote a textbook on the topic.

I feel sorry for those experts who are also motivated by the monetary rewards to find faults and blame other pathology colleagues. The process of pathology slide review is so unfair. These medical-legal slides come to an expert with a red tag saying this is a "special case."

No cases in routine pathology offices arrive with a red tag during non-stop busy days of their practices. Hundreds of cases arrive with multiple flats, each flat having 20 slides, in non-descript ways while the pathologist is bombarded with constant interruptions of phone calls, frozen section calls requiring immediate attention from operating rooms, teaching the residents and fellows, signing out and looking at cases as emails pop up that require immediate answers, people walking into the office to request urgent answers, timely human biological needs of visiting a bathroom or the cafeteria.

Most of the time, my bladder is uncomfortably distended which exaggerates all urgent matters as more urgent. I tell myself *be human* and go to the bathroom and eat food for nourishment because my biological needs are the last thing I have time to deal with. To focus on every slide, every case with full attention so that I make a correct diagnosis (to hit the homerun 100%) is exhausting.

Coffee becomes necessary commodity to serve the patients well. And cold temperature (in my case 68 degrees Fahrenheit) in my office is necessary to make my mental status utmost acuity. Most people who walk into my office complain how cold it is, so they circulate crucial information among themselves to make sure they wear a sweater when they need to see Dr. Choi for more than 10 minutes.

My fingers are freezing and I shiver at the end of the day, but this is what I do to serve my patients. I never intend to make a mistake. Mistake is a disaster! I practice the Hippocratic law "do no harm" to all my patients. But at times, I do make certain mistakes, mostly spelling or grammar mistakes in my reports and I am somewhat relieved these are not life and death type of mistakes.

Forgiving oneself is the hardest thing to do. Humiliations I face by lawyers are nothing when compared to my own torments and rebuke. My mentors had told me that if I do not make any mistake, that means I am not practicing medicine.

Medical practice is named *practice* because this is what we do. We must learn from our mistakes and keep practicing to become a better doctor. The only way we escape making any mistake is not to practice medicine at all.

Also, I do not emphasize or give sufficient credit for 99.999% correct diagnoses I rendered over my 20 years of practice. Instead, I focus on one incident where I made a mistake because of the lawsuit which focuses and magnifies that incident only.

And with my luck, that case had to be with Dr. Kline's friend, who happens to be one of the most prominent medical-legal trial lawyers in town. My only encouragement comes from the defendant expert in placenta pathology who is equally famous in Boston. "This diagnosis is extremely difficult and rare, with most cases of placental choriocarcinoma are only diagnosed when either the mother and/or baby manifest clinical symptoms at a later time, a signal for the pathologist to go back and reexamine the placenta."

The defendant's expert stated, "More than 51% of the community pathologists will certainly miss the placental choriocarcinoma diagnosis from the initial slide examination, and therefore, this case is not a slam dunk case of negligence." The hospital (defendant) had a second expert placenta pathologist review the case and a similar comment is reported, adding, "The choriocarcinoma may have been originated from uterus, and not placenta after the delivery. The fact that the patient had bleeding symptoms for months supports this argument."

My hospital lawyers tell me I should not have admitted my mistake at the beginning, even saying "No doctor should apologize to patients who accuse them of making a mistake because the court of law will decide whether it is a mistake or not." Since I already claimed that I did make a mistake, it will be much more difficult for them to fight the case for me.

My lawyers also criticize my decision that the patient should not pay for all the pathology services including the placenta and the liver biopsy charges. Because of this act, it appears to the public that I was admitting my mistakes by canceling the hospital charges on the pathology side. At the time of the financial incident, I had decided to remove the pathology billing charges because I was merely following our hospital patient liaison's recommendation not to charge the patient.

The lawyer's argument is that removal of charges must go through the proper hospital policies and channels, especially if the case becomes a legal matter as a medical lawsuit. But at the time, there was no medical lawsuit filed.

The hospital medical-legal committee accentuates my embarrassment when I present the case in front of 15-18 diverse medical field doctors, all colleagues of mine. After my presentation, I am asked to walk out so that they can discuss the case and anonymously vote whether the case should be settled or fought in court.

They look for the odds of winning the case to decrease monetary damages and protect the image of the institution. No one looks at the actual doctor's case, reputation, or image, right or wrong again, and simply discuss the probability of winning in terms of a dollar amount and damage control.

This presentation is in addition to a quarterly morbidity and mortality meeting where any doctors, medical students or nurses can come and listen and hash out their opinions in public. It would be more tolerable if one of the rookie doctors had made a mistake and presented the case, but as the interim chair of the department presenting my own mistake it is even more embarrassing.

The point of all these open discussions is to learn from the mistakes of each other.

Due to our efficient staff who organize the morbidity and mortality meetings, I cannot escape my duty to present the case before the lawsuit is filed. Once the lawsuit is filed, the case cannot be discussed in public and would therefore not be presented in a morbidity and mortality meeting.

During all these processes, I have many sleepless nights. I begin taking sleeping pills to just function the next day. I sleep only 2–3 hours, constantly interrupted at nights with anxieties and turmoil in my heart. No sleeping pills can take over my stormy mind at nights.

Lack of sleep is definitely affecting my acuity at work. I dread the service work which requires my accuracy at 100%. I feel like I am shortening my life span, dealing with crushing pressure of the lawsuit, and playing the games with upper management. I am unable to answer my own questions of why I do this to myself.

This reminds me why doctors are the highest level of professionals to commit suicides. The demands to be a perfect doctor who never makes a mistake is an impossible task and yet the society and even the doctors themselves buy into this nonsense and unachievable goals to be superhumans or gods. I do not understand my own motivation to tolerate my circumstances and I need to be more sensible and forgive myself, to be just a human. Fear of failure should not be the only goal in life.

I only want this lawsuit to be over with, whatever that might be, either settlement or in court with the jury trial. I merely hang on to my dear life and try to do a decent job as an interim chair, play the politics with the dishonest and disgusting people who have no decency of being honest, all as I hold turmoil in my heart of losing one of my patients with my error in diagnosis.

My worst part is I have no person I can talk to, nobody to console with or get advice. The medical-legal issue cannot be discussed with anyone because it is the law. I cannot talk about the case while the case is active.

The political game Louis set into motion is just too complex to even start explaining to family or friends outside of work. It is just too much burden, and all I wish to do is disappear from the face of the earth. I only cry out to my God, who is mostly silent. I understand why I should not be a leader. It is not because I would be a poor leader but the title of leader would suffocate and slowly kill me. Even so, I am glad I am at least not harmful to others while being a leader.

Chapter Twelve

I need to speak with Gail Waisman again and call for an appointment. As our hospital risk manager for 20 years and an attorney herself, she is well experienced with the hospital and legal systems. Gail is described as a no-nonsense straight talker, strict and uptight in personality. I never saw her smile. Why would she smile at work since she deals with so many conflicts, bad outcomes, angry people, both patients and lawyers always showing the worst behaviors?

"Most malpractice cases never make it to the courtroom," Gail says, "and only 7% get to the point of a jury trial. The outcome is in favor of the plaintiff in 20% of those cases, which are one of five trial cases. The average waiting time for the patient is 16.5 months to file a lawsuit and another 27.5 months to reach resolution, a total of 3.5 years.

"But in this case, it took one week to file a lawsuit and the resolution most likely will be much sooner since the preliminary hearing in the court is scheduled only three months after the lawsuit was filed. This is a record fast time to expedite a lawsuit case, most likely because the attorney on the plaintiff side is Freedman himself, a senior partner and an owner of Grey, Zemke and Freedman LLC."

"They are very well-known medical malpractice trial attorneys, perhaps the best in town, maybe the whole state of California. The firm is powerful and pride themselves as *Earth Shakers*. These attorneys, especially senior partners, have private jets when they travel around the country and the globe. There is a total of 10 trial attorneys dispersed for this particular case, all incredibly known for their aggressiveness and this team is nicknamed *Shark*. Jeffrey Grey is a senior partner, one of the owners and known to make even male doctors cry during depositions and trials.

"They were involved in a previous case from our hospital only a year ago, and our hospital settled with an undisclosed amount, you know I cannot talk about the amount."

She cringes and continues, "After the lawsuit has been filed, one of the first formal legal processes is a discovery deposition. Have you had some experience in deposition? Well, here's the process. Lawyers for the plaintiff will ask questions about the case under oath in the presence of a court reporter.

"The first deposition is most likely a verbatim transcript of your words but sometimes it can involve video. It will be transcribed and presented to you by mail for review and it is very important that you review the deposition very carefully to correct and make any changes in order for the document to accurately reflect your answers. Deposition is incredibly important because it becomes the basis upon which the court case will be built.

"Remember, although the doctor is emotionally invested in the case, the plaintiff lawyers are not. It is strictly business for them to gain monetary awards and they are comfortable because it is their territory." She sighs.

"I've already done this, the deposition and yes, it was very uncomfortable," I add.

"Okay. To them, it is all about winning, not right or wrong. Their questions can be confusing, almost irrelevant at times but the lawyers use a method to their madness to bring you down into the rabbit holes with frustrated emotions.

"To the best degree possible, it is a good idea you become emotionally detached because the lawyers will attempt to confuse, irritate, and distract you to get your testimony on the record in such a way that it can be used against you. It is particularly important to listen to their questions carefully and answer only what they ask and not add any other things.

"Most doctors are brought up to be polite and answer a question to be helpful by adding or explaining, but you must not do that here. Ask them to rephrase the question and it is okay to say you do not understand the question. Do not rush into answering and refer directly to the medical record as much as possible.

"They will try to confuse you with introductory questions like, 'Wouldn't you agree that…?' Do *not* agree with them unless you really agree." She pauses and drinks some water.

"Expert witnesses may be obtained over the ensuing months from both sides, plaintiff and defendant. In this case, the plaintiff already told us that they want a jury trial and therefore, most likely we will prepare for the preliminary hearing.

"Negotiations may begin for the settlement. By the way, settlements can be reached at any time but it will require consent from the physicians to settle. If settlement is proposed, be sure to understand the consequences. If there is no settlement, then a trial date will be set.

"The most important part for you is to become detached from the case and pretend that this is not about you. But prepare by reading and essentially memorizing every page of the medical record that is pertinent.

"You will need to become completely familiar with the expert witness depositions as well. It is extremely hard to change your story or your testimony between deposition and trial without a good reason. Let your legal counsel guide you.

"Clear your schedule completely around the pretrial hearing date and the trial date so that you can immerse in the trial." She looks at me to check if I understand.

"Okay, I will do that," I answer. She nods.

"After the preliminary hearing and if we or they do not agree to settle, then, jury selection will occur. We will be given a list of jurors who are available and they will be seated in order. The number of jurors will be 12 plus a few alternates, and we must work on selecting jurors who can be fair and impartial.

"We have a few people who can sort out jurors who might support a defense verdict for you. During the jury selection, it is always the plaintiff's lawyer who goes first in asking questions to potential jurors, then the defense. It is our job to identify those jurors with predetermined prejudice.

"Then jurors will be *challenged for cause*, which means essentially, both sides rule out a juror who is unsuitable based on the perception of potential conflict of interest to serve. The judge will make rulings for cause, since jurors can be excused from service without specific reason.

"This process continues until the total 12 jurors plus alternates are seated." She pauses, looks at me to see if I still follow her. The information is already getting complicated but I appreciate her extensive knowledge.

"When you go to court, make sure you show up promptly and early. Sit erect and do not droop. Wear dark pants, suits and conservative, light-color blouses and shiny, clean, dark conservative looking shoes, not high heels.

"Do not wear overly decorative jewelry or large earrings that make distraction to focus on you. No heavy make-up also. Make eye contact with the jurors. You need to develop a relationship with them because they ultimately will decide your fate. Obviously, you cannot talk to them personally at any time."

Looking at Gail, I notice she usually dresses as she is now describing how I should dress. A big diamond ring on her left index finger is a little distracting but otherwise, she is pretty modest in her dress code.

"Opening statements begin after the jury is selected, first by the plaintiff followed by the defense. This sets the stage for the trial, which is essentially like Shakespeare theater. The plaintiff's attorneys will have the burden of proof and for a malpractice case, the standard is *preponderance of evidence* and not *beyond reasonable doubt* as in criminal cases.

"This preponderance of evidence means a jury believes that there was at least a 51% chance of reasonable medical probability that the doctor's duty of care caused the damages. The evidence of more than 50% certain on either side, 51% to be exact.

"Both sides will set the agenda for the trial; the plaintiff will state what they will prove and our defense lawyers will likely disagree with the plaintiff's statements and describe how the evidence will be refuted.

"The plaintiff's lawyers will make statements about you that will surely upset you regarding your clinical expertise, decision-making ability and judgment. It is very important you do not react outwardly, so watch your body language. The jury will read your reaction and make a note of you. The first impression is especially important.

"I need you to remain calm and collected at all times. Do not stare at the jurors but do make eye contact." Gail stares with a stoic demeanor.

"This is then followed by calling the first witness for the plaintiff; most likely it will be you. They are very skillful at upsetting you to fumble and their motive is to impeach you with prior inconsistent statements from your deposition.

"This is slightly different from your deposition, in that you will be given a chance to explain yourself, not merely answering the questions. The plaintiff's counsel may not allow you to explain much but we will make sure you get your chance to explain.

"Then the plaintiff's counsel will likely call their expert. The expert is not how you define the word expert in your field. The expert in the case is someone who has just enough expertise to express the opinion that supports the patient's case.

"Experts will say in their opinion, you did not use reasonable care, were negligent in some way and will clearly state that you rendered a diagnosis that was below the standard of care. You must realize that those experts are paid well by the plaintiff to express their opinions clearly by showing off their expert credentials and using necessary medical literature. This will be one of the emotional low points of the trial for the defendant." Gail observes my head is going down. I can already picture that dreadful day in the court.

"Then, it is our turn. We will call expert witnesses for the defense who will testify that you followed a reasonable course of clinical action and met the standard of care. We have two experts for your case who will defend for you, one from Boston and one local. The plaintiff's attorneys will have a chance to cross-examine our experts.

"You may be called as the last witness and finally tell your story in front of the jury. Make sure to engage them, I mean jurors, with your personality. Be calm, personable, respectful and convey the message that you provided the best patient care possible under the given situation.

"After this, there will be closing arguments, plaintiff first followed by the defendant. The plaintiff's side will use all kinds of drama, their best act, an exaggerated version of the loss to make sure the jury feels sorry for the patient and her family.

"Your counsels will bring out the facts and evidence that support your appropriate care. And that will end the course from the lawyers.

"Finally, the jury will be instructed in the law that pertains to your case and proceed to the jury room to deliberate the case. Unlike a criminal case, in a civil case the verdict does not have to be unanimous. When the requisite number of jurors decides for either side, then the case is over.

"If the jury finds in favor of the plaintiff, they will need to determine damages, which can be much more than the settlement amount. But remember, it is extremely hard to win a case over a doctor, and the defense wins about 80% of the cases.

"There might be an appeal from either side, but that discussion is for another day."

After this long lecture about the legal system, I am exhausted, but it is so helpful to see the whole picture. There are so many things I need to know and ask, but it is hard to clearly formulate my questions. Finally, I ask, "Why is Dr. Kline involved in this case?"

"Well, the plaintiff lawyers are arguing the point that he should have started radiation therapy immediately."

"I thought the father of the deceased is a close friend of Dr. Kline."

"Well, you know these lawyers are only interested in money. They are suing not just you but Dr. Kline and the hospital. The more targets, better chance to gather a larger profit."

"What about my decision to waive the pathology billings?"

"Well, that is going to be a little sticky for us to do damage control. By waiving the pathology bills, it looks like you are admitting your error. You did not go through appropriate procedures and policies of the hospital committees.

"We will simply defend your action as a naïve doctor who was trying to help the parents of the patient with their demands and ease their frustrations. Only thing is, the plaintiff lawyers will make fun of you and claim you are not so naïve after all, because you are the chair of the department."

"Interim chair," I reply.

"Is the same thing, you are the chair of the department. By the way, when are they going to announce you as the chair? I think it is coming soon, right?"

"No, I do not know. That is not the point here. I am just so depressed with this case. I cannot sleep at night."

"I understand. Most doctors are like you, but you need to be tough as a nail now. This experience will toughen you up more. It is not pleasant and most doctors dread malpractice lawsuits. Some quit medicine entirely because of the trauma they face in lawsuits. I am surprised you have not had a lawsuit so far. How many years have you been practicing?"

"Almost 20 years. I had one deposition on a case involving me only peripherally."

"You are lucky. Actually, pathologists are not commonly involved in the lawsuits. Mostly the surgeons, especially neuro-surgeons, OB/Gyn, internists and ER doctors are more vulner-able. Well, I will keep you posted of any update. But expect to have the preliminary hearing in the next few weeks and the trial date sometime after that."

"Thank you. By the way, do you know the amount of money they are asking?"

"No, they have not stated it yet. Are you willing to settle?"

"Yes, absolutely."

"Okay, good to know. I do not think Dr. Kline is willing to settle. He is going to fight to clear his name. There is much circumstantial evidence why he did not have the patient go through radiation therapy at the time. He claims chemother-apy was much more important at the time and we have several expert witnesses who agree with Dr. Kline."

"Can I have my piece of the lawsuit settled and let Dr. Kline fight for his case?"

"No, unfortunately the case is treated as a whole, and it is not separable. Also, you should not admit that you made an error in your diagnosis because most of the placental choriocarcinoma cases are found after the patient or the infant have symptoms.

"First of all, they are extremely rare and most are from the case studies published in literature. Most of the placental experts will say the slides are not conclusive. In this particular case, the patient had a brainstem metastasis that killed her. You should just watch what will happen and how the case will be ironed out."

"Okay, thanks for your time. I learned a lot from you," and I stand to leave her office.

My head is still down and shoulders drooping. I just want to die, right here, at this moment and never go through the process Gail talked about. *God, help me!* That is all I can say.

I admire all the doctors who went through medical-legal lawsuits, still came out, tough as nails and continue practicing their medicine. They keep their heads high and help many new patients with their best care as possible. The amount of courage it takes to keep on going astounds me.

I begin to respect all the doctors, especially the surgeons, who face all kinds of allegations and difficult patients in the frontlines. I can see why they have to tough it out and become somewhat nasty at times.

Chapter Thirteen

The legal processes in malpractice lawsuits are complicated. I am glad to learn many things from Gail, and grateful Gail is a woman who explains in such a thorough way. If I had a male counsel, it is most likely I would not have such a clear picture of the process in my head.

I wish that I recorded our conversations so that I could refer to her advice. I am also glad that I work among great lawyers with their intimidating and prestigious names under a powerful university hospital as they protect me and our physicians.

Within a few weeks, I read three depositions from the placenta experts, two from the defendants and one from the plaintiff side. Reading through their depositions, I realize how the legal system has so many loopholes and how imperfect it is.

Depending on the expert, the jury is given a specific impression of the standard of care. The expert witness may practice pathology in a setting so different from that in which the alleged malpractice occurred.

The jury may have a skewed view of the standard of care because an expert witness is the determination of whether the standard of care was met. Definition of the standard of care is a legal term and refers to how the average pathologist would have managed the patient under similar circumstances.

However, an expert witness is often not an average pathologist, but an esoteric academic pathologist who often practices in only one specific field such as a placental pathologist and often has written a textbook and published many articles in that one area.

An average pathologist would not write a textbook about placenta. None of the expert witnesses practice medicine under similar circumstances as I do. The slide reading on a routine case does not come with diagnosis made by another pathologist, or a red label reading MEDICAL LEGAL CASE accompanied by a phone call or email notification from attorneys. If a case came like that, any pathologist would pay more attention, seeking out what is wrong with the case and study more carefully.

In a routine practice in pathology, caseloads in one day may number 40-100 cases for each pathologist, without any red labels. An expert witness who examines a medical-legal case can in no way examine the case without bias.

Things look quite simpler and clearer when we have 20/20 retrospective vision and the hindsight of what happened to the patient. Expert witnesses who examine a medical-legal case face temptation to side with the person who asks for opinion. After all, a significant amount of money is given to experts for their opinion.

From the readings of my own case, the three expert witnesses all differ in their opinions. Two experts from our hospital side have similar findings. In their summary it states:

> Gestational choriocarcinoma occurs in 1 in 40,000 pregnancies and placental choriocarcinoma is the rarest and is usually diagnosed in symptomatic patients with metastases. There are only 21 articles with 32 cases of placental choriocarcinoma reported cases in the English literature. Macroscopically, the majority of placental chorio-

carcinoma is ill-defined and interpreted as placental infarct or intervillus thrombi which are very common in normal placentas.

It is only after metastatic symptoms occur in mother or infant that the placenta is resubmitted for further evaluation, and small lesions are identified microscopically. In the current case, the microscopic focus of placental choriocarcinoma is not characteristic and extremely subtle.

There is no confluent proliferation of trophoblasts distributed as a mantel around villi, necrotic or hemorrhagic areas to call for the diagnosis of placental choriocarcinoma. If there are additional sections able to be obtained from the placenta, it may be helpful to further analyze the presence or absence of such diagnosis.

Also, the patient may have developed choriocarcinoma in the uterus after the delivery of infant and placenta. Especially given the medical history of the patient with bleeding for months after delivery.

My report was addended months later that under the wet tissue preservation policy based on CAP and our hospital, we could not submit more tissue from the placenta to examine further after the patient's symptoms became known to us.

The expert witness for plaintiff concludes in the deposition transcript,

It is obvious that the pathologist misdiagnosed the placental choriocarcinoma which is present in one slide with significant proliferation of trophoblasts with partially circumferential around villi with central villi necrosis and intervillus hemorrhage. Gross examination of placental chorio-carcinoma is easily identifiable as yellow-white granular lesions and multiple areas of infarcts which the microscopic sections should have been taken from, especially given the clinical history of pre-eclampsia to the pathologists.

What would the jury believe after hearing these conflicting opinions from the different expert pathologists? Incidentally, pre-eclampsia and placental choriocarcinoma are not related, contrary to this expert. Typically, the jury will not have medical education and all the medical terminology and jargon will confuse them. It all will depend upon which expert witness is more convincing, more confident, has the biggest name or come across as an impressive speaker. Is this a true definition of the standard of care?

Many clinicians think that pathology is more black and white than other medical fields. This may be true but there are many shades of gray areas in pathology slide interpretation and sometimes subjective in interpretation. Even experts often disagree on controversial diagnoses. Thank goodness, the frequency of claims against pathologists is low but the stakes are high for payout because all treatment begins with a diagnosis, the consequences high-risk for allegations of misdiagnosis.

It is my understanding the average pathologist experiences a claim every 10 years, often causing a personal crisis for the pathologist, like myself. I feel paralyzed with my mental ability to read and sign out another slide from another case. I am the most incapable pathologist in the world at this point.

Do other doctors feel the same way as I do when they receive a subpoena delivered for an in-person signature? I am shaking all day with the envelope in my hands and cannot even read the contents of a subpoena after a FedEx driver delivered it to my office. I just sit for a while. I cannot function for several days.

From the very beginning I admit my mistake, and the medical-legal processes are hanging me out there to dry with slow choking maneuvers for me to suffer. I just want to get this over with and pay out whatever the plaintiff is asking with the medical insurance premiums my hospital paid for over 20 years and never had an opportunity to use.

What are my consequences? I might be reported and listed in the public records and my name will be forever tainted by that blacklist; a report filed by the hospital under the pretext of "protecting patient safety" in an Adverse Action Report (AAR) in the National Practitioner Data Bank (NPDB).

Negative consequences are many; inability to continue practicing in one's specialty, inability to obtain or renew medical staff privileges and/or medical license, inability to obtain employment as a physician, and termination of medical liability insurance or a significant increase in my premiums for medical liability insurance, to name a few.

Also, whenever I want to change my hospital employment, I will need to disclose the negative lawsuit filed against me on my application records, even though the case was not my fault or was dismissed. The Health Care Quality Improvement Act of 1986 (HCQIA) law makes it extremely difficult for physicians to successfully challenge an adverse action.

The damage inflicted by being included in this blacklisting is severe, including negative rumors, smears, blackballing, and tactics similar to extortion, causing physicians to have severe long-term stress, depression, and even suicide.

I, for one, am thinking about quitting medicine altogether at this point. I am exhausted with the tortuous selection process of being considered as department chair, and the intimidating medical-legal lawsuit.

Continual sleepless nights cause me to live in a hazy, tired brain that exacerbates my torments. With this rate, I will fall off the tracks, either involuntarily or voluntarily. Lack of sleep and appetite drags on, and soon I will lose immune system to fight even a mild cold. I can easily give up and die and maybe that is what I actually want to do.

The only way I even breathe and live is to rely on the strength of God. In the Old Testament Bible, there is a story about the prophet Elisha in 2 Kings 6:8–7:2, when the king of Aram was at war with Israel. Time and again Elisha warned the king of Israel exactly where the troops of Arameans were planning to mobilize and attack.

The king of Aram became enraged over this, thinking there must be a traitor. One of the officers said it was not a traitor, but Elisha, the prophet of Israel who told the king of Israel even every word the king spoke in the privacy of his bedroom. The king demanded the officer find Elisha so he could send troops to seize him. A report came back to the king that Elisha was in the town of Dothan.

So, one night the king sent his troops, chariots and horses, and surrounded the city. The servant of Elisha awoke in the morning and said, *"Oh no, my Lord! What shall we do?"*

Elisha replied, *"There are more on our side than on theirs."* Then Elisha prayed, asking God to open the eyes of his servant. The Lord allowed the servant to see the hillsides all around Elisha filled with horses and chariots of fire of the Heaven's Army.

As the troops of Aram advanced toward him, Elisha prayed to make them blind, and so the Lord struck them with blindness. Elisha then told the troops they were not on the right road or the right city, and he would lead them to the man they were looking for. So, he led them to the city of Samaria.

I pray to be able to see Heaven's Army with horses and chariots of fire surrounding me to protect and fight for me. Things unseen are a powerful reality, and having faith in God in this life is what sustains me from giving up.

Though I may fall, I shall not be utterly cast down, for the Lord upholds me with his hand.

IV: Martin's Story

Chapter One

I am mad as hell! How dare they kill my daughter Julie! All the sons of bitches have to pay for this and I will make sure they pay a hefty price! Slowly but surely, I will torment and destroy them one by one starting with the lab doctor.

How can the top hospital like Beverly Hills hire such an incompetent doctor who butchered up my daughter's case? Who is this bitch? What does she look like? I just want to meet her and see her face to face. She should not be mucking around being a doctor but should just have children and a husband to attend to. And leave these matters and important job of medicine to men doctors.

How could Dr. Kline, my trusted doctor, have done this to me, leaving such an important job to a woman doctor when I have been giving him a ton of money for his research? Not only that, but he also botches up my daughter's care by not giving her radiation treatment in time. Now I regret giving him so much research money after he helped my wife deliver all three of our girls.

I thought he was my friend. Doctors are all the same, they protect each other when there is a lawsuit. And those two must have been hiding something and not telling me the truth. Well, it will all be revealed in the courtroom. My hired guns will reveal their secrets and display them in daylight.

Let's see how these doctors look when we put them on the stand and see if they can extricate themselves out of the situations. I will make sure my lawyers bite them like sharks. We'll make them spit out all their mistakes with as much bleeding as possible.

They will get a dose of their own medicine by the time I get through this lawsuit. The jury will see how vulnerable doctors really are and I will bring them down from their high and haughty white tower, prideful egos and put them to shame.

Even so, I am not sure justice will be served. My Julie is still dead, and she will not be with us, forever. This pain of losing my child is so overwhelming and devastating. I can't think about anything else but to be hyper-focused on revenge.

I am her father and I did not protect her. Feeling like a failure torments me. I have not been talking to my wife or Jane, my second daughter. Luckily, June, my first daughter is at college and there is my excuse to avoid talking. I do not have to see her every day. But Mary and Jane, I must see every day and I have no idea what to say to them. They keep distancing themselves from me, and from each other, too. Everyone goes to our own rooms, closing the doors behind. We no longer have family dinners.

My wife does not want to see me anymore. She locks the master bedroom door, so I cannot even get in. She does not address me about the scene at a hotel, as if nothing happened. Sometimes I even wonder if she actually witnessed me standing with another woman in the elevator. I make several attempts to talk about this, but Mary won't budge. She avoids me and does not acknowledge I am in the house.

Right after the elevator incident with my paralegal Beth, my wife decides to give me cold looks. She will not even talk to me. I cannot believe Mary followed me into the hotel! I almost kissed

Beth in front of her. I saw Mary but it did not register I was seeing her right in front of me. I got caught. Guilty as hell. But I deny it, of course. And I will deny it all the way if Mary asks me.

Sometimes women can overlook and overthink, and I can fool them to think otherwise. I still have my charm and smarts to get out of a sticky situation like this. Over time, Mary will think maybe she thought she saw things that were not really what appeared to be. I never cheated on her before this time and we have a fantastic marriage. She will forget about all this because we have girls with us, a family.

I have supported my family as a bread winner successfully. They have a beautiful house, private schools and many vacations all over the world with my company's private plane. We have a beautiful lake house in Lake Tahoe we enjoy every summer.

I always provide for them spectacularly well. What more can anyone ask from me? I am more than a capable man and support my family in prolific abundance. Besides this little slip with the paralegal, I am a perfect husband and a good father.

With Beth, it just happened so naturally.

I spend a lot of time in the office, and still pull 70–80 hours a week as a senior partner. Making money can be a little addicting. As I make more and more money, I notice there is no limit to the amount that satisfies. If I make a half million dollars, then, I want to see if I can achieve three quarters of a million, then a million, and why not ten or hundred million? Sky is the limit.

Nothing is more exciting than to know my capability to profit my company and earn a good living. What is wrong with that? Regarding Beth, it is momentary fire and flirtation I could have resisted, but I said to myself "why not?" Why would a capable man like me settle to have just one woman for life?

Although I do not really believe women can be as capable as most men in my business, we are required to hire more attractive female attorneys and paralegals. Plus, they can be helpful in many of our cases. They somehow approach problems in different ways; shall I say more softer and at times manipulative ways, and some of our clients listen to their voices more than mine. We pay very competitively and can be choosy in selecting who will join our company.

Stacks of applications pour into our place every year and we can be very selective, and what is wrong with selecting only the attractive ones? This applies to both females and males. After all, it is a fact that attractive people are more successful and they get what they want more easily.

Beth is perhaps the most attractive lady in our company. She is a blond, blue eyes, tall, young and thin with figure. Her high heels make her body swing; her full buttocks, it is a killer especially with those long legs of hers crossing when she sits. She flaunts it because she knows she's got the looks. Among senior partners, we bet who will get her first. Well, not actual money but in a joking manner.

Competitive edge always serves me well. I never lose anything when I put my mind and priorities in place.

When I begin sleeping with Beth I do not think through things or how it will affect my family. I've just got to have Beth. What does she look like naked? She addicts me. I'm willing to do just about anything when a competition is set in front of me. Being first is important, but I have to think about the consequences, unfortunately. I never think about getting caught, to be honest.

Beth is becoming more demanding. "Why don't you buy me this or that? How come I can't see you in public? Why can't we go to Hawaii for a vacation together?" Her annoying lists become long, and I am tiring of her whining voice, straining to fulfill her demands. We go to Hawaii, and I lie that it is a business trip to my wife.

At lunch I stop by Tiffany's to find Beth something, open my wallet and there is not enough cash. My credit card works. Rushing back to the office, I realize Mary now pays the bills. I relinquished that responsibility to her just last month. Now I have to buy something else for Mary and cover up the first charge I just made for Beth. I forget it was from Tiffany's in Beverly Hills and a couple days later I pick up a necklace from Nieman Marcus for my wife, not thinking whether or not it is packaged in a Tiffany blue box. On top of this, I totally forget about our wedding anniversary. I just took a Hawaii trip with Beth.

"Oh, it's not from Tiffany's!" Mary screams.

I know I blew it, immediately. I have become an insensitive son-of-a-bitch to my wife. Why have I come this far? It is not fair for Mary. She has been a good wife and a good mother to my children. I feel remorse but she will not even face me, and I will tell her how sorry I am if I must. Maybe I have come too far to fool her to think I am not having an affair.

My only hope is to show her how much I care about her and the family by winning this lawsuit case. That will show Mary and my family how great I am to take care of matters with my own hands.

Not only do I pick five top-notch senior partners for my medical-legal team, I add five more associates who are aggressive, rising stars in our firm. I release hungry sharks to be free in the water for them to seek prey. They will have a field day as they destroy these doctors and that hospital.

Chapter Two

It is early November and finally Los Angles weather is consistently getting cooler. I work hard to get this case heard by pushing some judges, my old friends in the court system to get a prompt pretrial hearing. We get a fast-track date for early November, just two months after Julie's death. It is good to know some people and use some muscle to shift things around in the legal realm.

The day is upon us to meet all these doctors and defendant attorneys face to face. Of course, I know what this lab doctor looks like from her web page. I am mostly excited; and a little apprehensive to meet her and crush her.

I never get accustomed to courtroom drama, how it makes me nervous, especially in the beginning. *Butterflies in my stomach during my opening statements.* Although I am not personally involved in this case, my nerves are jittery.

In the preliminary hearing, the defense side only has two counsels, Mr. Harris and some young female attorney named Melissa Razi. The hospital always retains respectable liability firms, and today it is Harris and Sidman, LLC. Melissa Razi appears to be Persian, in her mid 30s, fairly attractive attorney with a slight Farsi accent. She will shrivel and cry, an easy target for the guys I hired. My attorneys will deliver sharp remarks and can be ruthless.

Karl Harris is another matter. He gained some weight and more gray hair over the years. He is very experienced, skillful and a smart guy we previously encountered with the same hospital a number of years ago. The outcome was really bad for us; we lost the jury trial. The damn Harris group and idiot jurors put us to shame and we are still paying the price for our reputation. We still made a profit from the plaintiff, who had to pay all fees for every hour billed by our firm, as we rarely take on pro bono cases. In the end, we always win by gaining monetary rewards.

Today is showtime. Our ten attorneys will crush Harris this time. He is stupid enough to show up with just one additional meek new attorney. Last night our side called Harris with a settlement amount which he should have agreed to pay. He should have accumulated more defense attorneys to at least take our side seriously and show us some respect.

We carefully calculate the amount in every detail. If Julie were to live and become a trial attorney like myself, she would have earned so many millions of dollars, minus her education fees. If she were to be just a housewife. minus education fees, her life might be worth a particular amount of lesser dollars. We make sure the figure lies somewhere in the middle to be perceived as realistic.

Suddenly, anger hits me. I am sure she would have been a star, wildly successful as a trial attorney, maybe even better than me, as I quickly recalculate her billings, bonuses, plus inflation.

I am still not satisfied with the final amount but I have to be reasonable. What I really want to do is ask for an obnoxious settlement amount that will push our case to a court trial, but my partners persuade me to be reasonable. Their interest, after all, is the money, not a jury trial.

Usually, the plaintiff's side requests pain and suffering be compensated, while the defense side wants their names to be cleared, and their attorneys are ultimately interested in money.

This is what the system boils down to in the end. In this case, plaintiff and attorneys are one, at least from my viewpoint. My partners still do not see it this way and are only interested in money.

I am not one of the counsels at the table, for a change. I take a seat behind the players, next to my wife and Jane. June plans to come from Berkeley, probably the last day of deliberation or earlier if she has to testify for some odd reason. I try to protect her from interruptions during her college classes.

Jane is somewhat thrilled and anxious, glad to skip her high school classes and witness every action in the courtroom and actually observe the outcome after her sister's death. None of my daughters have ever seen me in courtroom action. I never take them to my playground where I thrive and play hardball.

Too bad I am not a counsel contributing at the courtroom table. I want to impress my daughters and my wife how great I am.

It starts. I watch all ten of my attorneys walk in, all in suits. Dark navy blue, gray and black. There are not enough seats for my side. Mr. Harris shakes hands with five of my guys, Jeff Grey the lead, Tony Spiro second in command, and three others. Mr. Harris introduces his partner, Ms. Razi. Next to her is Dr. Sara Choi and Dr. Kline.

This is the first time I see Dr. Choi in person. She is tiny maybe five feet, four inches tall, shockingly attractive, Asian and appears very intelligent with her glasses, younger than her age. She looks to be in her mid-thirties, but Dr. Kline told me she is late 40s, almost 50 years old and chair of the department.

Dr. Kline spoke very highly of her once, when she read my daughter's liver biopsy. He said she is a top-notch pathologist.

There is something about her and why do I feel somewhat intimidated? She seems too smart for me. A coolness about her, perhaps an air of confidence I have never seen in any woman.

Her hair is deep brown to black, a little curly and long and she wears it straight down covering her shoulders. Her deep navy pants suit is pristine, perfect with her starched white blouse which is not low cut. No jewelry except a sleek smartphone watch with a classic silver band. Choi's black shoes have low heels, she's comfortable but dressy. Indeterminate emotion on her face, probably good in poker games.

Dr. Kline is next to her. They talk softly to one another, leaning in close and whispering into each other's ears. Clearly friendly, they like each other. Well, they have to be one team, working together for this case at least.

Inspecting Dr. Kline in his generic dark suit and necktie does not impress me or draw my attention. I do not care how he looks except to say he looks much more nervous than during our casual dinners at each other's places many years ago.

I certainly do not want to penalize him too much. *Just answer the question, why did you delay radiation treatment to my daughter?* I really am not out here to get his money or his reputation. If I had my wish, we would immediately drop our claim against him after hearing his answer.

I am here to get Dr. Choi. I will pull her down so that she cannot practice pathology any longer and confiscate her medical license to prevent this damaging medical care of hers that delays diagnosis and treatment to other patients.

This trial is about punitive damages. I am rather happy to have Virginia Chang, Esq. in my group, in case there are sympathetic jurors out there for Dr. Choi, an Asian descendant. Ms. Chang will slay her with one sentence and put her in misery.

Chang's sharp tongue and killer instinct has her disliked by every secretary in our group because of that nasty tongue and prideful attitude. I would hate to face Ms. Chang if she were not on my side.

When everyone is situated somewhat, we stand to greet the judge. The judge walks in; I am flabbergasted. Elizabeth Wayne, an African American woman in her 60s, the only black judge in our district. *What luck! Why do I have to get her!* My mouth is wide open and my eyes roll as I wonder if this is the reason why my partners never told me the judge's name for this case.

I personally requested a jury trial, made a deposit for it and requested judge Andrew Coulter. How could they switch judges at the last minute? My mouth quickly shuts as I get a text. It's Mavis Hill, one of the attorneys in the front row. *"We didn't know!!! Maybe Coulter sick? Heart attack? Wayne a substitute…We're in for a ride!"*

No! I cannot believe what is happening right in front of me. Did this judge even have time to read all the depositions and evidence we provided? Why is this happening to me now when I worked so hard with Judge Coulter and prepared him in advance? Our guys know Coulter disdains medical doctors with their pride. We benefit from Coulter on this case.

"Please be seated," Judge Wayne says. "We are here to begin the pretrial proceedings of Freedman vs. Beverly Hills Hospital and Drs. Sara Choi and Steven Kline. I read all the transcripts, depositions from both doctors and the depositions from experts. The defendant has filed an answer and a motion to dismiss the complaints.

"The plaintiff filed a pretrial motion and I am here to hold a hearing. Based on this case management conference, we can move this case to a jury trial today or set another date for a trial date. We have 90 people here on jury duty, enough to begin the process of jury trial. It is up to you, both, so, please proceed Mr. Grey and Mr. Harris, or have you come to settlement?"

Mr. Grey begins, "No, your Honor, we have not agreed to settle. We are proceeding as planned."

With that, attorneys on both sides briefly present their case. Huddles of heads nod and whisper, and shortly after their huddle Judge Wayne proclaims jury selection will begin today.

After 15 minutes, about 30 jurors walk in. Twelve of them sit in jury chairs, four are seated in alternate chairs. They're nervous. The 12 seated in the jury chairs are variable in ages, seven are white, two Latino, two Asian and one African American. Eight are men and four are women. The judge says her welcome speech to all jurors and quickly begins her interviews.

One by one, starting from juror number one she asks for name and occupation. The entire process is taking longer than one hour. Attorneys on both sides intently observe each juror and I am able to tell when each attorney formulates their impression of each juror. Most of the jurors have their subtle attitudes, and do not want to be here.

Our side has an expert who reads out jurors accurately and I am glad Mrs. Tomoko is here today. She is like a fortune teller in reading out personal characteristics on people very precisely. Tomoko can predict each juror's verdict by just looking at the person, listening to the voice. Her high salary for this is worth it. We always bring her to the courtroom during jury selection. This is definitely an advantage for us.

Mr. Harris and his side do not have such a person. Time after time, I become a believer of Mrs. Tomoko and her ability to pick out the best jurors. Selecting the best jurors and alternates will take most of today and at least a part of tomorrow.

I cannot emphasize enough how important this process is and why we need this time to read out each juror to benefit our side. We want no jurors in the medical field, and no health care providers, either themselves or their relatives who are likely sympathetic to their own professions.

Next day, attendance in the courtroom is limited to our side and the defendant attorneys handling juror selection. The judge is here to observe and occasionally asks questions to the jurors. Fifteen more jurors are here today, in case we run out of potential jurors. I give body gestures and make eye contact with Ms. Tomoko constantly. Even though I sit in the passenger seat, I am the one who ultimately decides how this courtroom will look like.

It is our best interest to also exclude Asians, and female jurors. They might be more sympathetic and empathetic to Dr. Choi. My target is to bring her down.

After interviewing those selected jurors from yesterday, we decide to let go of jurors #1 and #7 because they already made up their minds and appear hostile toward our side which is obviously undesirable. Unfortunately, one of the alternates from yesterday is chosen to replace juror #1, a retired male doctor who used to be a pediatrician.

My understanding is that we are not to have any health care workers in the jury but the defendant side argues that he is retired, and therefore, it does not fit the category of health care worker per se.

The defendant's side tries extremely hard to keep him. We lose that battle. We have a potential problem with this retired doctor. He's likely very accustomed to being an influential leader and other jurors may give him that authority. Other jurors may become deferential to him in their thoughts and verdict.

Thank goodness this is not a criminal case where everyone has to agree on a verdict. If we can just convince majority of the jurors, we can win the case.

Ultimately, we end up with 12 jurors variable in age, ranging from the oldest, 72 and the youngest, 39 years old; eight whites, two Latinos, one Asian and one African American. Seven are men and five are women. It looks good and favorable to us, except for the retired doctor.

The four alternate jurors are also chosen in case a juror is unable or disqualified to perform his or her duties at the time he or she is sworn in, especially important for a lengthy trial case like ours. It may extend up to two weeks.

The trial will start tomorrow 9:00 a.m. sharp.

It's showtime!

Chapter Three

The courtroom is packed, features ten sharply dressed counsels from our side and ready to fight. The defense side has brought one more attorney, an Asian American female introduced as Courtney Tan.

Looks like she appeared just out of law school. It just shows how the defense is scared to death about losing this case so they bring in another attorney. They got smart and brought in someone new, an Asian American person to defend their Dr. Choi.

They should have brought someone more seasoned into the courtroom, not a young attorney nobody recognizes. We, seasoned experts, know who is who, who is new and who is mediocre in court because we spend time winning inside this place.

Trial attorneys are very different animals and we know who is good. Other than Harris, his two females next to him to defend doctors are not at all impressive. These women are timid and I am pretty sure they will show tears when we attack them. It will not take much time until they fall apart and cry. I enjoy smiling as I think about it.

No experts from the defense show up today. Perhaps they will come tomorrow. From our side, we have Dr. Odze, a famous gynecological pathologist who specializes in placenta sits next to our case provider behind the barrier that separates them from attorneys. Odze flew in from Boston last night and is staying at The Ritz-Carlton in downtown Los Angeles.

The dinner is expensive. Our attorneys and Dr. Odze drink significant amounts of wine with dinner. I have to pick up the tab which is over $3,000 with tax and tips. Dr. Odze is a talker. He was born in Czechoslovakia and came to the US as a teenager and was educated in the states. He still has some accent when he speaks but is quite understandable. His ancestors are Orthodox Jews who lived in Czechoslovakia. Odze says his father was a rabbi, who died several years ago.

Anyway, my only concern is can he speak his technical language of medicine in an understandable way to lay people on a jury, slowly, and gain respect from them? But as the night continues, I notice he talks faster and faster with more accent.

Why do we not have a white, American guy who can talk without any accent in the courtroom so that no one has to worry about what is being said? In any case, Dr. Odze wrote a textbook in the field of the placental pathology and evidently, he is well known in this field; he is the best one for us.

Dr. Lee also joins us for dinner. He is our radiation oncologist expert who practices locally. He is rather quiet and does not speak much throughout our dinner time. He has just one glass of wine and a few small bites of his medium-well done steak.

He is very skinny, apparently not a great eater. A rather short, tiny man. His voice does not resonate and I barely hear him because I sit at the corner farthest from him. I wish his voice was more manly and deeper, but at least he seems to have no accent. His CV is impressive and he has extensive experience as an expert witness in courtrooms. *His calm manner sure will impress the jury.*

We, the attorneys, have to take some chances in choosing these expert witnesses and hope for the best. We pay these experts top dollars to appear in the courtroom. The experts are selected through word of mouth among many trial attorneys. I never saw either of these doctors and I carefully observe how they act during dinner.

Dr. Choi is dressed today in a dark brown pantsuit and her hair is down. She looks attractive even at her matured age. Well poised and impressive in manner, friendly with a warm smile. I am a bit concerned about her making a good first impression and personal connection with the jury.

It would be nice if she acts more like Dr. Kline, displaying a more pompous and prideful personality. He does not bother to make eye contact with the jurors. He sits next to Dr. Choi, and looks respectful with his receding white hair, neatly dressed in a dark gray suit and solid blue necktie.

Normally I see him wearing a white long coat. Today, with his suit, he looks more distinguished. His presence is much more intimidating because he exudes confidence without even trying. The profession of medical doctors should belong to such a person, not clouded by women and an Asian American doctor like Dr. Choi.

Regardless, we need a sacrificial goat, and she fits perfectly. This case will be over before we know it with millions of dollars in our hands. At least this is what I can do to alleviate some of the pain our family endures, losing Julie. Surely justice will be served.

Almost all seats in the courtroom are filled by friends and family members and some spectators I do not recognize. Judge Wayne walks into the courtroom and we all stand to greet her. After some introductions and guidance of the courtroom rules, the case begins. The opening statement from our side comes first. Lead counsel Jeffrey Grey rises, calmly walks toward the jury and begins to speak.

"The evidence in this case will show that hospitals cannot expose a patient to an unreasonable risk of injury and death. If a hospital's doctor chooses to expose a patient to an unreasonable risk of injury and this case death, the hospital is responsible for the harms and losses caused.

"In this case, who are we suing and why? We are here to hold The Beverly Hills Hospital, and Dr. Choi seated at the trial table responsible for delaying the diagnosis of Julie Freedman, which caused her suffering and death. And I represent the estate of Julie Freedman, her father Martin Freedman, her mother Mary Freedman, and all her siblings June and Jane Freedman.

"During the trial, we will explain the medical term *placental choriocarcinoma* which is really just a fancy term for a deadly but very treatable cancer by chemotherapy if detected early, which was right after the delivery of Ms. Julie Freedman's baby boy, Gregory Freedman.

"Julie successfully delivered her baby boy, and because she had a condition called pre-eclampsia, which is just a fancy medical term for high blood pressure during the time of pregnancy, the placenta was sent to the hospital's pathology lab. Dr. Choi who is seated there at the trial table had examined the placenta, but because of her negligence, she failed to provide a correct diagnosis which led to a critically long delay in time before treating this horrible and aggressive cancer." Jeffrey Grey pauses and looks at Judge Wayne.

"Your honor, in this trial, you will be hearing how Dr. Choi's irrevocable negligence allowed this deadly cancer to spread throughout this young girl's body, and I will remind you again, that this cancer is extremely curable because it is exquisitely sensitive to a specific chemotherapy that kills every cancer cell; if only Dr. Choi had simply detected the cancer in Julie's placenta.

"These deadly cells were right in front of her; she had the glass pathology slide in full view using her own microscope, but she failed to recognize these deadly cells. Mind you, Dr. Choi is a trained gynecological pathologist and interim chair of the pathology department. She was responsible for the case, making a diagnosis and reading the placenta while her patient, young Julie Freedman was comfortably recovering in the hospital after delivering her healthy baby boy.

"What happened over the next few months is stunning and is why we are here today. Because Dr. Choi failed to detect deadly cancer cells in the placenta, numerous areas throughout Ms. Freedman's body became sites where cancer cells began to lodge, which is called metastasis.

"One of the body sites included her brainstem, along with multiple sites in her brain, both her lungs, liver, spleen, her abdominal organs including ovaries, fat around her belly, her uterus and everywhere else, killed her which we will provide by evidence, and testimony from other expert doctors.

"These professional health care providers and the evidence will show that Dr. Choi did not use the degree of standard of care, which a reasonably competent health care provider engaged in a similar practice, acting under similar circumstances, would obviously use.

"All this really means is Dr. Choi was negligent, and Dr. Choi is responsible for the harms and the losses that her care caused, and the evidence will show that she is.

"In this case, there are two allegations of negligence. One, she breached the standard of care by not identifying and naming the deadly cancer cells in the placenta; and the second, she did not even do further studies to simply confirm the diagnosis even after admitting she initially thought those cancer cells were a little strange.

"Furthermore, she negligently thought it was 'nothing to worry about' because she had an important meeting she needed to attend. Dr. Choi failed to do her job. How can this doctor take an oath to protect and do no harm to her patients and then behave in this way? This is the real question in this case.

"Another important aspect of this case is another doctor, Dr. Steve Kline. He was Ms. Freedman's attending physician, but failed to treat his patient's brainstem tumor with radiation therapy which is widely known to be effective in decreasing the size of a tumor. Dr. Kline then failed a second time and chose not to take this enormously urgent case to his weekly tumor board meeting where other expert doctors, which would have included a radiation oncologist, likely would have suggested this potential radiation treatment in time to relieve the painful and horrifying symptoms Ms. Freedman suffered from due to swelling and obstruction of the brainstem, which eventually caused her death.

"We have a pathologist here today who looked at these same slides and found the tissue from the placenta removed at the time of delivery had enough material to diagnose numerous deadly cancer cells. Dr. Odze, who is a board-certified pathologist and has written many respected articles, is the leading expert in this field and will explain the process of making a diagnosis of placental choriocarcinoma, which Dr. Choi missed.

"I also have Dr. Lee, a board-certified radiation oncologist, and he will explain how timely radiation treatment could have shrunk the tumor size, thereby saving Ms. Freedman's young life when followed by the standard chemotherapy for this particular cancer.

"I want you to be aware that Ms. Freedman was in the hospital under the care of these health care providers for two weeks before she passed away. Two weeks is enough time to treat appropriately and she lost this critical time to be treated with life-saving radiation therapy.

"I will remind you, that this particular tumor is highly sensitive to the standard chemotherapy and this young mother's life did not have to be lost if these doctors in the hospital were not negligent in their standard care of medical practice.

"Now, in this case, Your Honor, we will explain there is a preponderance of the evidence and will instruct you at the end of the case, in order for us to prevail more likely than not of Dr. Choi's inability to diagnose placental choriocarcinoma caused Ms. Julie Freedman's brainstem tumor to grow so large to cause her demise, which are the elements of the burden of proof for us. And, we have Dr. Kline's failure to urgently treat Ms. Freedman with radiation therapy to gain the critical time needed to treat this tumor which is extremely sensitive to chemotherapy and radiation therapy.

"Both of the health care providers, Drs. Choi and Kline, have failures amounting to a breach of the applicable standard of medical care, which was the direct and proximate cause of all of the Plaintiff's injuries, damages and death.

"Now, we are here for an additional compensation for all the harms and losses caused by the hospital's negligence due to the doctors. It is called pain and suffering and mental anguish, not just the death.

"For the family members who are here today, their suffering is crushing. The father and mother lost a child, and the sisters lost their young sister. Here is a little bit about what Julie Freedman did during her short life.

"She was the last child, lovely, fun and free-spirited one who brought much of the happiness and laughter for her family. She went to Beverly Hills junior and senior high schools, achieved good grades, and was an honor student who was blessed with the cherished values of compassion and love.

"The whole family are devout Catholic churchgoers and a model family in their neighborhood. The family had three girls and now only two. When they go home, they will see an empty room and bed for Julie Freedman. She is not there anymore. She could have been a mother to her beautiful child, Gregory Freedman.

"Ms. Freedman was only 16 years old and had her life open to her with so many opportunities to become someone significant. She could have become a doctor, lawyer, an accountant, a teacher, a banker, you name it, she could be any one of these, perhaps a trial attorney just like her father who is a very prominent attorney. She could have earned so much money; she was a bright, intelligent, very smart kid. The whole life was ahead of her.

"And when you hear the testimony from this family, you will know at the end of this case why the fair and accurate compensation we are going to ask for is fifteen million dollars. Thank you very much."

With this powerful statement, Jeffrey Grey walks back and sits. His face is glowing. He knows he did a marvelous job opening the case.

Our jury is convinced that my poor girl could have lived, if only the doctors had made a correct and timely diagnosis, this death would have been prevented. And when Dr. Kline and the rest of them knew our poor child had the proper diagnosis, they still botched up by not giving her appropriate and standard of care treatment.

I already feel vindicated. Kudos to Jeffrey Grey! I knew I can always count on him.

Chapter Four

Giving the opening statement for the Defendant, Attorney Karl Harris rises to speak. "Good morning, members of the jury. My name is Karl Harris. I represent Dr. Sara Choi, Dr. Steven Kline and The Beverly Hills Hospital. Both doctors are sitting at the counsel table today.

"There is a difference from what you just heard from Plaintiff's Counsel and what you are about to hear from me. And the difference is this. During the course of the trial, you will hear medical terms. That is why Your Honor said, 'Do not Google these terms because we are going to explain the terms to you.'" He pauses and looks at jurors.

Harris continues. "The placental choriocarcinoma is what killed Ms. Julie Freedman. Two expert witnesses for the defense will show how difficult it is to make that diagnosis in the placenta. The diagnosis of such is usually made only after the patient already has the symptoms with metastasis all over the body, not unlike this case.

"Dr. Choi was *not* found to have error in diagnosis and did *not* practice below the standard of care. Most of the pathologists, greater than 51% of the time, would have arrived at the same diagnosis as Dr. Choi. In Julie's case, the tumors were found all over the body, including her brainstem where it governs breathing and life in general.

"Because of the tumor location, the natural course of the disease is death. No matter what could have been done by the doctors, her life would have ended and there is nothing any doctors could do to save her life. Dr. Kline had done the best he could to save her life but Julie's life could not be saved.

"Even if radiation treatment were given simultaneously with chemotherapy, the edema, which is swelling, caused the mass-like effect in the confined space of her brainstem and she would have died, perhaps even earlier than two weeks that she stayed in the hospital. It is the natural cause of her death, no matter what the doctors would have or could have done.

"It is a tragic story of Julie and a sad loss for the family. The facts show she became pregnant at age 15, an unmarried teenage girl. This eventually led to her death because she happened to get a deadly cancer, not because of any delay in diagnosis.

"Expert doctors on our side will tell you that deadly cancer may actually have been in her uterus after the delivery, not necessarily within the placenta. This lawsuit is not necessary and should be dismissed."

He sighs and adds, "It is heartbreaking to see a child, a 16-year-old girl, die with such unfortunate circumstances, with such a highly unusual and deadly cancer. It is natural for all decent human beings like you, jurors, to sympathize and want to do something for the suffering family. You want to do something about it and maybe compensate the family for such a loss.

"As you actually hear and see all the evidence, you will realize all the doctors seated here today did their best, and none of their medical care led to the death of Julie Freedman, except her own fate which no one has any control of nor any fault.

"The doctors and the hospital did their best to save her, alleviate and comfort her during pain and we should not seek scapegoats because there are no doctors who performed below the standard of care. The burden of proof is on the plaintiff's side.

"You will hear from their expert who might say this diagnosis is a slam dunk and an easy case but the medical literature will say otherwise. I want you to hear them out carefully, but in the end, you will go back to your room and think, and conclude this death of Julie Freedman had really nothing to do with the two doctors, but she died of her deadly cancer.

"And this deadly cancer is not caused by anyone else. It was a natural death of Julie Freedman, and was induced by her pregnancy because this cancer happens commonly after pregnancy.

"If only Julie did not have metastasis in her brainstem, she could have been cured but because of the location of the tumor, it is sad that she lost her life. With or without the care from the doctors, her death would have been inevitable."

With that, he slowly sits down. All the jurors appear confused. Some nod their heads. They just heard a very contrasting point of view from the same story. Harris did a respectable job. Always impressive. Too bad he does not work for me.

The judge asks to resume after lunch. Everyone is getting dispersed to have a two-hour lunch. I want to have lunch with Jeffrey Grey and the expert witness Dr. Odze who is next up on the witness stand this afternoon. I hope he will not have a drink with his meal. I plan to walk him through the scenario including the cross examination from the defense, and tell him to speak slowly, calmly without getting ahead of himself.

I am disappointed in his dress code today. We told him to dress conservatively but here he is, in a bright orange dress shirt, black tie and black suit. He looks ready to go to a Halloween party. Sometimes, these doctors are really not paying attention to details and never listen to our suggestions and recommendations.

I should have expected this from Dr. Odze because he appeared a little nerdy, esoteric and bookworm type without much common sense. Odze is definitely an odd person. He must be very bright, one of those genius scientists but far from having good social skills.

The defense experts look much more reserved, respectful and authoritative in somewhat more normal attire and appearance. There likely will not be time for them on the witness stand today. Will have to see what they wear tomorrow when their time comes to appear on the stand.

Chapter Five

My team walks out to the parking lot to drive to the restaurant, and I hear my wife Mary running after me, calling my name. I just totally forgot about her! Mary and my daughters are here today in the courtroom. I am so focused on coaching Dr. Odze and completely forgot to tell them I cannot have lunch with them.

"Martin, I need to talk to you," Mary says.

"Will talk tonight. I am so sorry I cannot have lunch with you and girls. Can you take them to eat around here? I am really busy and tied up. This lunch meeting is about strategizing our next move for this afternoon." With that, I turn and sit in the passenger seat of Jeffery's car. Behind is Dr. Odze with a silly grin, seated and already buckled in.

"Martin, I want a divorce!" raising her voice in front of all these spectators. There are other attorneys parked near our car, including Mr. Harris and his two female attorneys. I am embarrassed our domestic issues are displayed in public. I am also shocked. *Why does Mary have to deal with this now?*

"Honey, we will talk about this tonight, I promise."

"No, I want you to listen to me now. Not just divorce, I want you to drop this case RIGHT NOW!" She is shouting at this point. All attorneys stop what they are doing and all eyes stare at me and Mary.

"Honey, what are you talking about? We are in the middle of the lawsuit. We can win this case easily, it's millions of dollars."

"Martin, listen to me! I don't want the money! I do not want this lawsuit to continue! Listen to me for a change. You never listen to me. Julie is my daughter as well, not just yours. You will not do as you please this time. I have my rights and I want you to drop the case, right now!" and she looks deadly serious.

"Do you remember Martin, right before Julie passed away, she said she was in peace. She met Jesus and told us not to be angry at the lab doctor. She did not knowingly mean any harm. It was not her fault but God's plan to have Greg in our arms and let go of our daughter Julie. She even said we should comfort the lab doctor because she feels so bad because it was not her who did anything bad to us. She said it is God who decides who lives and who dies. Julie was going to a beautiful place to rest. She died with a smile and told us to be in peace." Mary is now crying.

"This lawsuit is wrong. Julie is sad to see you doing this. This is not meant to be. You need to let go of this dispute and have peace for once in your life. Please stop this, please!"

Mary is in tears and bending her legs, crouching on the parking lot. She obviously does not care how she appears. My two girls run toward her, try to lift her up to stand but Mary just sits there, sobbing and pleading. Both girls give up and sit with her on the parking lot, crying together.

What a scene, I look like a fool. All eyes are on me. I look at Mr. Harris and shake my head. I feel like my own family is destroying my reputation. I was never embarrassed like this my entire career, especially in public.

I get out of the car and walk toward Mary and the girls. I help her to get up, and walk my family toward her car to let her sit. Her car is parked not too far from the scene. Everyone is still watching us.

"Okay, okay, honey, I heard you now. We will talk about this tonight." I tell June to drive and get some lunch. June drove all the way from Berkeley last night to be at the courthouse and is skipping her classes.

I tell June I will ask the judge for a recess and request she postpone afternoon court activities so I can discuss things with Mary tonight. I explain my team must talk to the judge and get her approval for this.

"I will call you soon so that you can drive Mom back home after your lunch."

All I can think of are the expenses we have to pay, especially for Dr. Odze to appear an added day in court which is a substantial amount. If we do not win this case, all these expenses are billed, and paid for by us.

Not only that, but the most important thing for me is also the public embarrassment. They will wonder why I did not have consensus with my own wife, my own family, to pursue the lawsuit. I look like an idiot! Not only does my wife not want this lawsuit to continue but also said she wants a divorce—in public.

Women are so selfish. They do not care about saving faces for their husbands. Their emotions get in the way and they express whatever they feel and wherever they are regardless of the situations their men are in.

There are so many nights I was with her and she would not talk to me. I tried so many times to talk about Beth, an affair I had recently, but Mary would not talk.

But now, she has to talk about it, in the courthouse parking lot, a display in public, in front of my daughters and all the attorneys. The shit hit the fan today and definitely landed on my face in broad daylight for everyone to see and enjoy the scenery.

One thing for sure, I cannot control women.

All eyes still on me, I walk to Mr. Harris who is still standing nearby.

"I'd like to ask the judge if we can recess for the afternoon. Would you be willing to do so?"

"Yes, absolutely. I have Judge Wayne's phone number. Do you want it?" Mr. Harris says.

"Yes, please," I meekly respond.

He texts me the number. I am embarrassed not to have the number myself. Supposedly a well-connected trial attorney and no phone number for the judge in my hand is another embarrassing point. Not my day for sure. Might as well bring every possible embarrassing thing to me today, all at once.

The judge happens to answer my phone. I briefly explain what is happening and ask her permission to recess for the rest of the day. She said she will let this happen only once and advises me to talk it over seriously with my family tonight and not waste all the peoples' time and resources.

"We will meet tomorrow 9:00 a.m. sharp and better have your act together attorney, as to how you want to proceed." She is very firm. Another strike against me today.

I thank her. I tell Mr. Harris we will see him tomorrow morning and I walk over to Jeffrey and tell him the same, and to cancel our lunch because I must go home and address this mess with my family.

I find my car and drive away, fuming. I realize I must control Mary and the girls. I text June so she knows I will be home in a couple of hours to see them. Court is adjourned for the day and we need to discuss a few things together. I stop at In-N-Out Burger, get myself a lunch and drive to the Beverly Hills park.

I sit on some bench to eat the burger and fries with a cold drink. I am the most overdressed person in the park eating lunch in my three-piece suit. But no one cares to look at me.

I chew my burger and begin to think how pitiful this site of myself actually is. I am the respected attorney who built the empire of Grey, Zemke and Freedman LLC. I am an owner of this law firm, the leading member of this prestigious firm.

We own two jets, a couple yachts and a portfolio of vacation houses all over the world. We have more than one hundred top attorneys, the best in town, every cream of the crop attorney in Beverly Hills.

How did I get into this situation? I sit here eating a burger, put to shame by my own family. How did I get here?

I look up. It is a bright blue sky without hint of a cloud. A spectacular day! Another sunshine day in Southern California. How small I am, compared to the endless blue sky.

Suddenly I know how small I actually am. This must be how God sees me. Just a tiny creature. Just another human being out of billions of people living under the vast sky. No matter how big I feel about myself, how proud I am with my own achievements and the money I have, I am just another creature to God.

I miss my daughter Julie. I wish I can just hold her again and tell her how much I love her. Why am I not in peace as she was? Julie told us that she is in peace, and hence, we should be in peace. She told us not to get angry, for she is in heaven with Jesus, sitting on His lap playing with Him in heaven.

Here I am on this park bench, fuming, in anger for losing her, looking for faults from someone else even while God is in control. God must have known what He is doing with my daughter. I certainly have no control over Julie's life, let alone my own life. I cannot control my wife. I have no control over anything, in fact.

Why am I so angry? Who am I angry with? I am completely lost and have no answer.

Death is the inevitable part of life. Death is true as the life itself. We all die at some point. Then, what is the meaning of all that I am doing? I was merely trying to support my family to have a roof over their heads, food to eat and providing comfort for their lives.

I did my job well enough as a man of the house. That is all I ask of myself. I should have peace then, within myself. It is not my fault that Julie died. I should not feel guilty about her death since I had no control over that. Maybe I did not actually fail to protect her as her father.

I have not finished eating the burger and I hold the cold, half-eaten thing in my hand along with a couple of cold, floppy fries and begin to cry. What a pitiful sight I must be, again in a public space. It must be several decades since I last had tears flowing down my face.

I trash the rest of the food and wipe my tears with the napkins. I better get hold of myself before someone walks close to me and sees this pathetic sight—a grown man in a three-piece Armani suit, eating a cheap hamburger crying.

I give myself a slow walk around the park to gather some thoughts; what I should do and what I am going to say to my family. Come to think of it, I never had time to myself like this—being alone and just thinking about what I am thinking. I was robbing myself to take time for myself.

Chapter Six

Even though I have a great temptation to rebuke my wife's behavior of punishing me with embarrassment in front of a public courthouse, I decide to just listen to her when I get back home.

They are already in the house, cleaning up their salad lunch partially left on the kitchen table. Mary hardly touched her lunch. I have no clue what they talked about during my absence, but I hardly care about that.

I ask the girls to be excused for a few minutes while I talk to their mother. They quietly disappear into their rooms.

"Darling, let's talk. It is well overdue," I begin.

"Martin, I'm sorry I made a scene in the parking lot, but I could not wait any longer."

"It is water under the bridge. I wish you would have talked to me beforehand. We had so many nights together and I wanted to talk to you too," I plead.

She already has tears in her eyes. "I'm really sorry, Martin. I know how important your image is but I need to get you out of your world and get the attention shifted to me. I deserve to be heard."

"Of course, honey, please talk to me now."

"Like I said, I want a divorce and I want you to drop this case. It is not all right Martin and you know it. This is not what God wants us to do now. Do you not remember what Julie said to us in her dying bed? She said we need to comfort that lab doctor. This is not the way we should act, this is not comforting her for sure."

"Mary, think about this for a moment. Listen to what you are saying. The lab doctor is the one who caused our loss. Our daughter could have lived. Today she could be running around the house, bugging both of us to listen to her stupid new wave music and watch her dance movement. Right here at the kitchen table! Remember Mary? She used to make us laugh. I miss her so much!" I begin to cry too.

"Martin, you know it is not up to this lab doctor to let our daughter live or die. She does not have that kind of power. It is God who decides who lives and who dies. No human will ever have that kind of power.

"The lab doctor is merely a servant of God. If she missed the diagnosis, it was God who made her blind at that moment to miss the diagnosis. Maybe she blinked at that time.

"You read the depositions from the defense expert doctors who said that diagnosis is almost impossible to make until the patient has metastatic tumors all over the body." She breathes hard.

"Yes, the other doctors said it is quite a treatable disease, but it is God who made Julie to have the tumor in her brainstem that killed her. You know, Martin, Dr. Kline told us repeatedly that he was going to do strong doses of chemotherapy first before radiation therapy because he thought it was our best chance to have the tumor cells killed.

"Radiation therapy was scheduled the following week but our daughter died. She died so fast before they could even pump another cycle of chemotherapy.

"How can you fault Dr. Kline? Isn't he your friend? How can you sue your own friend doctor who tried his best to save her? He delivered our grandson Greg and all my girls." She pauses to catch her breath.

"You wanted a cesarean section, so Dr. Kline did a cesarean section. If Julie did not have a C-section, the placenta would not have reached the lab doctor. Did you not hear that a normal vaginal delivery would not have sent her placenta to the lab for evaluation?"

"No, her placenta would have gone to the lab doctor because Julie had a pre-eclampsia, gestational high blood pressure. It was not just because she had the C-section."

"Okay, okay, whatever. Still, the expert doctors said the diagnosis would be extremely difficult to render."

"Not my expert. He said it is a slam dunk case."

"Okay, we will agree to disagree. You have your thoughts and I have my own. Whatever it is, I am asking you to drop this case. I will not have it. I want you to call me to the witness stand tomorrow morning and I will have something I want to say to both doctors."

"You are not scheduled to be on the stand. Dr. Odze is. You are not taking the stand at all!"

"Yes, I am. I am calling Jeffrey Grey, right now if you don't, and I am going to stand there and deliver my wishes."

"Honey, be rational about this. You are being emotional again."

"Martin, you belittle me, in fact, you belittle all women. I am tired of listening to your chauvinistic attitudes toward women in general. Remember, you have three daughters and they are listening to your nonsense about women-this and women-that. You should be ashamed of yourself.

"So what if we women have extravagant ways of expressing ourselves with emotions? What is wrong with that? It is men who define what is appropriate and what is not. You men are scared of emotions and you simply don't know what to do with that.

"Just because you men don't know how to react, does not mean that emotion is not an appropriate thing to express in public."

"Honey, Mary, calm down," I say, and reach out to calm her down. She violently resists my outreached hand.

"Is that why you had an affair with a young paralegal? She shows no emotion and is cool as a cucumber? If that's what you need from a woman, go ahead and live with her!" Mary shouts at me.

I am sure the girls hear this. I am devastated with embarrassment again. I do not want my girls to know that I had an affair.

"I want a divorce. I do not want to spend the rest of my life wasting it with someone who never listens to me, and you do not even listen to or honor the last wish of our daughter before she died.

"How can you be so insensitive? What kind of father are you? I can forgive you for being a terrible husband to me but I cannot forgive you for being a terrible father to Julie."

Mary walks out to the backyard after saying this. She sits on the beach chair near our pool, breathing hard. We need some time to reflect on what we said to each other.

I need to digest what she said. Sitting on the couch, I consider what just happened. June and Jane suddenly stand in front of me. I look up.

"Dad, did you have an affair?" June asks.

No clue what to say, I just look at her for a while.

"Dad, I am asking you, did you?" she shouts.

"Well, your mother and I…"

"This has nothing to do with Mom."

"Well, yes, I did, and I'm sorry."

"When did this happen? Was it during when Julie was dying?"

I have no answer. I try hugging her. She resists my arms.

"How could you, Dad? How could you do this to Mom?" she says and runs out.

Jane follows her big sister and says, "You are disgusting, Dad."

I sit back, dumbfounded. I feel out of place. All these women are killing me today. One moment, I am their hero and another moment, I am a scum. I need to compose my thoughts and sit a while.

Humiliating day, indeed. Humiliated by my own family and rejected by the beloved women in my life. I go back to my study room. This seems more real to me and I sit down, now in deep thought.

I will call Jeffery Grey so my wife can take the witness stand and talk out her thoughts.

What will Mary say or do there on the witness stand? The only thing I can predict is that she wants to drop the case. Maybe I should have a brief meeting tonight to settle the case with Mr. Harris, instead of dismissing the case. What is the point of having Mary stand there on the witness stand to say what she needs to say?

I should try and settle the case tonight with Mr. Harris, maybe for half the amount of money. It will still be a good chunk of money we can all stash away.

I head outside with a cold sparkling water with a wedge of lemon as Mary always likes and sit next to her.

"I will call the defense tonight and settle the case. Okay, honey? In that way, we will not have to go to court anymore."

"Martin, you still do not hear me. I want to go to the court tomorrow. I need to tell those doctors something. Put me on that witness stand. I will not settle the case. I want to drop this lawsuit." She uses her determined voice without even looking at me.

"Okay, I will do what you ask," as I hand her the drink.

"Martin, there is one more thing, I want you to pack and leave this house, now."

I go back to my study, call Jeffrey and ask him to put my wife on the witness stand tomorrow, first thing in the morning. He is not only extremely upset at the last-minute change, but also wants to know what she will say.

He threatens by telling me if the case gets dismissed, I must pay all the expenses, which so far total tens of thousands of dollars. He then adds, "Get control over your women!" and hangs up.

Apparently, Beth is venting to others and claims I was her lover who recently broke it off with her in such an inhumane way and not even returning her phone calls. Evidently my nickname these days used by Beth and her close friends is "The Bastard."

Come to think of it, I never returned Beth's phone calls, texts and emails after that hotel incident. I just left her at the hotel and walked out. That was the last time we saw each other as lovers.

I sometimes see her at the office but I ignore her completely. I do not want to face her. I do not know how to end that relationship. I never meant to hurt my wife or divorce my wife in order to be with someone else.

Mary is my life, I never wanted to lose her. What an asshole I am! I thought I would never get caught while having some fun.

My daughter's death jolted me. I never imagined I would lose her. And the thought of losing my wife now with divorce scares me. For the first time, fear is invading my heart.

I never meant to live like this, losing my daughter and separated from my wife, a broken family. Even though I downplay women's significance with my wife and daughters, they are all I have and they are who define me. I will not exchange anything for them.

I heard Mary's last words, actually a command to leave the house. I thought I heard it correctly but ignored it as usual. She does not really mean that. Why should I leave this place? This is *my* house!

She is just terribly upset and said it without really meaning what she said.

As I refocus on some work at my computer, I hear a suitcase roll across our wood floor, then stop at the door of my den office. Mary opens the door and I hear, "I packed your stuff. Please leave now!"

"Honey, where am I going to go? This is *my* house!"

"Well, I am not leaving and the girls are not leaving. So, *you* have to leave!"

"I don't understand. Can we talk about this?" I am almost pleading at this point.

"No, Martin, no more talk. I do not want to talk, please leave." She stands there and I suppose she is waiting for me to get up and leave.

"I cannot believe this, Mary. I hope you know what you are doing," I say as I pack my laptop computer with all the entangled cords.

"I don't believe this," and continue shaking my head. She is just standing there, waiting for me to get up and go.

So, I leave. I check into the Beverly Hills Hotel. It is expensive, especially without a reservation, but what can I do? I have no friends or family around who have a place where I can stay.

I wish my vacation house at Lake Tahoe was closer for a time like this. I know one thing, and that is when Mary decides to do something, she will do it. *Stubborn woman!*

Chapter Seven

Mary is dressed in a black suit as if attending a funeral. Actually, she is wearing the same skirt suit she wore at Julie's funeral. She even wears dark sunglasses in the courtroom.

All the people are here, attorneys from both sides, expert doctors from both sides, Drs. Choi and Kline, the jurors and Judge Elizabeth Wayne. The rear of the courtroom is also packed with people like yesterday. Among them are my two daughters sitting on each side of Mary.

"Your Honor, we call Mary Freedman as our first witness," Jeffrey Grey says.

Judge Wayne looks down, lowers her reading glasses to her nose bridge as if she wants to make sure she heard correctly.

"Counsels, approach the bench, please, both of you," pointing at Mr. Harris and Mr. Grey. They gather closely and talk quietly among themselves, probably discussing why Mary Freedman is called to testify instead of Dr. Odze, as planned.

I look back at Dr. Odze who is gesturing "What is going on here?" I shrug my shoulders as if I have no idea what is going on. Fortunately, Dr. Odze is dressed much better today. He wears a dark navy-blue striped suit, a white dress shirt and bluish-purple polka dot necktie. Jeffrey Grey must have given him a dress code lecture yesterday. Thank goodness.

After a brief time, the judge says to Jeffrey Grey, "Please proceed."

Jeffrey Grey calls for Mary Freedman again. Mary walks across the courtroom and steps upon the witness stand. She places her hand on the Bible and her right hand is raised.

"Do you swear by Almighty God that that the evidence you give to the court in this case shall be the truth the whole truth and nothing but the truth, so help you God?" the bailiff asks.

"Yes, I do," Mary says.

"Please be seated."

Mary sits down in the witness box.

Jeffrey Grey approaches her. "Mrs. Mary Freedman, please state your name and spell your name for us."

"Mary Freedman, M.A.R.Y., F. R. E. E. D. M. A. N."

"What is your relationship with Julie Freedman?"

"Julie was my daughter, my last child."

"And what is your purpose for sitting in the witness stand here today?"

"I-I want to convey a message to Dr. Choi and Dr. Kline today."

"And what is your message?" Jeffrey Grey asks with a some-what irritated voice.

"I want to say the whole thing without any interruption. I prepared what I want to say to them on this piece of paper and I am going to read it, because if I speak without reading I might forget to say something important because I am very nervous right now. May I do that?"

"Please proceed," Jeffrey says, looking at me for an approval. I bend my head down for the okay sign.

"Your Honor, members of the jury, and my family and friends, I stand here to say to you all that my heart is broken beyond your imagination losing my child Julie." Mary is already tearful but she gathers her courage to finish reading the letter she wrote, clears her throat and wipes her tears with a tissue she brought.

She continues, "As a mother, losing a child before my own demise is something no one can fathom, the pain I must endure. This is not supposed to be like this. The child should die after I pass away. That is the natural way.

"But my child, Julie died first. And the pain is like nothing that I ever experienced. It is as though a piece of my heart is ripped apart and taken away from me.

"Julie was a special child, our last one, with free spirit, and such a giving person. She made our family laugh and gave us much joy. She was just 16 years old when she died. Her death was related to her pregnancy. She began to love this boy from her school. They were in love.

"At first, I was frustrated at my daughter sleeping with him at such a young age and faulted myself for not keeping her pure, a Godly woman. I felt embarrassed about her pregnancy thinking I must have failed to be a good mother. I kept her hidden from neighbors as their source for gossip. I wanted my child to keep her reputation and avoid mean and cruel comments spoken to her from nosy people." She pauses.

"The world is so cruel to girls and women when they are pregnant without husbands. The society has this double standard for women. So, in her last six months of pregnancy I spent time with her far away from home. I lied to everyone that she was sick.

"During this time, I was with her, just two of us, hidden from the reality. I realized I was doing this for myself, not for her. I was embarrassed, ashamed that my daughter got pregnant at such a young age without her husband, and I wanted to avoid those rumors. I was seeking a fake sympathy from friends, coworkers and family.

"I became lonely. I had no one to talk to or console with. When I am not in truth, I can't seek true sympathy or empathy from others. I was rejecting my daughter for a long time because of her behaviors.

"But Julie accepted me even when I was embarrassed about her to present to the world the truth. She comforted me day after day. She is the one who hugged me in our silence when I was feeling like a failure. She is the one who told me everything is going to be all right. 'God will bring out goodness from all these pains,' she said. She told me she is sorry to cause such a heartache and burden to me." She turns the page.

"Julie eventually died, but she left her son Greg to us. My grandson Greg has her eyes, her lips and her hair color. When I see Greg, he reminds me of Julie when she was an infant.

"Now my heart aches from the joy he brings to our family. A gift from God. God gives and takes away. How can any one of us argue with God when He is the Creator and we are just His creatures?

"Our lives are not our own. We are not able to plan our own course. God is the potter and we are the clay. All of us are the work of God's hand. So then, it does not depend on a person's desire or effort. It depends entirely on God, who shows mercy. And we know that in all things, God works for the good of those who love Him, who have been called according to His good purpose."

She raises her head and looks toward the jurors. "I want us to examine and be honest with ourselves. Do we have power to control the life of Julie? Did any one of these doctors have any kind of power to decide who lives and who dies?

"I believe not. I believe they did their best for my daughter. My daughter, before she died, she told me and my husband Martin that the lab doctor, Dr. Choi must be in pain and lonely and we should comfort her, because she did her best and she must feel so bad."

Mary turns her head toward Dr. Choi and says, "I want you to know, Dr. Choi, my daughter not only accepted her death, but before she died, she asked us to comfort you. She was worried about you having a peaceful mind.

"It is because of that, we also forgive you. Not just forgive you, but we thank you for your work and your heart, suffering for losing our precious child, Julie. I want you to know that you are not at fault for Julie's death because you do not have such power. Only God does. It is His will that Julie go to heaven at this time.

"We had a beautiful 16 years with Julie. She was a gift from God that we all enjoyed while having her in our family. I do not care if you missed the diagnosis or the diagnostic material was not there in the slide to begin with. I will not continue with this dispute because it is meaningless for me and Julie. The end result is the same. Julie died. She is not here with us." Mary cries.

"Dr. Choi, go in peace and know that we forgive you and God is with you. May God give you peace beyond your comprehension. And know that you were a part of God's plan in relation with Julie."

Then, Mary turns to Dr. Kline and says, "And as for Dr. Kline, you hesitated to give the C-section for my daughter since it was not indicated. If you had your way, Julie would have undergone normal vaginal delivery and there is a chance you would not have sent her placenta to Dr. Choi because Julie had just a mild hypertension during her pregnancy.

"You did exactly the way my husband asked you to do, bending your better knowledge of medicine to accommodate our demands. And I thank you for all your efforts.

"To not give Julie the radiation therapy, you must have used your better judgment to make your medical decisions. Julie died in such a brief time, before anyone had a chance to do anything. Her death is not related to your lack of medical judgment, as this lawsuit states.

"Julie's life belonged to God, and not you, Dr. Kline." Mary stops and looks up at the people in the courtroom.

"It is no one's fault, and I solemnly believe we need to let Julie rest in Jesus's arms peacefully. When we are not at peace with her death, she will not be at peace in heaven. I believe Julie is watching us from heaven, even now. This is her last wish that we all be in peace and forgive doctors for they did nothing wrong intentionally. It is not their fault she died.

"God gave us another precious gift, Greg, in our arms, a part of Julie, reminding us and continuing the times we had Julie as our child. Therefore, I want this case to be dropped, for we all need to be at peace.

"No money can substitute for Julie's life. This lawsuit should not have happened. It is partly my fault because my husband and I did not talk carefully, and I am terribly sorry to put you all through this. I was in so much pain, and could not see other people around me. Please forgive me."

Mary is crying through her entire talk, but manages to finish without losing any part of her speech. She said it all very clearly. The courtroom is deadly silent, a pin drop will be heard. There is no one without wet eyes in this courtroom.

Dr. Choi is sobbing, putting her head down, drenched in her tears the whole time. Even Dr. Kline has tears, which he wipes with his fist. The entire jury has tissues in their hands, wiping their tears. Judge Wayne is in tears as well. Looking back over my shoulder, I see my daughters crying, holding on to each other.

I am in shock. I did not realize Mary had in herself such a confidence to talk in public. She had the entire audience in her hand. This is not a courtroom sight I ever experienced in my long professional career as a trial attorney.

Jeff Grey is astonished, perplexed and opens his arm into the air, shrugs his shoulders, looks at me for what to do next.

Judge Wayne raps her gavel three times and says, "Thank you, Mrs. Freedman. You may step down. The court will recess for 30 minutes. Both counsels and Mr. Freedman, please come to my office." She gets up and leaves the courtroom, wiping the tears that she can no longer hide.

Chapter Eight

I do not want to look at anyone's face, especially my wife Mary. I avoid her at all cost. Somehow, she makes me feel like I am the less significant partner in this marriage.

Jeffrey Grey and I walk down the hallway to take the elevator up five floors to Judge Wayne's office. As we walk down the hallway to the elevator, Mr. Harris is right behind us. We all take the elevator in silence. I look down the whole time. I hoped to talk to Jeffrey but Mr. Harris is here, so I do not speak. As we enter Judge Wayne's office, she is taking off her robe.

"Please sit, counsels." She points to her round table with four seats. We all sit around the table but she sits at her desk chair, leaving some distance between her and us.

"What's the next step? Mr. Freedman, why don't you talk to us," she says.

"Well, I did not know my wife was going to do this."

"Well, if you do not govern your own household, I don't know what to say to you. You gentlemen, you usually like to control women? Why don't you tell us the next step right now so that you do not waste anybody's time?" She says with sarcasm in her tone.

"I am sorry about all this. I don't know what to say, I need some time to think about this."

"Well, would you like us to give you the rest of the day to think about it? Do you need to talk to your wife now, and then come back to us? By the way, I was impressed with her today. For my entire lifetime working at this courthouse, I never heard such intelligent and heart-filled words spoken until today. You have married up and I don't know if you deserve her, Mr. Freedman."

"I just don't know what to say. I need more time," meekly comes my response.

The judge says nothing and I am so humiliated and irritated with myself for not communicating with my wife. I should have talked to my own wife in our private times and not displayed the dysfunctional part of our relationship in the courtroom. Women have their ways to take men's pride away in public without trying or sometimes even knowing.

"Okay, Mr. Freedman, I can let you have the rest of the day to sort it out. Mr. Harris and Mr. Grey, do you have anything to say?"

"No, we can wait until Mr. Freedman has some time to think it over," Mr. Harris responds.

"Yes, I want to talk to Mr. Freedman to maybe settle. We will get your answer by tomorrow morning," Jeffrey hurriedly says, almost getting up from the chair.

Judge Wayne stares at Mr. Grey like a disgusted 8th grade school principal and says, "I guess you two did not hear anything this morning from Mrs. Freedman. She talked the truth with mercy, clearly stating the fact that both doctors are not at fault. What is the basis of settling? Are you not gentlemen, not afraid of God looking down at you?"

"But we can't just drop the case. We had so much effort put into this case. What about all the expenses?" Jeffrey pleads.

"Shut up, Jeff, let's talk outside!" I blurt out.

"Well, gentlemen, please discuss among yourselves. I will ask the court to recess until tomorrow morning. I need to hear from you this afternoon by 4:00 p.m. One of you shall contact me, so that I can decide what to do for tomorrow's session.

"If I do not hear from you by 4:00 p.m. sharp, I will decide what to do for tomorrow. I will see you at 9:00 a.m. sharp. Thank you all, please get out of my office now, so I can get my other work done," she coldly orders.

We quickly leave her office and walk down the hallway.

"Let me know what I should do. You have my number," Mr. Harris says as he takes off to use the staircase. I guess he did not want to join our dispute in the elevator.

"What the fuck?" Jeffrey says, rolling his head and eyes in frustration when Mr. Harris is out of sight.

"Shut up, Jeff, it is not your decision. It is mine. I need to talk to my wife first."

"Now what? At this rate, we cannot even get a million, let alone $15 million, not even halfway at seven!"

"It's not always about the money Jeff. Wake up to reality."

"What is that reality Martin? To walk away from seven million just because you could not handle your wife?"

I am ready to punch his left cheek. "You watch your filthy mouth, Jeff. This is my last warning!" I turn to take the stairs and will not bear the pain talking to Jeffrey any longer.

"What now?" he says and shrugs his shoulders.

"I will call you before 4:00 p.m. today," as I close the staircase door. I call Mary's cell phone. She does not pick up. I leave a voicemail that I need to see her at home ASAP. I have about six hours to sort out this situation and I desperately need to see her.

Chapter Nine

Driving home, I quickly slow down and sit idling in my car with familiar LA traffic. No car is moving on Wilshire Blvd. It must be due to an accident. Stupid traffic! What the heck are all these Los Angeles people doing on the road, always jamming up the traffic? Why don't they just stay at home or stick to their office at this hour so I can get home?

Using both hands I open my traffic apps and see solid red lines for the next three to four miles, and all the surrounding streets are all red. I turn off the engine of my silver metallic Porsche. The traffic has literally stopped for the past five minutes. Someone must have been killed, maybe one of those lousy motorcycles passed between the lanes and got hit by a car, throwing the body up in the air which then landed on the road with the brain splattered on the street. *Another attorney's heaven,* I imagine.

In the silence, with nothing else to do, my memory of Julie's last words pop into my head. I hear her voice very clearly. She has incredibly peaceful, gentle, and joyous eyes looking at both of us, Mary and me. Her eyes are indescribable, as if I am looking into Jesus's eyes through her.

She tells us to be peaceful, for she is at peace. She saw a dream that she was with Jesus, she was sitting in His lap playing. She told us not to be angry at the lab doctor. No one means to do any harm to the patients knowingly.

How can she talk about the lab doctor when she is dying? But she really worries about the lab doctor who must feel so bad for the pain and suffering she caused to our family. The lab doctor needs to be at peace, so, we need to comfort the doctor, forgive and let it go.

God is using the lab doctor in His infinite designs and it has to be this way. Everything will work out and Jesus will take care of everything. All we have to do is just trust Him. Live one day at a time knowing that He sees everything we do and think.

She is going to a beautiful place, the Heaven where we all belong, and we shall see each other there one day and embrace each other once again.

And my wife's words today saying what can we do about our lives when the key of living and dying is not up to anyone else but God. The lab doctor was just an instrument that God used and she had to be there at that time for His work to be completed.

So, why am I so angry? Who shall I really be angry at? Am I actually angry at God Himself? I feel God is looking down at me right now, feeling sorry for my loss of direction in life. *"Come to me, all you who are weary and burdened, and I will give you rest. Take my yoke upon you and learn from me, for I am gentle and humble in heart, and you will find rest for your souls. For my yoke is easy and my burden is light."*

I melt down with these words. Why do I think of these words? I heard these words from my Sunday Bible session in the Catholic church when I was a toddler growing up. These are Jesus's words.

I begin to cry, out loud, pouring out all my anger, stormy passions, and hostility toward life in general. I do not know what I am doing with myself and with this case. I did not even honor my daughter's last wish from her death bed. What kind of a father am I? What kind of a husband am I to Mary?

I was not listening to either of them. Why am I dismissing their voices?

My daughters and my wife are everything to me. I am nothing if I do not have them.

What did I work so hard for?

Why am I always in disputes and conflicts all the time, just to be in complete control and strive to win? To win for what? Just an argument? For my pride?

What does that matter anyway, when we all just die in the end?

Will God say to me, "Good job for winning the arguments all the time?"

Why did I not see the futility in my behaviors and my works?

Why have I not paid attention to see Greg, God's gift through my daughter Julie?

Why was I irritated with his cries at night, when he was asking for my attention to take a look at him?

Mary said Greg has Julie's hair, eyes and lips. I didn't even realize that. I must go see him and actually look at him.

I can't wait to get home and hold him, to see and appreciate what he looks like. I haven't opened the gift box God left for me at my own home for such a long time.

I never had a son. I always wanted a son. Finally, Julie gave me a grandson for me to raise.

There are too many regulations set by well-meaning people saying we should get married and have children; no teenage pregnancy allowed; we should have a mom and a dad raising children in a household. The family has to look a specific way to be accepted in the eyes from society. But the truth is, all the families have dysfunctional aspects in their lives. Nothing is perfect.

Greg is a child out of wedlock, from a teenage girl who sinned. But God made something beautiful about Greg. He is precious to us, and he is a perfect gift from God, indeed as Julie said in her last words. He will bring joy to our family and much laughter as she did.

I can't wait any longer to see Greg. I turn at some sort of street and park the car. I walk, actually I begin to run, the four miles home and to hell with this traffic. I take my necktie and jacket off. It feels good to do some exercise and breathe cool November air in LA.

Chapter Ten

By the time I get home, I am drenched in sweat. My daughters look at me as if I am some street bum looking for food. They never saw me unkempt like this—ever. I am usually in a three-piece suit holding a leather briefcase. I did not bother to bring my briefcase when I ran. It is still in the car.

"What happened to you, Dad?" says June.

"I ran here. How did you guys get here? There was traffic on Wilshire."

"Yeah, we took the freeway most of the time. Did you walk?"

"Yeah, where is Greg?"

"He is sleeping. He is with our nanny. Don't go in there, you will wake him up. And you are filthy, Dad!" she says with her nose pinched, waiving her hand to dilute my sweaty unpleasant smell in the air.

"I am sorry. Your mom here?"

"Yeah, she is outside, the pool area."

"I got to see her now!"

"Dad, I think you need to listen to her. I know how you think about the lawsuit, but you really need to listen to her and Julie. I think Mom did a fantastic job today. We are so proud of her.

"Why don't you take a shower first, Dad? I don't think Mom wants to talk to you smelling like this."

"Okay, thanks," and I rush to the bathroom. The cool water over my head is indeed refreshing. I have just over two hours before I need to call Jeffrey and Judge Wayne.

I haven't the faintest idea how to start the conversation with my wife. The girls must have the same thoughts as Mary and they must agree, since June said they are proud of Mom.

After a quick shower, I fix a turkey sandwich with two bottles of soft drinks and go out to find Mary, who is still sitting near the pool. The water sparkles like a million pieces of diamonds under our clear sunshine day.

"Honey, you did a great speech. I was proud of you," I say gently.

"Where did you go? You had no lunch yet?"

"No, I ran four miles. Wilshire was stopped. I saw eight or nine police cars and a few ambulances. Someone must have been severely injured."

"Yes, we saw Wilshire had a fatality accident, so we took the freeway. You know how these young people use their smartphones for traffic information. They are really different from our generation. I got a benefit from their cleverness today."

"Well, Mary, we need to talk."

"My talking is over, Martin. You need to leave this house. I said what I need to say in the court today."

"Yes, about that…"

"Martin, did you hear anything I said today?" Now she looks directly into my eyes.

"Yes, I heard you. And I remember what Julie said on her death bed. I was thinking a lot the past few hours. First, I need to say I am sorry I put you through all this while we both have not processed the loss of Julie. I should have listened to you. I need to call the judge by 4:00 p.m. today to let her know our decision. Do you want this case to be dismissed?"

"What do you think, Martin?"

"Well, before I say what I think, I really want to hear from you first."

"You heard my voice this morning in the court. Why are you asking again now?"

"Okay, I heard you loud and clear. You want to drop this case. No settlement, and no money."

"Yes, that is correct."

"Okay, your wish will be done. Your wish is Julie's wish and, therefore, my wish also."

"Thank you, Martin," her face showing relief.

"I will call the judge."

We sit there without talking for a while, watching the water dance under the mild breeze. "I want a divorce, Martin," Mary says when she breaks the silence.

"I know, you said that before."

I wanted to say much more than that. I wanted to tell her how sorry I am for all these years, putting her through a life tolerating my continual disputes and anger as I lived preoccupied with the concept of winning, long hours of absences from home, inability to attend to her loneliness, insensitivities in understanding raising children and to top that off, my infidelity. I can see she has had enough.

But I want to tell her what I felt this afternoon, driving home today, how I broke down under the cross of Jesus, repenting my shortcomings and why I ran to home. For some reason, I did not have courage to say all this to her now. I just finished my sandwich and left her at the pool.

My body and soul ache as I walk back to my car and drive to the hotel. I need to get a more permanent place, for it might take a long time to settle things with Mary and me.

Too bad I have to do the work and find a place to live for the next few months. My secretary could search for my apartment.

I am spoiled and taken care of by all the women around me. I even feel violated that I have to pick up the phone and make calls for a place to stay.

Chapter Eleven

The Motion to Dismiss paperwork is signed by all the parties involved. The judge reviewed and agreed. "I am glad that you came to your senses, Mr. Freedman," Judge Wayne says, and cancels attendance for jurors, the doctors, and the expert witnesses for the next day.

All we have to do now is to get the signatures on the final paperwork by Mary, myself, Jeffrey Grey and Mr. Harris tomorrow in front of the judge. Then, the case is dismissed. Zero dollars exchanged.

I do not get to hear from anyone, how they felt when Mary spoke from her heart describing how she felt. I want to hear from the lab doctor, how she felt, and why did she cry so much. What is her story? Why did she make that kind of mistake? How does she feel about it now, and off the hook?

Some part of me still wants revenge. I want to see the defeated face of the lab doctor. But I know this too is meaningless, because in truth, she was used by God. Like Mary said, no human being has such power to control another person's destiny.

One thing I must do is pay tens of thousands of dollars for lawsuit expenses of this case, out of my own pocket and pay to my own company. I also need to absorb humiliations that I did not win the case. I owe a big favor to Jeffrey Grey who I am not sure will ever forgive me for this case. It will be a defeat on his personal record because of me. He is not used to not winning, either.

My own wife humiliated me in public, then saw that I am just a powerless man behind her. Well, I just have to man up and face all the attacks. It is after all, my fault for not listening to my family's wishes and acted on my own desire of revenge. As a man of the household, this is the only thing I know how to do well in all of my life. I thought I was doing the job I needed to do and focused on acting my part. This is the way I should protect my family, the girls.

I was caught up by worldly expectations of what a man should do and be; wealthy, protective, decisive and powerful. But now, what I care most is to find the direction for Mary and me to continue. She wants a divorce. I do not want that. We need to sort that out carefully.

Maybe I will convince her to get a temporary separation for a few months and then decide what we should do. Hopefully, she will be amiable to this suggestion. I just need to gather my thoughts and speak to her with clarity. I am very well equipped to do so in my job and argue effectively, but when it comes to my wife, I am not sure how to speak or get my thoughts across and communicate to her. It has been so long that we talked this way.

Have we spoken this way before? We were busy raising kids and doing our respective roles in the house. I need to engage with her, back to two decades ago when I was courting her. We came so far from then.

Chapter Twelve

I rent a one-bedroom condo in Century City close to my office and home. Not that I foresee going back home soon, but just in case Mary calls me to perhaps babysit Greg some night, I will be close by. I brought more clothes and kitchen stuff Mary packed me for this new place.

It is so unfamiliar living without my daughters and my wife cooking for dinner, making all kinds of noise in the process. I am alone, sometimes a welcoming time to be quiet and reflect, but at times, saddened by loneliness. No one to talk to and no one giving me a nice warm homemade dinner. The kitchen was always warm with ovens on, smelled wonderful with a pot roasting and bread cooking. I miss that.

I miss seeing Greg. He is growing so fast. Every day seems different when I see him. He stands up and falls to the ground to swipe the floor with all his extremities, smiling and trying to come toward me when I sit on the sofa. Thank God the floors are always clean. Greg drools all over the place, slapping on his own pools of saliva on the floor with a big smile.

Life is messy. Indeed, very messy, but so beautiful. If it is not messy, it is not real life. I hated that drooling part from all my daughters when they were infants. I hated all the messy parts in life. I just wanted to have a clean, well-organized house with my wife. But life is never that ideal. It is messy, unorganized and tangled with all kinds of misunderstanding.

Now, finally, I miss that. Kitchen with a half onion rolling around, cutting board with sticky starchy potato cuts, apples cut and oxidized, banana half eaten, the yellow outside turning black in color. All the messy things I hated and constantly telling my family not to do; now, I miss all of them and all the scenes as well.

My place now is empty, clean and organized, just like what I wanted. But I am not happy. I am not smiling anymore. Today is December 1. Soon, Christmas time approaches. I am here all by myself. I just want to go back to our home with the family and Christmas dinner.

Having no Julie is sufficiently sad for this Christmas. But I am here all by myself. I am not sure Mary would want me to be there for the holidays. What can I do or say to make her change her mind? This separation definitely is sufficient suffering for me, but how long will Mary require me to be not seen?

Having all the money in the world does not make me happy. I could have another woman's company if I want to, but that is not what I want. It seems unfair that I paid for the house while Mary and my daughters live there happily without me.

Why is the man always the victim in loneliness? *They are still not paying a dime for the house. I am!*

But if I could only go back, I would tell Mary I am sorry and I would do anything to be with her. This is the day I receive Mary's letter. I unfold her letter. This beautiful handwriting makes me cry.

> Dear Martin,
>
> You have wronged me in a way that should not be overlooked or minimized. Whether you like it or not, forgiveness is needed on my part,

for you. When I forgive, I am absorbing the cost of your wrongdoing. This blank check on my part should not become foolish enablement or willful naivety.

In my anger, and while still licking my open wound, there is nothing I want to do but to hurt you back equally. But I am realizing this desire of mine to pay back the pain I have received only hurts me further. Jesus taught us to pray, "Give us today our daily bread, and forgive us our debts, as we also have forgiven our debtors." And in Matthew 6:14-15, He says, "If you forgive other people when they sin against you, your Father in heaven will also forgive you. But if you do not forgive others their sins, your Father will not forgive your sins."

I see the need for me to forgive you, not for your sake, but for my sake. Forgiveness is also needed for me; to not be a victim of you as a perpetrator constantly hurting me again and again in my thoughts.

And to forgive is not seeking restoration, for not all forgiveness will result in restoration. I am only able to assume the debt of your sin against me because God has assumed my debt against Him and He promised to cover whatever losses I incur by forgiving others.

I am sorry to say, I still need some time to recover from relinquishing the blank check of trust to you again. I will not do this from naive amnesia. I am fully awake and for my sake to live in trust once again. When the time comes, when my forgiveness is seeking redemption, I will ask you to come back home. Greg misses you and so do our daughters.

For the Christmas family dinner, it has been our tradition for you to cook a ridiculous and tasteless fruit cake and I would not want you to miss it this year for the kids. Greg needs to learn this tradition for the first time too.

Come home for Christmas, Martin.

Yours truly,
Mary

V: Dr. Choi's Story

Chapter One

Going to the court is like getting pulled with a rope by my neck to get slaughtered as an animal. It is my darkest moment in life. No one can imagine how I feel every day, and how humiliating my experience with this whole thing is.

Even though everything about the lawsuit is confidential and no one should talk about it, the whole department and other departments, especially oncology and surgery, knows who is sued and why. I am the topic of their gossips and that is not supposed to get discovered or discussed. The frequency of the doctors getting lawsuits are increasing, and it depends on what fields or subspecialties doctors are practicing.

In recent years pathologists get a lawsuit every eight to ten years on average. There is significant variation across specialties in malpractice lawsuits, ranging annually from 19.1% in neuro-surgery, 18.9% in thoracic–cardiovascular surgery, 15.3% in general surgery, 15.3% in OB/Gyn, 5.2% in family medicine, 3.1% in pediatrics, and 2.6% in psychiatry.

The *New England Journal of Medicine* in 2011 says that one in 14 doctors face a malpractice suit every year. Moreover, almost every physician will face a malpractice suit more than once during their career. This is the 2011 data, and expected to be much higher currently.

The 2008 data shows overall annual medical liability system costs, including defensive medicine, have been estimated by some investigators to be $55.6 billion dollars which is estimated to be 2.4% of total health care spending. Nearly two thirds of claims are dropped, withdrawn or dismissed despite this staggering total numbers of malpractice suits.

Only 10% of claims are decided by a trial verdict, and nearly 80-90% of those are decided in favor of the physician. To avoid malpractice suits, a majority of physicians order confirmatory and sometimes extra tests and/or consultations simply to avoid the risk of litigation, which profoundly increases the cost of care. This is called defensive medicine.

Among doctors who face malpractice suits, the most common effects from the lawsuit are burnout, decreased career satisfaction, and personal distress and suicidal ideation, which is exactly what I am currently experiencing. The amount of stress that I face in making the correct diagnosis 100% of the time is enormous and cumulative. To be expected to be a superhuman when we doctors are only humans is an unrealistic goal that society expects from us to do every day of our career.

I know this fact, but when I face the malpractice lawsuit myself, I cannot expect to be just the numbers. I am suffering for possible error in the diagnosis causing a young girl's death, and the pain that I must have caused for her family. This is unbearable.

Forget about the 99.9999% of the time when I did make the correct diagnoses and helped the other patients in my career. The one case of possible error is magnified and broadcast to the degree in the courtroom and during the deposition as if that is the only case I ever rendered a diagnosis.

I just want to kill myself and disappear from the face of the earth due to shame. Those trial attorneys are so skillful at making me feel small that I feel like I should just shrivel and die.

The most painful part of all is me not forgiving myself. Because of this unforgiving of my own self, all these humiliations from the trial attorneys and other doctors and patients seem justifiable and I must bear everything and anything they say to me and I have nothing to say back. The verbal diarrhea to cause me shame and humiliation from the plaintiff's attorneys feels justifiable and even my deserved portion of the deal, because my internal anguish in unforgiveness of myself is even more unbearable.

How do I express the remorse and regret to the family of Julie? How do I begin to trust my own self to continue practicing another day? I feel unworthy to be a doctor and even a human. The fact is every single doctor makes mistakes without exception, and whether the doctor admits or denies it is up to an individual doctor. If any doctor says they never made a mistake is a liar. The only way a doctor can truly not make mistakes is not to practice at all.

When mistakes happen, the next step is to admit it, take the responsibility and move on. This is the healthiest way to cope as a doctor but most doctors including myself cannot do the last step well: move on. Mistakes can be paralyzing, causing disempowerment, and loss of confidence even if I accept and understand the fact that all doctors are human and fallible.

We as the doctors do not imagine receiving forgiveness from the patient or the family of the patient. To hear what Mrs. Freedman said to me today in court is so shocking and unexpected, that I cannot control myself from shedding tears.

The sound of forgiveness when I am not even forgiving myself astounds me. It is as if I am hearing God's voice through her. God Himself is consoling me. And to hear that the young girl, before she died, was even worried about me because I must feel so sad about the situation is unfathomable.

It reminds me of the verses, in Romans 5:8 in the Bible, "*But God demonstrates his own love for us in this: While we were still sinners, Christ died for us.*" And in John 4:10, "*This is love: not that we loved God, but that He loved us and sent His Son as an atoning sacrifice for our sins.*"

I feel undeserving to receive such love, beyond just forgiveness from the young girl before she died. How can she worry about me when she was taking her last breath? Generous mercy was already given to me by a young girl who saw her Savior Jesus before she gave her soul to Him. How precious this story is to me? When I was still a sinner, my God delivered me from my destined and deserved penalty. What a redemption story!

In this courtroom, there are no dry eyes. I have no courage to look at Freedman family's faces. I felt so guilty and so bad that I wish that they just crucify me as fast as they can. Yet, the mother of the young girl looks straight into my eyes and relays what her daughter said toward me in her last breath.

They could have multiple millions of dollars after the jury trial because the jurors usually feel sympathetic to the loss of a child's life. For me, it is not about the money, or my loss of reputation or facing humiliation, or even the right and wrong, but it is about the guilt that I may have caused the patient's death.

But the mother of the young girl reminds me to think and ask myself to say, "I do not have such power; to live or to die is not up to me but up to God." Isn't that the truth?

Why do I even think for a moment that I have such power? It is not me who caused her to die but God took her and reclaimed her life because that is His ultimate and infinite plan for her. Ultimately, I do not have such power or intention to begin with. But I did want to say to the family, "I am sorry. Truly sorry!"

The society and the system do not allow me to say that to the family, but I am indeed sorry. If I could just meet them outside the system, I want to apologize for the loss and that I may have something to do with it. If only I did something about it, if only I detected before she had the disastrous symptoms, if only I had more suspicion at the time, and if only…time clock never returns, the damage is done and forever gone for a chance for me to change the fate. And this too is out of my control.

The only thing I can do now is to remorse. But now, I received the grace beyond my understanding. Now, I must achieve the hardest thing to do which is to forgive myself, and let it go.

I talk to no one, including Dr. Kline afterward. When Mr. Harris tells both of us the case is dismissed, I just say thanks, and walk from the room. It may appear cold, thankless and insensitive, but I need to walk away from the incident to reflect and heal myself. There is no time to feel celebration in jubilee for I just received enormous amount of mercy in exchange of someone else's life and pain of loss.

It is like we people do not dance and celebrate our joy for gaining our eternal life in heaven when we are faced with the cross of Jesus's death. It is a somber and holy moment to see Jesus's dead body, a lamb of God who took upon Himself to absorb all the sins of humanity. I know what it took for me to get that mercy when I deserve to get the wrath.

Chapter Two

Louis has decided to hire a different person altogether, someone who is much older, a former chairman at another institution in a different state, a friend of his—instead of starting a new search for the chairman of our department.

His sudden decision is less than a week after he announced in our faculty meeting. "I need to start a new search for a molecular research pathologist as the new chair. We need an expert in molecular research."

Oddly, Louis hires a surgical pathologist. This is another one of his own promises he does not keep. There is no new search, just an announcement. The whole thing is so irresponsible, disrespectful and disgusting from the beginning.

There was never any advertisement for the position through any national search. His promise has been broken that either me or the other candidate from Houston will be the next chair. Apparently, Louis added the requirement of "molecular research expertise" because of his current predicament, so that I would be disqualified.

These erratic decisions come after he openly announced, "We need more women chairs for several departments," and yet he hires another old white dude. His actions are outside of his original context and are against the institution's goals that were created for the future of the institution's image. His words carry no actions. It manifests to all that Louis changes his mind daily depending on what new circumstances he faces; a sure way to lose respect.

Today, Louis and I exchange text messages.

"You will *love* the new dollar amounts in your revised contract so you can continue as the interim chair," he writes. He promises to get this new (old) person as the chairman, but it will be well beyond my contract expiring at the end of December.

His manipulation to attract me so that I will continue my interim role until he fills the position is so evident and disgusting. He must think I am stupid enough to not notice what he is doing.

And for him to think any dollar amount will satisfy me and shut me up, to do the job I need to do before someone else takes over to receive everything that I have laid in place — it is obscene. One thing is for sure, I cannot trust Louis.

I feel exhausted to work for and with him. I'm foolish not knowing the true intentions of Louis, used and abused by him for not knowing his manipulative tactics to use me for his own benefit, and then I allow myself to get trashed at the end. At this point, I am no longer interested in his schemes and plots.

"Thanks for the new dollar amounts, Louis," I text, then quickly follow with, "Is there a bit more compensation you can look into providing me?" My texts send him on a goose chase to look for ways to pay me more money to continue the job of interim chair, while I fully well know that I have no intention to continue beyond the end of December. All I want is Louis's honesty, but he keeps hurting me with his manipulations.

During my last 1:1 meeting with Louis, I ask point blank why I am not chosen as the final candidate for the chair position. Louis is unable to answer my direct and simple question.

"You are doing a great job, in fact, fantastic job!" and, "Sara, I couldn't ask anything more from you." So, it is not my inadequacies, incompetence, lack of judgment or performance that he does not choose me. The reason is also not the lawsuit ordeal, especially since the case is dismissed.

At any point in time, doctors are being sued at this institution. Maybe Louis himself is involved in a lawsuit, for all I know. With a long pause from Louis, I notice this must be God's plan for me not to be named as the next chair of the department.

I stare into Louis's eyes for a long time, maybe two to three minutes. Quiet and speechless moments grow more noise in my mind, clearly allowing me to see that Louis is used by God for me: to move on from here.

One of our faculty members has emailed Louis, concerned about the instability and all the changes in our department leadership within a year.

"Dr. Bernard, I am surprised you chose to demote our existing chairman, then you appointed Dr. Choi as an interim chair, and now you are changing plans again? I am disappointed you abruptly started afresh with a new person. Your new choice for our chair was not even on the original candidate lists." Louis replies to the email by explaining the new person is coming next year and he is fast-tracking the new hire, and "The faculty better talk only good things about the department to the new chairman, and not scare him away, *capiche?*"

This is not received well by the faculty member, who explains to a couple colleagues the word *"capiche"* is like a mafia gangster demanding a particular act, "or else" type of situation. My colleague did not share this information with me for my benefit, but just to express his insecurity and lack of leadership in Louis.

From this ordeal I learn everyone looks for their interest only. Everyone has a different position and perspective. The needs are completely different based on one's own position. The faculty members seek their own security and stability, Louis is utilizing his power to put someone in place who he can control easier and patch the hole as quickly as possible.

He does not act for the benefit of the entire institution, and his best solution is fast-tracking to fill the position so he can avoid losing his own reputation. And for me, I lost a sense of why I need to sacrifice myself and my life for the people that I do not trust. All individuals have to do what they have to do in order to survive. At the end, no one can be faulted.

Our mission and purpose statements include "dedication to medicine by offering excellent care with integrity and transparency, to transform the future of health care by science and innovative research, and to teach the next generation with knowledge, leadership and compassion."

These statements are clear, but it is too often I see our leaders compromise their integrity, fill their own needs with quick reflex responses, put out fires only to save their reputations, and in the end, they do not follow our own institution's policies. Their major decisions are often done under the table and never transparent.

It is true that throughout the centuries, women are seldomly seen as chefs, conductors, pilots, chairmen of the department, presidents, CEOs, deans, astronauts, captains of ships, sports coaches, or any other visible leadership positions. Even though men may intuitively understand that when they work side by side with women, they might benefit and widen their own perspectives and understandings, men still shy away from being inclusive to women in leadership positions.

They like to keep the position of power to themselves. I understand certain physicians even recently have said, "Medicine used to be all men, and women ruined their careers." Even now, specialties such as orthopedics, thoracic and neurosurgeons are pretty much exclusively men, secretly and sometimes outspokenly against females joining their exclusiveness. White old males dominating key positions perpetuate through time and their defense is to say, "Bring us the qualified women!" without intention to actually hire them.

Even though Louis himself outwardly spoke that we need more women chairs, and repeats what our male leaders clearly state, "We want women to advance." Still, he cannot help but hire another man. Chairman as the title itself emphasizes it needs to be a man, an implicit bias. The position does not say Chairwoman. Women are just as well educated, talented and hardworking as their male counterparts but they face more resistance and obstacles when it comes to advancement.

Women outnumber men in college and medical schools now — they account for about 55%. Women tend to have higher grades and drop out less frequently than men. Yet according to a study sponsored by the Rockefeller Foundation, women hold only 4% of leadership positions in Fortune 500 companies.

A woman often faces a "double bind" as she is labeled a bitch for being too aggressive, but weak if she is too sensitive, as I experienced in my interview with the CEO. I tend to prefer humane and collaborative leadership styles over charismatic leadership styles, and this was regarded as inferior.

My style of leadership such as integrating connection, empathy, emotional cue-taking, consensus-building, mutuality, and questioning are often misconstrued as "less-than or weaker" leadership traits, which clashes with the dominant male culture of leadership. Someone told me to "never cry in public" as a leader because women leaders need to have an appearance as a strong person.

In general, I would agree with this in that I do not want to portray that I am flimsy, but what is wrong in showing the emotion? Whether it is crying, smiling, laughing or shouting, what is wrong in showing what it is that we women feel in public? Just because most of the leaders are white men does not mean we as women have to act like them, dress like them and meet the same expectations in social behaviors.

One of our faculty members told me that he likes and appreciates a top-down, authoritative style of leadership even when he is being reprimanded. This is reflective of our social and family culture; he respects his father's authoritative voice and he runs to his mother for consolation.

Women lack in role models of leadership because there are so few examples of women in leadership to look up to. Women already experience imposter syndrome if we feel not good enough, underqualified, things are over our head; or if we don't come from a high pedigree or riddled with self-doubt due to systemic oppression or directly or indirectly told by others throughout our whole life we are less-than or underserving of success if we begin to achieve things in a way that goes against a long-standing narrative in our mind.

How can women enter into a leadership position when men are not providing opportunity into their exclusive club? Most men are not even aware they are not inclusive, are selective in their circles, and may wonder why women are not joining into their club called leadership. Secretly, however, men must enjoy the privilege and seek to prolong their positions.

I also think, due to affirmative action and the image they need to portray, Louis and other men need to include women or at least persons of color in leadership positions to be lauded and to fulfill their public image, and to meet a diversity quota.

I do not want the job as a leader for the social sympathy and endure suspicion that I was in the inclusive program project. I want to be a leader totally based on merit and talent. As Ruth Bader Ginsburg said, "I ask no favor for my sex. All I ask of our brethren is that they take their feet off our necks."

America gives the illusion that anyone can accomplish anything today if one sets their mind to it. If one cannot obtain the opportunity, it is one's own fault. But is this really true for women today? Even in modern time, women are considered to be "the other sex," the "second sex," the sex to be further explained. Men are considered the normal human being and women are "the other," to be compared to the male.

To start off, when I was in medical school, the classic anatomy and physiology established the male body as the model and norm. Entire organ systems were studied with a male body over 90% of the time. Interestingly, an erection state of penis is considered as normal anatomy and named ventral and dorsal sides of the penis, as if a normal male always should be in erectile position as a normal state of existence. No wonder why some men have penis consciousness and insecurity if they have difficulty having an erection.

Woman's body was introduced as the "different reproduction system," as if women's ovaries, fallopian tubes, uterus, cervix, vagina, vulva, and clitoris are aberrant organs. This concept of male normalcy prevails in most fields including medicine, science, history, law, economics, literature, and art.

After defining a normal human being as male in all these fields, women are defined further by ever-so-growing phenomenon of syndromes, with mostly problematic connotations attached such as premenopausal syndrome (PMS), menopausal syndrome, superwomen syndrome, imposter syndrome, battered women syndrome, etc. The number of syndromes related to females recently increased with the so-called Queen Bee Syndrome. It is suggested to be prevalent within medical professions including medical schools, residency training programs, and even in clinical practice, in which females compete with one another and withhold opportunities from other women.

The implication from all these listing of syndromes is that women are deficient and should measure up to what is considered "normal."

Man is still the standard against which woman is judged. A woman leader who acclimates well to the male norm of being outspoken, decisive, assertive, self-confident, independent, abrasive, self-centered, logical, rational, and courageous is often described as a bitch, lacking feminine qualities such as loving, kind, considerate, caring, warmth, gullible, selflessness, soft, pliable, and a gaudy display of emotions.

No wonder many women are struggling to find balance in the workplace as a leader. They have a double standard. Women in general already lack self-praise in valuing her own effort at work and self-humbles herself to the degree of doubting her own success, and attributes her success to the team and to luck, not due to her own abilities and competence.

There's a natural tendency of women to question, "What have I done?" when things do not yield satisfactory results rather than a typical response of the male leader who will express anger and question others or the system and asks, "What's wrong with *them*?" My own lack of self-promoting when appropriate confidence was needed in public situations has been a disservice to my own career advancement.

In general, males are more conceited than females, men overvalue the work they do, are not realistic in assessing their abilities, better at self-promotion, and naturally confident. The values of females become "deviant" when the measurement definition starts from males. No wonder why females often fail to measure up.

There are so many books and multitudes of conferences on how to "fix women" in their inferiorities and publish lists of their problems. If women did not fit, it was their own fault.

Simplistic view from society evolved after male researchers used questionable data from scientific papers. These include conclusions such as men are better than women in spatial ability, which leads to a quick conclusion that perhaps women are deficient in spatial skill and that they should not try to become engineers or architects. Men justify and adapt this as a God-given reality, and it infests themselves by excluding women from joining their careers of men.

This concept extends further by saying since women are "hormonally dependent on their mood" with a monthly cycling problem, they should not take leadership positions which includes the US Presidency. God forbid she push the button for atomic bomb or missile on the enemy country when she has a severe PMS.

Ironically, none of these speculations are tested to be true; that hormonal imbalance will lead to irrational behaviors. In fact, it is not hormonal dependency nor imbalance, but rather, natural cycles in women's bodies. But some women join the conclusion that they should not entertain the possibility of becoming engineers, architects, or leaders.

They settle with the idea that a woman is not complete until the prince comes to save and rescue her as in ancient fairy tales like *Cinderella.* If she is not beautiful or unwilling to give up her identity for a prince, she is doomed to a life of struggling. This is the typical story a young girl grows up to.

No wonder women have less self-identity, self-confidence and independency because it requires a prince to fulfill her identity and her dreams to live happily ever after. Lowering one's ambitions to be completed by the prince and admitting her own lack of power is expected of women, which perpetuates powerlessness. It places the burden of adjustment on the woman.

The other set of more courageous women who challenge their once defined sex as fundamentally different and inferior to men in many ways and copes with the concept of "the other sex," these women instead try to prove that they are as good as, as competent as, as intelligent and capable as the men who set the norm, and then hear repeated criticisms of working too hard, too uptight and unable to have fun at work.

The very definition of superwoman who can juggle both work and family responsibilities draw attention away from the actual culprits: husbands, employers, division of family obligations and structure of institutions. It places the burden of adjustment on the woman, thereby, eliminating the need to make adjustment elsewhere.

The society's value system could flip, and emphasize what is wrong with males and their problem lists: inflated or overly confident, unrealistic self-esteem, rigid, selfish, offensive sense of humor, insensitive, aloof, too autonomous, uncooperative, angry, linear in thinking and their pathologic inhibition in expression of their emotion, suppression of pain, guilt, shame, remorse and fear.

When asked, a few honest men admit they are afraid of crying in public from fear of not knowing how others will respond, what might happen, and their lack of control in the situation. Fear of losing control is ultimately why many men do not express emotion, so they play Mister-up-tight-in-control role and are actually inarticulate about what they feel.

It is not because I need to be the leader or wanted the job so desperately, but I liked to get the title to show the world, "Yes, women can do the job and here is how," to many women in the world. I also want to see if what men emphasize and preach can actually happen when they say, "We want to see more women leaders." I also wanted to prove to myself I can actually do this job, not just do the job, but do it very well.

Ultimately, I wanted to challenge myself to learn how to be better, and to become a more effective leader.

But as time passes, and the fights prolong, I see futility in inner struggles and I need to decompress the pressures in life. My interest in fighting for the women's rights and be a role model is rapidly diminishing as the price is too high for me to bear. I decide to see the other half-full side of the cup.

Being selfish to escape and dodge the pressure is the preferred way out for me at this point. I ask a question to myself, "What is the most important thing in life when I already lived more than two thirds of my life expectancy?"

So far, I ran as fast as I could without any rest. It was not merely jogging to run a marathon but a fast sprint. I push myself to excel in whatever I do, not satisfied with a good grade; I must be excellent. I aced all tests, and never failed any courses or tests. Everything I did and touched had outstanding scores, even the unknown territory as the interim chair. I ran tirelessly without reservation.

Now the question to me is, "Why am I still running so fast?" I have no regrets and if I have to do it all again I would do exactly as I did, but it came with a price. I had no time to eat, think, and enjoy the gift of life. I ran breathlessly without taking a break.

Yes, I am enjoying all the peripheral benefits such as financial security, medical degree, social respect, prestigious titles and the materialistic comforts. But I lost the sense of pleasures, grace, and joy in life as I rush though the hours of my life.

Lunch is always while I read hundreds of emails and type away my necessary responses, and chewing food is a mere chore. Dinners are usually a takeout from the neighborhood restaurants and eating while watching the late news of exaggerated and dramatized sad and violent stories. The weekends are spent catching up with the paperwork, long overdue email responses and academic writings which leave me with just a few precious minutes to wonder what I should do for leisure, always alone.

I never had an opportunity to stop and think what shall I do next, what defines pleasure for me, and what is the meaning of all these works I do. The waves of responsibilities came to me to accept, digest and perform the duties as I went along my professional life. I never even asked myself, "Do I like this?" and, "What do I really like?"

The interim chair responsibility is no joke. As the institution grew exponentially within the last ten years, we ran out of space capacity and the lack of parking spaces became a nightmare even to our patients.

We are constantly challenged by meeting the annual goals set for us, but the CEO, President and a few senior leaders get distracted by the next shiny object in their immediate future that appears attractive to them, then leave all the works to their people below, including the department chairs.

Dictatorship is the leadership style, without providing the proper funds and time to fulfill their own dreams to look good. The next chair of our department will have to face monumental challenges and stresses. Even a seasoned chair with experience and who knows the ins and outs of the department will have substantial amount of stresses.

The favored candidate, who rescinded his application, was the smart one in not accepting the position. In my case, the decision was made easier for me because the leadership decided not to give me a chance. This rejection is perhaps a blessing in disguise. To think of doing all those tasks gives me chills to my spine.

The countless sleepless nights, getting aged beyond my age, and attempts to fulfill insatiable goals from senior leaders who do not have specific and targetable goals will be incredibly painful for the next chair. For what glory is sufficient enough for that much sacrifice at the workplace? The only way I can envision the next chair becoming somewhat successful is to remove himself from all these nonsenses and carry on with being who he is with his own goals and identity priorities with clear end dates in mind.

There is a philosophic country song about successful gamblers who know when they should hold or fold their cards, when to walk and when to run from a game, what to throw away and what to keep. I know this is my time to walk away and I lost some of my cards and now I see that my loss will be the size of a moun-tain if I keep going.

It is the first time in my life I am facing myself directly and ask the question, "What do I want to do for the rest of my life?" The question to myself is no longer "Can I do this?" Sacrifice for the group, delay in gratification, suffer and bear the pain to gain at the end, strive to live by endurance, patience, and perseverance; these are not the words I would like to use in my professional career life any longer.

I will no longer sacrifice any of my time, efforts, intelligence and energy to the organization which does not recognize my greatness.

Chapter Three

Come to think of it, I never really asked God what I should do. There is a story in the Bible, 2 Samuel when David asks God if he should attack the Philistines. This is the period when God always gave David the victory to take over surrounding lands whenever David went out to fight.

The Philistines regrouped and the natural step for David was to just go and fight again. But David always asked God for his next step, even though it appeared obvious for him to move forward.

God told David not to proceed but to circle behind them in front of a section of poplar trees and wait for the Lord. *"As soon as you hear the sound of marching in the tops of poplar trees, move quickly, because that will mean the Lord has gone out in front of you to strike the Philistine army."*

I feel at this time, I am supposed to wait for the Lord, take a breath and stop everything. Think and reflect what I am supposed to do for the rest of my life. I will have to hear my Lord's voice to wait for Him.

For this moment of the great interruption in my life, I am able to see how God used Louis in my life, and for this, and for the first time, I am thankful for Louis. Maybe Louis is being used by God in my life, to stop and think what I should do for the rest of my hours in life.

My gravestone will not boast that I was at one time the chair of the department of a once well-known academic institution and the long hours I worked there. The stone will list my name, the date of my birth and date of my death. Maybe someone honored me by adding "Beloved" if I am lucky enough to have my own family that I never had thus far.

Life is not all about the professional career. But today, I decide to celebrate my own achievements in my professional career. I ran the race fully in my career with integrity, keeping the pride without shame, and not eroding into my own value and doing the job as best as I can.

I did not sell myself to cynicism and sarcasm and reached the highest title anyone could have in the field of pathology. My evaluator of my performance is no one else except God who says, "Well done, my servant and friend," and I will say, "My Lord, it was because You gave me the strength, opportunities, wisdom, endurance, patience and blessings."

Chapter Four

With many thoughts and prayers, I decide to resign the position of interim chair and leave the institution by the end of the year. This morning I write a short letter stating such and give it to Louis and Dr. Bruce Drysdale (we called him Dr. D) who is the medical group president. I send it by email, and a hard copy by mail. Louis soon sends me an email and asks me to keep this in confidence for at least another month and I just reply, "I will."

Once again, Louis tries to rectify the situation in secret and I agree to go along with it. But within an hour, the email I sent to Louis and Dr. D is sent out as a public announcement. I am not sure who in HR did this and how it happened. Louis is in chaos and sends a second email in less than an hour with his transition plans to all the leadership and department heads.

Louis calls me and vents his frustration to me about "this person in HR who sent that blasted email" to everyone without his permission. He thinks it was handled very inappropriately and unprofessionally without his knowledge and his approval. It is obviously very upsetting to him personally.

I feel sorry for him not because he had to deal with his spilled beans. Sadly, he tries to control everything and every person with his hidden secretive ways in handling situations, always trying to look good. The truth always reveals in time.

To hide for over a month the fact I resigned and will leave the institution is strange and absurd. Everything must revolve around preserving his image and to minimize the damage control for his reputation and benefit.

Louis sends a third email. "I have accepted Dr. Choi's resignation," he begins, then concludes the brief email with an unremarkable accolade. I did not realize he has to accept my resignation.

I thought it is entirely my freedom to leave the institution. In our employment policy, it has a 60-day no-cause policy of termination by either the employee or employer. This too is giving himself the significance.

A few days later, when the faculty members are digesting this news after much gossip, much surprise, and criticism that my decision is too fast and drastic, my former chairman Dr. Daniel Ross walks into my office and tells me he fully understands my situation and decision.

He also tells me that Louis probably was not prepared for me to leave the place; Louis might assume that I am disappointed, but not leave the institution. By me leaving, Louis had a lot to lose and his reputation is damaged. Louis lost his credibility as a leader by losing me. Departmental people had expected his announcement would state that I am to be the next chair. This is what Louis had stated to staff—not my resignation announcement.

Other people assume I would be appointed chair after Louis demoted Dr. Daniel and appointed me as the interim chair. Colleagues and other leaders know I have been doing an excellent job, not just a good job, and believed that perhaps Louis had reasonable judgment and character. With this announcement, I am not just stepping down as the interim chair but leaving the institution altogether, and this highlights Louis's lack of leadership capability and damages his reputation.

To my surprise, countless female staff, faculty, students, and residents come by to support me.

"Dr. Choi, you are an incredible leader!" and one young staff member, in tears, "Dr. Choi, you are our hope for the future, knowing there is someone out there in the leadership position who is not a man."

"This gave us confidence and hope that the world can be fair after all, and that some of us who are young will be able to keep our dreams and visions to be a leader one day in our lifetime."

All staff understand that no one has ever been a department chair who did not identify themselves as a man. "Women leaders are so hard to come by," they say.

I have been the representation of women's hope for the past year, which I had not known. I am touched by their sincerity and most of all their tears, which cannot be faked.

Tim Cobalt enters my office and closes the door. "I am going through a grieving process, to fill a huge vacuum, a space devoid that you were occupying, providing leadership with calmness and confidence."

Our department indeed had undergone many changes, having two chairpersons within a year, which is unsettling to say the least.

The majority of faculty come to the same conclusions:

1. Louis wanted Dan out.
2. Louis put me in charge.
3. Louis said he wants a female chair.
4. Louis will appoint a chair in July or sooner.
5. It will be either me or the other young male candidate from Houston.
6. Louis changed his mind and will do a new search for a molecular research pathologist.
7. Louis did not do a new search but appointed someone who was not a molecular research pathologist, nor a person in the candidate pools.
8. Louis asked me to extend my time as interim chair.

9. Louis now receives my letter of resignation.
10. And finally, Louis had no plan B and lost his two top candidates.

Looking at it this way, I know people see what happened and how damaging Louis appears.

My challenge is to continue the business as usual until my last day of duties as if nothing happened. Often it is best for both parties to disengage as soon as we know we are not meant to be together. Daily business of dealing with unhappy people continues.

But most disturbing is that Louis calls Tim, essentially seeking any dirt he can gather to find fault in me. He asks Tim to check and see if I had indeed improved the turn-around-time of the pathology reports from our cytopathologists in the department, and to learn of any gossip about me.

Further, Louis asks Tim if I had not given a certain doctor in another department the opportunity to join our department. This doctor had reportedly requested to sign out pathology subspecialty cases in hematopathology.

The person Louis may be referring to is a research scientist who had not gone through mandatory credentialing processes for professional medical practice privilege, a legal policy for any institution including ours. On top of this and more recently, this physician also had behavioral issues toward a female colleague in the research lab, something to do with sexual misconduct and was fired from the institution immediately after the incident.

I am disappointed that Louis is personally looking to see if he can dust me off to find any weakness of mine to place blame and save his reputation.

Louis is not asking only Tim about my conduct. He emailed other physicians in different departments to verify whether I had indeed improved the turn-around-times. These colleagues expose Louis by adding me on their reply to Louis's email, praising how well I improved and shortened the time of diagnosis from the pathology department, and congratulate me for my effort.

Louis once said to me he is dealing with 40 other tasks and juggling countless things and not just handling the decision on who will be our next pathology department chair. Now I see that he is personally digging into finding any dirt about me to publicly say I was perhaps not an ideal candidate after all. This act by Louis also damages his reputation.

Throughout the day I meet with various leaders including Dr. D as part of the exit interview process. Leaders inform me things done by Louis were not according to the book, and not the policy for recruiting the chair of our department. Independently, others express the entire process was chaotic, riddled with irregularities and haphazardly done, partly due to the aggressive and unrealistic timeline.

Search committee members are upset and did not agree with the candidates chosen by Louis for the second interview. Louis made these unilateral decisions which led to a loss of respect among search committee members. Louis redirects his blame and pours it upon the chair of the search committee who is also a surgeon. Louis had numerous opportunities to work with me and patch things up by speaking truth, but he chose not to do so. In the end, he lost both candidates.

Dr. D spoke with me during my final weeks. "Louis will not be successful if he continues to act this way. He is trying to simulate his previous institutional model into ours, disrupting the culture and value system from our institution.

"Sara, you have performed a superb job as the interim chair, especially given the contentious and difficult personalities in your department. Your departure is a tremendous loss."

The fact no one asks me why I am leaving or tries to retain me is a bit surprising, not that I would stay if they tried. Dr. D must have known this, not to even try to retain me.

Attending all the necessary meetings including our chairmen meetings which Louis conducts until the end of the year is challenging to me. But I must finish the term and the job given to me without missing a beat to fulfill all my responsibilities and duties.

It is awkward when I attend the chairmen and other meetings as if nothing happened. People around me know about it, but most pretend nothing has occurred. Business as usual. I can tell, however, other people around me respect the fact I am finishing the job given to me without a complaint or bad-mouthing Louis.

Yet, day by day, I know my emotions detach me from work slowly and surely. This detachment from emotion comes with a degree of fresh and welcome freedom.

Chapter Five

I schedule time to see a psychologist for my mental health balance. Whether I admit it or not, I am grieving during the entire time of this prolonged process of getting rejected. Grief, resentment, anger, growing self-doubt, and the necessary emotional detachment are the things I am facing.

The psychologist asks me to write a letter to Louis to release anger. It does not matter whether I send this letter to him or not. The important thing is writing my thoughts to him on a piece of paper. So, I do.

Deep inside my heart, I notice that I am angry, and I want to get rid of this anger which haunts me at nights. During the day, I do not notice this emotion of anger has been affecting the daily business. But late at nights I awake, and think about things, especially Louis and my despair of rejection I can no longer deny or block.

I get noticeably hot; my heart rate increases, and I feel the anger toward him. Sometimes, I cannot go back to sleep for three, four or even five hours and finally fall asleep at dawn and get up late for work.

A realization enters my mind that I have not completely processed my thoughts well enough to brush off the anger to move on with my life. My decision to leave the institution is all I can do to manifest my pain and hurt which is not enough to damage Louis.

My heart is bitter, and I want to hurt him somehow. I feel helpless there is nothing more I can do to hurt him back and give back the pain and rejection I still feel.

I always felt proud of myself to compartmentalize my emotions into the boxes in my head and trusted my capability to brush things off as if nothing bothers me.

This too is the denial mechanism of brushing away the pain with which I am dealing. I am surprised. Why do I feel this way and afraid of my own feelings; the desire to revenge? I come to realize my hurt is much more, and deeper than I care to admit.

In Romans 12:19, God says, *"Do not take revenge, my dear friends, but leave room for God's wrath, for it is written: 'It is mine to avenge; I will repay,' says the Lord."*

And Deuteronomy 32:35, God says, *"It is mine to avenge; I will repay. In due time their foot will slip; for their day of disaster is near and their doom rushes upon them."*

But my desire is not ready to wait for the Lord to revenge. I want to see for myself how Louis is getting hurt. I am disappointed at myself letting go of my ego and allowing Louis to walk all over me and control my destiny with his hand.

I should have rescinded the application a long time ago. I feel like I did not do a decent job protecting myself, to let Louis dismantle my ego and pride, in rejecting me.

I knew better not to let him hurt me repeatedly. I must let him go in peace and not let him control me, residing in my anger, for my own sake. I cannot let him hurt me again and again in my thoughts for the rest of my life.

I will not let him get hold of me in this betrayal, hopeless and helpless version of me. The irony is Louis will not even think of me while I am preoccupied by him in my own anger.

Yet, I know I am able to handle my emotions with so many sophisticated methods: intelligence, education, degrees, titles, past experiences, maturity, mindful weapons, arguments; and most importantly, my God who provides Heaven's Armies to protect me. I do not need anyone's approval for my values and confirmations on who I am and what I am capable to do.

Whether I am a burden to other people or not is no longer my worry or issue. Other people may burden me including Louis, this is the problem. As my strong emotions subside because there is no need for me to have emotion toward him, he will no longer have control over me, and he will not afflict me any longer. I must let him go. It does not matter whether he understands me or not. His reality, whether through his narcissism or as a psychopath who is unable to feel empathy toward me or anyone else, is no longer important to me.

The letter I write in one setting is as follows:

Dear Louis,

I am writing this letter to you for my sake. I am letting go all the negative feelings including betrayal, abandonment; used, discarded, and rejected because you are not worthy of controlling my thoughts any longer.

You may not even know how I felt throughout this year when you treated me poorly and you may deny all these things, but you cannot deny how I feel, my portion of the reality. Whether you have a different viewpoint and reality does not matter to me.

What matters now is I tell you that you lack integrity, virtue, and leadership. Your lack of leadership is manifested by losing both excellent chair candidates, and in the end, you lost a loyal interim chair who worked for the department, institution and for you tirelessly for a year.

In your own words when you nominated me for the EXCELLENCE award, you wrote,

> *She has performed wonderfully in her interim role of department chair with great passion, integrity and inclusion to those around her. She exudes care, sympathy and friendliness and considers her role to be of utmost importance to our patients. She is excited to embrace our vision of Precision Medicine which is critical because Pathology is at the heart of our new initiative. She delivers excellence in every challenge she and her team take on. Our leaders appreciate her novel ideas, problem solving, and ability to lead. She brings joy to those who are fortunate to work with her and we appreciate the impact Dr. Choi makes to our teams and our patients.*

Louis, a good leader in most people's minds is someone who is visionary, approachable, humble, selfless, inclusive to others, good listener, fair, takes all perspectives into consideration before any major decisions, team builder, works for the betterment of the group, good communicator, appoints and selects suitable persons for the right kinds of jobs, provides full potential to the employee to be more/better than they may see by motivating and providing resources; honest, personal integrity with virtue, and transparency.

You lack nearly all these attributes. You only trust yourself, that you are the only person who can solve all the problems and know the best, and therefore, you exude secrecy in decisions, exclusiveness, and disrespect for others.

In the end, the truth reveals from your foolishness and dishonesty and as a result, the people around you will lose motivation to work with you.

As for me, you misled me from the beginning to end. Your words were: "I will hire the new chair in July; it will either be you or the other candidate." Then abruptly, "I will start a new search." You offered me a new salary, hoping to attract me into continuing the interim chair role.

Your processes had no fruitions. July came and went. You never did any national search from the very beginning, violating our institutional policy in how we search for the chair of a department. The actual chairman you chose comes out of nowhere; patchy problem-solving to fill the position when you told my faculty your goal is to be transparent.

You lack clear and consistent criteria for the chairman of the department. First, you sought someone who would fire people, then sought for a good leader, then someone young, then someone a research pathologist and now someone of years well beyond me, missing your own aggressive timelines, misleading, and deceiving me so that I would continue my interim role until you could personally find another warm body to sit in the chair position is disappointing, to say the least.

You surely know how to demotivate someone like me who really works tirelessly for the noble cause—a sure sign of lacking leadership skills on your part.

I remember you mentioned to me that in your prior institution, you as the chief executive eventually brought profits of 275 million dollars to the program from 6 million when you started, but no one said "thank you" at the end.

Instead, there was constant jealousy, competition and others looking to take over your job. No wonder why people at your old place did not say thank you, even when you exited.

Your repetitive behavior pushes blame to others, continual deception to reveal only flowery situations, while choosing not to reveal the true, good, bad, and ugly parts of all matters so that other people like potential chair candidates can decide for themselves.

Some of us, like myself, like to take on the challenges of a job when we know the bad and ugly sides of the work, if you reveal all in truth. This also can create trust in you, if only you welcome honesty in the relationship. At least we are informed of all scenarios without feeling trapped with "switch and bait" situations you tend to create.

Above all, a good leader takes the blame, responsibility and accountability in all situations and never pushes someone under the bus when push comes to shove. And a good leader respects and values someone who has guts to say, "Emperor, you are naked" when you are indeed naked.

Your pride works against you. I am surprised by your naivety, lack of virtue as a human and your demand for loyalty so you alone can look good. But in the end, your decisions and choices will be respected because you are the current president.

During this process, I want you to know that you hurt me. I decided to let go of everything including the position, title, glory, my retirement, job security, all my friends at my workplace including you—out of my reach in invoking any of my emotions because you do not deserve this from me.

My only regret is I shall lose this opportunity to work more with my great staff and friends I made during the process.

—Sara

After writing the letter, my heavy heart and burden are lifted somewhat. I am somewhat able to distance myself from anger at Louis. I met the statistic that most people leave their boss, not their job.

This reminds me of a friend from residency training who decided to pursue another job because he could not tolerate his boss. We met recently at a medical conference and all he talked about was his prior boss. His perpetual pent-up frustrations and negative words were about his boss, saying she was a controller, tyrannical, a sociopath who must win all battles at all costs, who must say the last words all the time.

His angry voice echoes into my ear. While he was saying all these things, I saw how he was re-living hurtful and painful times, consumed by his anger and continues to carry his heavy burdens in his heart. He could not stop talking about his boss.

He could not let it go. He wanted to unload his burden to whomever had time to listen. In doing so, he was letting his boss hurt him again and again, afresh, even when he is out of that workplace, not realizing he is victimizing himself repeatedly.

His anger snowballs into a larger and bigger monster, eroding joy out of his new life and becoming consumed by it. And he does not even know it. The funniest thing is that his boss does not even think about him that much. Maybe occasionally when his name surfaces by others, she might think about him.

Nor will Louis think of me. The perpetrators are nonchalant and go about their business, live well, while the victims are obsessed with thoughts of the perpetrators. I was in the same position where I can join the choir talking about Louis (which I do not). The specifics of Louis, how it happened, who Louis is, how deadly and destructive a sociopath or psychopath he really is.

But it is not important. What is important is how I will not let him consume me in my thoughts, repeatedly defeating me again, and again. Beginning to think less of Louis is not letting me forget the importance of this experience. Yet as I considered giving it away, it felt like it is a sign of weakness and vulnerability, so I kept forgiveness sealed and locked tight away in the depths of my heart.

The futility of repeating the hurtful and painful experience in my mind and in my head over and over is astounding. Why would I allow myself to harm me, when I know hating Louis and regurgitating my anger will not heal me? Forgiving Louis is not for Louis, but for me. Acknowledging the anger toward Louis is important but the more important thing is not letting thoughts about him invade and consume in my mind.

So, how do I begin to forgive him? It is not by me getting a more successful job and position of a department chair in a better and more prestigious place or living my life in a dream world or striving for more money or better titles.

No one cares what I do, actually. They are busy living their own lives. No one thinks about me when I am not in their sight any longer. Out of sight, out of mind. People are too busy living their lives.

There are generally seven steps to forgiveness:

1. Identify the hurt, start by pinpointing the source of the hurt,

2. Acknowledge the hurtful emotions,

3. Forgive yourself and let go,

4. Breathe in compassion,

5. Forgive unconditionally,

6. Be grateful and

7. Love again.

These are neatly packaged, good for conference talks and the peripheral education materials but how to really live in it? For me, it is for the practical purposes. When I am in anger, consumed by the thought of Louis, I am not in peace as my mind is poisoning the prospect of my future. I want to be free of this poison. I want to feel free and love again. I want to trust in people again. I want to smile again.

People say time will heal everything. Time truly is a powerful method to forget and heal. But humans tend to forget the pleasurable times more easily than painful times. We tend to over emphasize, talk about, remember and grab hold of the hurts and pains more than any other emotions. Time is a powerful drug for sure but that is not the only antidote for forgiveness.

As for me, the practicality of spending any minute longer of my life, wasted in thinking of someone like Louis is simply unconscionable and useless. I come to realize that forgiving Louis is for my sake, not for his sake.

People often are mistaken that if I forgive someone like Louis, then he is off the hook, and it is not fair for Louis to escape pain and suffering. My reality is if I hold on to Louis, it is myself who will endure and magnify pain and suffering. Louis will not think of me and suffer. I will be a thing of the past for him quickly.

It is extremely difficult to let go of my anger toward Louis but the sooner I let go of it, sooner I will be healed. Forgiving myself to let go of it all is the hardest thing to do but I must do this for me to love myself. All the actions of forgiving are not humanly possible.

So, I must ask God to intervene into my life to perform His miracles. I have a deep faith that God who sees and knows everything including my deepest heart, what really happened, and that I was treated unfairly. And to know that my Lord has space to perform His will and to perform vengeance in His time, is sufficient for me. I may or may not know if, how and when God will perform His vengeance. I may not be able enjoy the scene of how specifically Louis will get paid by God and it is fine with me. In fact, I wish the best for Louis.

Forgiveness is not a humanly possible thing. It has to come from the power of God. Without God, forgiveness is impossible.

For me, it is the grace I receive from my patient Julie who freely gave me freedom to live in her forgiveness that I can let Louis go out of my mind with God's help. I have received forgiveness from Julie and my God, that when I was still a sinner, she and my God forgave and loved me.

I am forever grateful to receive such mercy and grace, and from this knowledge gives me strength and freedom to know that I can love again. Most importantly, I can forgive myself, and I can love myself. Only then, I can love others.

I have been forgiven by Julie and now I can forgive Louis. And, I forgive myself.

Chapter Six

It is late December, a few days before I leave the institution and I am hosting a big farewell party for myself, inviting only a dozen people from the workplace and their spouses to a Christmas/Farewell party in a plush restaurant to enjoy a private room with 3-course meals.

I am providing a gift for each person who means so much to me. These people vary from those with important titles who truly helped me to do my job better, and assistants who only saw me infrequently and peripherally but who gave and still give me strength to work here, knowingly, and unknowingly uplifted my spirit every day, and when I have a difficult day.

I give each guest my gift, with a card explaining why their presence is so important to me and what each of them mean to me. Farewell parties are often given to the person leaving the workplace, but I chose to give it to myself.

Events such as birthday parties, weddings, and funerals are an important aspect of our lives. This celebration is an important one for me. It is finishing this chapter of my professional life in a tangible way. I feel extremely lucky to have a dozen staff and colleagues with who I truly enjoyed working together. And I receive their love and warm hearts through this dinner tonight.

The time is filled with laughter, joy, and good memories that I hope to remember for a long time.

My last meeting with Louis is today, just he and I for 40 minutes and I assume he will cancel. Surprisingly, he arrives on time for the meeting. First five minutes or so, we chat about our family plans for Christmas.

"I'll be terribly busy with weddings next year for my two daughters. I am even thinking about semi-retiring. I've served our CEO for enough time." I wonder whether he talks like this to anyone else. "Sara, I admit the new chair I hired might not work out and will deal with any damage to my reputation at that time."

"What is your reason for not hiring me as the chair?"

Louis looks at me for a long time. I sincerely think he has no idea, or he cannot utter his reason to me. Whatever it is, I am confirming again that it is God who controls Louis and all the circumstances, and God must have some other plans for me. This fact frees me tremendously, knowing Louis is under God's plan. Knowing this fact also helps me to forgive Louis in all his weakness and incompetency.

"Louis, I am leaving because of you. You lied to me on several occasions and your words do not carry any weight. I cannot distinguish which words you speak are true and which are not true, and as a leader, words from a leader must always mean truthful, and accountable."

"Dr. Choi, I've never lied to you."

"There is a difference in the reality, we will have to agree to disagree. You have discriminated against me to have a fair chance. There is nothing you asked for me to do that I failed to achieve. I have met every goal and task you asked me to do, which were not easy by all means," as I remind him. "Louis, it is your lack of leadership and also your lack of vision as a whole, and so I cannot continue to work with a boss like you."

"Sara, you're making an emotional decision, a hasty one." He finally speaks, repeating, "I will not stay here at our institution for a long time. I'm thinking about semi-retiring in the next year or so."

He must be tired of working, fulfilling all his responsibilities and hearing all-common and never-ending criticisms as a leader which comes with the territory of being president.

Louis repeats a couple times how much I am respected by all the people he has been talking to, and strangely asks, "Sara, please have dinner with me, or even better, with me and the pathology faculty to say goodbye."

"No, thanks." It is all he deserves from me. His invitation and offer seem disingenuous and intended to salvage his reputation. I will not feel obliged to be political with Louis any longer.

As Louis leaves, he looks down at me and asks, "Sara, are you going to work someplace else?"

I decline to answer.

The next morning, I click on an email from Louis. He has documented vastly different things than what we had discussed.

He denies the fact he ever lied to me and asks me to talk to HR about the processes of hiring the chair for our department. Near the end of his note he awkwardly adds, "Sara, I'd love for you to stay beyond this year, and I spoke to the new chair about you — who by the way is coming next year — about how talented you are and about the possibility of you staying. Perhaps you can speak to the next chair about this."

How unbelievable! Louis has twisted and misinterpreted our conversation about why I decided to leave the institution. Especially after I articulated my intentions and thoughts so clearly to him.

This cover-up or make-believe document is to protect him from possible accusations from me if I decide to pursue legal action against him or the institution.

Or Louis is a person who cannot hear clearly or chooses to interpret a reality into his favor and his own reality, and to protect his position. This again reinforces to me how far our realities differ and how glad I am to walk away from a person who chooses to be deaf, like Louis.

He is destructive and detrimental to others. Not only does he not know how he affects others, but he is absolutely not remorseful or guilty. A true definition of a psychopath, and he is beyond hope for remediation. I feel deep sorrow for my institution who has someone like him as a leader.

Chapter Seven

It is not my desire to be the center of the attraction, but my faculty and staff are giving me a surprise farewell party on my last day and last couple hours here at work. I had known of this a day before the event.

Tim has told me so that I could dress up a bit because I usually show up to work in scrubs, the most comfortable piece of clothing in my opinion. The event is attended by approximately 200 people during our busy lunch time. It was designed to be a walk-in and walk-out, so people are not pressured to stay the whole two hours.

Louis modestly enters and gives a short speech about how much he appreciates my accomplishments during the interim time. He then says I had declined his dinner invitation with faculty and that I had told him, "I am not too popular, and no faculty will show up during the Christmas season."

"Ohhhhh…" pours out from people in the room.

Contrary to what I had thought, attendance here shows me maybe I am not so unpopular, and I hold back my tears.

During the rest of Louis's speech I sort of tune out what he has to say because he is a phony person, and it is not important to me what he has to say any longer.

Our interim surgical pathology director speaks next and says, "Dr. Choi told me she is attending this party as her last undesirable service to the department because she hates to be center of the stage." She smiles, people laugh, and some have tears.

Tim follows after her, and slowly and proudly says, "Dr. Choi has been a great leader. A leader with integrity. Honesty. Fairness. And the truth."

I think he purposely lists each of these attributes of great leadership to contrast how these have been absent in Louis, without really saying it in this public place.

I have not prepared any speech but somehow, I know what I want to say as I walk to the podium. I stand at the lectern and look at all the people, astonished that they bothered to show up amidst their busy schedules. I speak less than three minutes.

"I no longer seek personal accomplishments such as writing yet another paper, getting recognition or awards but I count for whom I loved in my life and who loved me in this journey called life. I gave you and me a vision why we are here in this place — for the patients who are suffering from their illness, and we all have a special gift to contribute hope for the patients who are in this hospital.

"We function as a body, some are being their hands, feet, heart, or brain, each with special talents and skillsets, an ambassador of hope to the patients. Please, keep doing what you do, with vision of being one body to provide hope for others who are in need in their time of desperation. What each of you do is so important, so important.

"I love you. Thank you for letting me be your leader."

People are in tears at the end of the speech. I barely dodge my own tears as I step down. Lines of people come to me, in groups, as individuals, as teams, and say my speech is heartfelt to them, and many tell me they do not really understand why I am leaving the institution, and some think they have not done enough for me and then maybe I would have stayed as their leader.

I am surprised and discover certain people still think like a kid when their parents are divorcing, and the kid thinks that they did not behave well enough and caused the separation. My reason for leaving is very much complicated, and I cannot share the truth why, at this stage.

I receive so many gifts, heartfelt cards with words of love, and hugs. So many people line up to take pictures with me, as if I am a celebrity. This is a lavishing love, and respect, and maybe I have made some positive impact or touched some lives or hearts to be admired this much.

Louis stays and glances at me while I am getting all this attention and love, and a thought comes to me. *What was it like when he left his previous institution? Were there people who would miss him, a farewell party?*

My last chair meeting, and Louis again tells everyone how much he appreciates my accomplishments and a successful job done in a rather difficult department. Around the table or standing against the wall, the chairmen and some guests give me a round of applause. After the meeting, he sends me another strange email.

"Sara, the newly appointed chairman of the pathology department is coming for his final meeting to sign the deal and you should meet him."

I am told Louis spoke to this new chair by encouraging him: by telling him I might stay. Something like, "As the new chair, I think you may be able to retain her." Again, Louis pushes his responsibility to others. That should be his job to retain me, not that I would change my mind, but I would like to see Louis's desperation with my own eyes.

Moving out from my office is complete. The chair's office is empty and echoes when I breathe. My exit interview with our HR liaison is rather brief. I could have talked about the gender harassment for the record. But what is the point?

Gender harassment is defined as "verbal and nonverbal behaviors that convey hostility, objectification, exclusion, or second-class status about members of one gender." In undermining a woman's road to professional and educational development, gender harassment is a leading cause for destructing the mental and physical health of women, and finally their burnout.

Medicine is a cruel place for women. And it is okay to be exhausted and even to leave. But I will not leave wondering if I was not the right person to be the chair due to lack of competence. It is entirely their loss.

I look around my office and know that I poured out my heart and soul to this job and have done all I could. I leave quietly during the holiday season, leaving my ID badge, parking pass and a laptop computer on my desk.

After all things are said and done, I have mixed emotions of defeat and celebration of my success. My heart is filled with vanity and meaninglessness, and I wonder if my life will feel as such when I take a last breath.

So many tasks that need to be done overwhelms and clouds the purposeful life and diminishes joy. The chores of everyday life such as eating, the tasks one needs to fulfill doing inconsequential things and talking nonsense fills the precious time in life.

Fading memories, even the significant events make none of life moments lasting because the next meal becomes the more important thing to consider. The power of forgetfulness is undeniable; what is past is merely past, a mere faint memory of significance flickering in one's mind without anyone's recognition.

The power of time overrides all meanings in its significance. What is lasting is the faith I have in God that carries all my burdens, memories, events, and my cries out to Him. The Lord is the only thing that really matters to me.

Chapter Eight

All people will have to stand before God and be judged for what they have done in this life. We will not be able to use the inequalities of life as an excuse for failing to live properly. I cannot use all my possible excuses, saying it is because I was an Asian American, female, short, Louis was unfair, etc., to stand before God why I had lived the way I lived my life.

People might say I lost in the battle and gave up. I was too weak, feminine, a meek woman who did not deserve to receive such a title in the end because I decided to get out and not fight back.

I am another number in the pool of women who gave up instead of fighting for a woman's right and stand in the position of power for the betterment of women's equality. And it may be true, and I will admit it.

My choices are to live freely with peace; or fight the battle in the workplace to gain equality and make a better place.

I chose the first, simply because I am at the age where my health is not able to tolerate countless sleepless nights and high blood pressure. I decided to choose a life for me, at least for now.

My only regret is to let the dominant society with selective white male leadership continue, another opportunity missed to display a different viewpoint to show injustice, diversity, and democratic values to all members of society who choose not to admit and recognize their privilege and position.

God created millions of different species, all equal in their value, connected to an ecosystem for balance. Not one species is accidently placed on earth by mistake. If one species becomes extinct, the whole ecosystem collapses eventually. Just like nature, I believe humankinds with all our differences are made by God's purposes and intentions to bring balance and equality.

Still, leadership is currently occupied primarily by only one kind of species in this country. Charity is not what I am asking for to become a woman leader, but merely a chance to address the root causes of social injustice that persist due to lack of diversity, disturbing the ecosystem in leadership, leading to avoidance of listening to those who are in the midst of injustice. By not having a small still voice of difference, the society in medicine once again delays the hope of the future for one more generation, a hefty price to pay for the women in medicine.

Yet, I choose to trust in the dilutional principle that other women, smarter and more fortunate women will carry the baton to run for the cause. I decide to live the remaining hours of my life in peace. I recognize that the life is much more than just working.

I am traveling the world, seeing things I never imagined. God's creation in nature, different cultures, food, and people are widely variable. So many varieties, so many colors and so many ways to live.

I only know my way to live in America; work hard, long hours; buy a house, a nice car and make a home for myself. If I am lucky, having a husband would be a nice addition. But I am not that lucky. After my first love, I did not pay attention and had no time for any other man.

When I took away the heavy burdens from the workplace by leaving the institution and as a practicing medical doctor, I feel free and calm. Though I may not know how to describe who I am anymore, I feel relieved. All the burdens and worries subside.

I find myself wondering why did I suffer so much and for what? I am sure I will face other burdens and worries of life in my new chapter because life itself is full of hardship whether I like it or not. But to be free of the old life is a good thing.

I can honestly say, I have done all I could and wanted in this life, without regrets.

All the plans, dreams, and wishes are made today not knowing when is the last day of my breath. How foolish this may appear to my God who sees and knows everything.

The only thing that my God asks of me is to breathe today, enjoy what I have and praise Him for who He is and who I am today because I am forgiven by Him and therefore, I forgive all including myself.

Epilogue

I am on a tour bus along the coastal highway from Marseille to Monaco where Princess Grace Kelly died. She was driving her British Rover 3500 on the snaking road at Cap-d'Ail in the Cote d'Azur region when she lost control, plunged down a 45-foot embankment, and died.

I want to emulate her sophisticated fashion style—I have a long white thin silk scarf over my head and a deep blue silk blouse with blue jeans.

I step inside a corner coastal coffee shop for a late afternoon café latte and a buttery peach and blueberry scone. Wearing huge sunglasses, I stare at the sparkling ocean that is much brighter and bluer than the Pacific Ocean. Maybe the Pacific Ocean is beautiful as this Mediterranean Sea, but I had no time to look at the water when I was in Southern California.

What a luxury it is to have a cup of my favorite coffee, enjoying the aroma of the coffee and stare at this beautiful scone in the middle of the day. I cut to reveal soft creamy texture of butter, beautifully yellow-white, with flaky crumbs. As I spread butter onto the scone, slowly it melts into the warm pastry.

The first bite is heavenly.

When was the last time I had a moment like this to savor?

A man of his 60s is approaching my table, smiling at me. A part of me inside says not now while I have this heavenly moment, and another part of me says, why not?

He also is wearing dark sunglasses and I cannot quite determine his eyes, whether they are blue or brown. Thin for his age, wears a white pressed shirt, a dark silk jacket and blue jeans, rather fashionable. Perhaps an Italian, rich, a little flamboyant for my taste when this man in front of me says, "May I?"

I gesture yes, with a smile.

What a different life this is. I do not know what I am going to do tomorrow. For that I am a little afraid but also excited what tomorrow will bring.

Final Thoughts

Life is not created to have the goods, comforts, titles, power, and worldly security, but to find and live with the faith in God.

Why did Jesus teach us the Lord's prayer? *"Give us today our daily bread. And forgive our debts, as we also have forgiven our debtors."* Forgiving is as important as eating daily. Forgiving is to sustain our spirit and eating bread is to sustain life. They are inseparable acts that we must do every day. God in His infinite wisdom must have known what His creatures need. God also must have known how hard it is to forgive one another and ourselves. And hence, He taught us to pray this Lord's prayer.

No power, no money, no prestige, no status, no position, no royal finery, no family, no friendship, no spiritual heritage, no education will be able rescue oneself from the misery of life in unforgiveness. And the power of forgiveness comes from God Himself.

Acknowledgements

Thank you, Charles Johnson, for your ever-present prayers and love. Your encouragement and mentorship are deeply appreciated. Dr. Elsie Koh, you postponed a personal trip and lost sleep and gym time to read my first two books. Your generosity is abundant and your shared experiences as a female physician and leader are valuable to me. To my husband Hal, thank you for being by my side every single day. I love you.

Special thanks to my patients, who I serve with gratitude and love. Your courage inspires me to keep writing.

About the Author

Sophia K. Apple, MD, is an expert in breast cancer, Professor Emerita at the David Geffen School of Medicine at UCLA, and practices pathology in Southern California. She is an author of over 70 peer-reviewed medical journal articles and primary editor of *Breast Imaging,* a seminal textbook correlating imagery from pathology and radiology. Dr. Apple is an internationally recognized speaker and current Editorial Board member  of the pre-eminent medical journal, *Modern Pathology.* Dr. Apple and her husband currently live in Southern California.

About the Cover

Pacinian Corpuscle is a major tactile sensory mechanism in mammalian skin, discovered by Italian anatomist Filippo Pacini. It detects pressure changes and vibrations in the skin. When the external pressure such as touch is applied to the skin, it senses the vibration by deforming layers of lines until the nerve ending in the center processes the touch. The Pacinian corpuscle can be described as oval-cylindrical-shaped, 1 mm in length and consists of 20 to 60 concentric lamellae (like onion rings) connected by nerve endings at the center.

This microscopic image is chosen for this book cover to depict the inner struggles we as humans experience via external stimuli, especially when it is negative. Natural reaction when the core of the structure is sensed as unfavorable is to recoil, retreat, shrink, flee, and finally fight if necessary.

Act of forgiveness, whether it is given or received, requires unnatural process of action. The power of the unnatural process of forgiveness is perhaps not possible by natural selection of human ability. God needs to intervene, so that humans can live peacefully with others and our own selves.